LONG
WAY
GONE

Center Point
Large Print

Also by Charles Martin and available from
Center Point Large Print:

Thunder and Rain
Unwritten
Life Intercepted
Water from My Heart

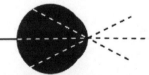

**This Large Print Book carries the
Seal of Approval of N.A.V.H.**

LONG
WAY
GONE

Charles
Martin

CENTER POINT LARGE PRINT
THORNDIKE, MAINE

This Center Point Large Print edition is published
in the year 2016 by arrangement with Thomas Nelson.

Scripture quotations are taken from the
King James Version. Public domain. The Holy Bible,
New International Version®, NIV®.
Copyright © 1973, 1978, 1984, 2011 by Biblica, Inc.®
Used by permission of Zondervan. All rights reserved
worldwide. www.zondervan.com. The "NIV" and "New
International Version" are trademarks registered in the United
States Patent and Trademark Office by Biblica, Inc.® The
New King James Version®. © 1982 by Thomas Nelson.
Used by permission. All rights reserved.

The text of this Large Print edition is unabridged.
In other aspects, this book may vary from the original edition.
Printed in the United States of America on permanent paper.
Set in 16-point Times New Roman type.

ISBN: 978-1-68324-202-4

Library of Congress Cataloging-in-Publication Data

Names: Martin, Charles, 1969–, author.
Title: Long way gone / Charles Martin.
Description: Large print edition. | Thorndike, Maine : Center Point
Large Print, 2016.
Identifiers: LCCN 2016040403 | ISBN 9781683242024
    (hardcover : alk. paper)
Subjects: LCSH: Fathers and sons—Fiction. | Christian fiction.
Classification: LCC PS3613.A7778 L66 2016b | DDC 813/.6—dc23
LC record available at https://lccn.loc.gov/2016040403

To everyone who's ever known the pain
of watching a loved one walk away
and then stood on the porch
staring down the road.

And to every loved one
who's reached the end of that road
. . . and turned around.

PART I

1

I'd seen him before. Old guy was probably seventy-five. Maybe eighty. Gnarled, arthritic fingers. Four-packs-a-day voice. Cottony-white hair with yellowed ends. Wrinkled ebony skin. A high-mileage chassis. He wore threadbare, blue-and-gray striped pants that had previously belonged to a wool suit and a soiled white buttondown that he'd fastened clear to the top. To complete the ensemble, he wore two-toned classic oxfords. The white was dull and cracked, but what remained of the black had been polished to a spit shine.

And his guitar was as road-worn as he. It was an old Gibson J-45 and he'd strummed holes both above and below the sound hole, exposing some of the bracing. At some point he'd slapped duct tape around the back and sides. His tuners were different colors, and even at a distance his strings looked rusty. But when that old man cut loose, both he and his guitar came alive. His feet tapped in rhythm with his strum hand, adding a percussive beat and suggesting he'd also played drums somewhere. The smile on his face spoke of the memory of who he'd once been. Or believed himself to be.

I'm not picky about much, except guitars. Six strings are a passion. A polyphonic concert in which each majestic string has a voice. Truth is, I am mesmerized by the idea that we can glue together disparate pieces of wood into an hourglass-shaped box, wrap it in bracing, binding, and phosphor-bronze strings, and then apply a little of the right pressure to give rise to a voice— the sum of which is exponentially greater than the pieces it comprises and as distinctive as the hands that play it. Deep, throaty, boxy, punchy low end, scooped middle, accentuated highs . . . I can make an argument for each.

That old man's guitar had lost its voice. It was played out. So was he. But while his mind might have forgotten more music than most would ever know, his fingers had not. Where most folks saw an itinerant drunk, I tasted the residue of musical genius. At one time, this guy had been somebody.

The last few Saturdays he'd set himself up on Leadville's Main Street, sat on a bench, and played until the tips carpeted the bottom of his guitar case. Then he closed his case and disappeared inside a bottle until about Thursday. Come Friday, he was thirsty. Parched.

Like now.

I slowed with the traffic and pulled over to park. The sidewalks were crowded. He'd do well today. I parked, tucked my notebook between the small of my back and my belt, took a swig of Pepto-Bismol, downed two Tums, grabbed my guitar, and heard him before I saw him. He was sitting on a bench across from a well-known biker filling station.

Leadville is a hot spot for weekend warriors out of Vail, Aspen, Steamboat, Breckenridge, even the Springs and Fort Collins. Expensive, chromed-out, low-mileage, no-muffler bikes driven by midlife men flaunting well-decorated, siliconized, tucked-and-lifted toys. It's an old mining town and one of the highest towns in the US, as it sits above ten thousand feet. Once a prolific producer of silver, today it's a shell of its former self. The population ebbs and flows with the seasons. In the summer it's a destination spot for folks on two wheels, both motorcycles and bicycles. It's home to the Leadville 100, a grueling all-day mountain bike ride; to High Mountain Pies—some of the best pizza in the Rockies; and to Melanzana, a small, privately owned company that makes the world's best fleece jackets and sweaters right out of its shop on Main Street. The "Mellie" is standard-issue among serious Coloradans. You see one and chances are you're dealing with a native. Or a wannabe.

The old man sat just across the street from the saloon so his sound projected into the bar. Smart. He had picked a good spot, but he had two problems. The first was the smell. He hadn't showered or thought of deodorant in weeks. Possibly months. The second was the inharmonious sound coming out of both his mouth and guitar.

11

He might make some mercy money, but little more.

My next move was a little dicey. For all intents and purposes, this was his fire hydrant and I was the new dog sniffing around. The trick was to come in alongside him, or underneath him, and make him feel like he was riding on a carpet of notes. I wanted him to like my being there before he even knew I was there. Working in my favor was the fact that he was focused on his next bottle, so his peripheral vision didn't extend too far. Working against me was the fact that he was focused on his next bottle, and he'd probably want to fight if he thought I was a hindrance to that.

I knew the song he was playing, so I matched the key, and since he was strumming (or banging on the strings pretty hard), I picked around him. To the ear I was a complement, not a distraction. After about sixty seconds he noticed me, stiffened a bit, turned one shoulder, and began to sing and play louder. The sound coming out of his mouth wasn't in the same key as the sound coming out of his guitar, and shouldn't have produced the smile spread across his face. He was definitely lost in the memory of what it once sounded like.

My gamble was this—I had the feeling he'd played with other musicians before and he'd know when somebody was making him sound better. He was loosely playing in the key of E, so I sat just off to the side and continued to flat-pick an answering lick underneath him. He frowned, raised an eyebrow, and started hammering out a few riffs his fingers knew but his mind had long since forgotten. I clamped on a capo and filled the air around with a percussive strum that gave beat and timing to the old blues riffs he was sporadically hitting.

Irritated, he switched keys and began barking out an old ballad he'd probably sung ten thousand times. I adjusted the capo and played an embellishment around him, lightly filling the air with color and melody while not taking the spotlight. This was a delicate dance. His dramatic increase in volume told me he wasn't quite sure he wanted to be my partner. Not if it meant sharing his tips.

He was pivoting on his backside to stare me down when a guy in black leather dropped a twenty-dollar bill in his case. The old guy saw it, glanced at me, and actually stopped strumming to reach for it. But when I slid ever so slightly away from him—and from his case—my message must have registered somewhere in his foggy mind, and he returned to his song.

By the time it ended he was staring at forty-five dollars, and I could see the panic in his eyes; he'd hit the jackpot and was weighing the decision to cut and run.

Seeing I was about to lose him, I stood and

dropped two twenties in the case. "Mind if I play along?"

He hooked the guitar case with his right foot and pulled it closer between his legs, then pointed his right ear at me. "Huh?"

I leaned in, pushing past the smell. "I won't be any trouble."

He stared at me, at the growing crowd, back at me. Finally his eyes settled on my guitar. His words were garbled. "J-forty-fi'?"

I nodded.

He pointed once with his strumming hand, directing me back toward my post, out of his limelight. I did as instructed.

When I was a kid I had a box of sixty-four crayons —the kind with a built-in sharpener in the back. I was so enamored of all those different shades that I thought it'd be neat to melt them and see what swirl of color would result. Bad idea.

This old guy reminded me of my experiment. What was once beautiful and distinct had lost its brilliance. All the colors bled into one muddled mess of dark brown. But people are not crayons. And where wax melts and can never be recovered, the color of people is part of their DNA. We're more like stained glass in a cathedral. Somewhere along the way, something dark had been thrown over this guy, preventing the light from shining through.

In a rather inexplicable phenomenon, music makes up a small part of the frequency of waves we see with our eyes. That's right, music and light are part of the same spectrum. It's just that we hear part of that spectrum, suggesting that the angels both hear and see light, which adds a whole new dimension to the idea of daybreak, high noon, or sundown.

My job was to shine light on old glass. And when I did, that cathedral window shone glittering blue, crimson red, and royal purple.

The old man came to life.

Twenty minutes in, he glanced at me and then at the space on the bench beside him. I accepted the invitation. One of the mysteries of music is that two can achieve together what one never could do alone. The effect is exponential. It's also the only activity on Planet Earth that can transport those who hear it from place A to place B in about two beats. It can shift a mood from laughter to tears to I-can-conquer-the-world to what-if and hope. It's the original time travel machine.

The faces of the growing crowd around us spoke volumes. Moments before they had written him off as a faceless drunk. Now they were asking, "Who is this guy?" That look wasn't lost on him. The old man stood on the sidewalk and belted out melodies I doubt he'd thought of in thirty years. In his mind he was standing on the stage, and it wasn't long before his laughter mixed with his tears, proving that glass can't lose its color. It can become darkened by shadow, or painted in error, or dimmed by drink, but you can no more take the music out of a man than you can peel apart the fibers of his DNA.

Soon two girls in dresses were dancing and twirling in front of us, and when the old guy launched into "Over the Rainbow," folks started singing along. He fed off the smiles and tears and stared in amazement as bill after bill fluttered down into his case. Finally he broke out an a capella version of "What a Wonderful World" that would have made even Louis Armstrong smile.

At an hour he had run out of tricks. And breath. He was played out and huffing. It's always better to leave the audience wanting more, so I stood, signaling my time here was done.

His bloodshot eyes were having trouble focusing. Must have been several hundred dollars piled in his case. He asked, "You don't want none?"

The crowd was clapping. Whistling. I knelt in front of the old guy.

"You paid me plenty." Then I placed my guitar in his case on top of the bills.

To some, a guitar is just wood and string. To others, it's a shoulder, a jealous mistress, danger, sabbath, a voice in the wilderness, a suit of armor, a curtain to hide behind, a rock to stand on, a flying carpet, a hammer. But sometimes, in moments where light meets the dark, it's a stake we drive in the ground and the darkness rolls back as a scroll.

As I made my way through the crowd, a little kid wearing a cowboy hat and a buckle almost as big as the hat tugged on my shirt. "Mister?"

I turned. "Hey there."

He held up a piece of paper. "Can I have your autograph?" He looked up at the man next to him. "My daddy says I should get your autograph now 'cause even though you look like you live way back in the mountains, you're gonna be somebody someday."

"Really?" I signed his paper, handed it back, and knelt beside him. "You play?"

"Yes, sir." He stood a little straighter. "Banjo."

"You practicing your rolls?"

He nodded, then pointed at the scars on my right hand. "Does that hurt?"

"Not anymore."

"What happened?"

I held it up, opening and closing my fist. "When I was young and foolhardy, some stuff fell on me."

"Like a barbell or a brick or something?"

"No, more like the ceiling."

He pointed toward my voice box. "You always whisper when you talk?"

"Unfortunately."

"Why?"

"I got caught in a fire."

"A fire made it sound like that?"

"Actually, the flames weren't too bad, but the heat mixed with some toxic fumes and did this." I smiled. "Makes me sound like I'm angry all the time."

"Daddy says he'll blister me if he catches me messing with matches."

I laughed. "You should probably steer clear."

As I started to stand, he tugged on me again. "Mister?"

"Yeah."

He touched my beard, allowing his fingers to tell his mind that I was real and not the scary man behind the scars. "I don't think you sound angry."

His words filtered down and into my heart where they met the welcoming echo of my father's voice. *Out of the mouth of babes you have perfected praise so that you might silence the enemy and the avenger.*

I liked that kid. "Thanks, pal."

When I turned around and looked back a block later, the old guy was playing my guitar. His eyes were as wide as his open mouth, and the smile on his face was worth a lot more than that pile of cash.

2

I drove south playing the kid's words over and over in my mind. The rearview reflected me back at myself, speaking a truth I'd long tried to bury. Shoulder-length, dirty blondish hair. Darker beard showing some gray. *Scruffy* would be one impression. *Mountain man* might be another. *Homeless* wouldn't be a stretch. Over the years I'd tried to hide the scars on my chest, back, neck, and right ear. When I "covered up" I found that people reacted more favorably to me. That said, I did look a bit scary. My right hand on the steering wheel caught my eye. I straightened my fingers and then made and remade a fist. Other than wearing a glove, there wasn't much I could do about that. Some things you just can't hide.

The Jeep was thirsty so I stopped for gas on the edge of town. Ambient noise filled the air around me. The slosh of gasoline filling the tank. Trucks on the highway muffled with the hum and *womp womp* of snow tires. A couple arguing as they came out of the mini-mart. A semi driving over a steel manhole cover, first the front wheel, then the back. A bulldozer and an excavator working in tandem in a lot behind me. A siren several blocks off, followed by a second. Kids playing basketball somewhere over my shoulder.

Given the mix of noise, any single sound was tough to follow. Like gnats at a barbecue. But every few seconds the noise would thin, and above it hung a melody. Someone was singing.

I looked down the road and saw a woman standing in the dirt, just off the highway. Thumb in the air. Too far away to see her features, but I could tell she wasn't young. Peroxide-blonde hair falling out of a purple beanie. Sky-blue Patagonia puffer jacket. Faded jeans tucked into scuffed cowboy boots. A backpack at her feet. And a guitar case. A little thin. Looked like she could use a cheeseburger.

I would not say her voice was overly strong. In fact, it sounded tired. But weary or not, it possessed one thing that most did not. Near perfect pitch. Not to mention she had canary-like control of her vocal cords.

There was something oddly familiar about it. But just as quickly as I latched onto it, it ended. The wind swirled, brushed my face, and brought the memory of a smell I once knew.

As I watched, a rusted-out, green, long-bed Ford with a snowplow attached to the front pulled over. Not unusual for late September in Colorado. Three people sat in the front seat, two in the bed. I saw the woman nod, then lift her pack and her guitar into the bed and climb over the tail-gate, displaying strength, grace, and a distance-setting amount of self-confidence. The truck descended into the valley in a cloud of smoke.

Lost in the distant residue of something familiar that I still couldn't place, and trying to gather the last of those notes as they faded off into the air, I was suddenly snapped back to earth by gas spilling out of my tank and sloshing onto my shoes. Up here the veil is thin, and it's easy to get lost.

Plus, I've always had a thing for girls who can sing.

I pulled back onto the road and stared out into one of the more majestic windshield-framed settings in all of Colorado: the road west and south out of Leadville toward Buena Vista. Through the glass in front of me the sun had set behind the snowcapped peaks of La Plata, Mt. Elbert, and Mt. Massive. The sheer enormity stretched beyond my side mirrors. Between them lay the deep scenic and historic cut of Independence Pass that led into the jet-set lifestyles of Aspen and Snow Mass.

Colorado is like a girl I once knew. Beautiful in any light. When the light or angle changes, some-thing new is revealed. Something hidden rises to the surface. In late September and early October, the light in Colorado shifts. Snow dusts the peaks. The color in the trees has peaked and begun draining out. Colorado in the fall is a peek into the throne room. Colorado in winter is majesty defined. A declaration.

When God carved this place with His words, He lingered.

I pulled into Buena Vista forty-five minutes later to see blue puffer girl sitting on the curb. Head in her hands. Feet in the gutter. One shoulder leaned against the pole of a parking meter. Her Patagonia jacket was torn and one side soiled with skid marks. Small down feathers spilled out of a hole in the shoulder and a few fluttered on the breeze or snagged in her hair. Her jeans were ripped at the knee. The guitar case was gone, and scattered about her lay the pieces of what was once the guitar. The green truck was nowhere in sight.

I sat at the stoplight, my Jeep idling, and stared at her. The light turned green, but traffic this time of evening was pretty light. I sat through the light cycle, watching as she stood and tried to shoulder her backpack. Her right hand was bloody, badly bruised and possibly broken. She brushed the hair out of her eyes but the beanie had fallen down, slanting at the same angle as her body. Blood trickled out from underneath it. Unstable, she clung to the parking meter and tried to catch her balance.

I kicked the emergency brake on and hopped out of my Jeep just in time to see her eyes roll back and her head slump forward. She lost her grip on the pole and toppled.

Into my arms.

I stood on the sidewalk holding a bleeding woman I did not know. I grabbed her pack and walked her to the Jeep, where the intoxicating smell of her wafted up and wrapped itself around me. There it was again. The same fragrance I'd smelled while pumping gas. I sat her up and pulled the beanie off her head because it was covering up her mouth, and I thought she'd do well to get some air. Only then did I see her face.

I stood up straight. *No way. Can't be.*

I leaned in, tilted my head to match the angle of hers, and looked a second time. The hair color had fooled me, and like me, she'd aged. But then there was the smell, and there was no mistaking Coco Chanel. Especially when she wore it. I spoke out loud. "You've got to be kidding me."

I drove three blocks to the hospital and came to a stop in short-term parking while she bled on my seat belt. I doubted her injuries were serious, but the lump rising on her forehead indicated a pretty good thump. I lifted her off the passenger seat and carried her through the front door.

The receptionist was a sweet, plump woman who liked fuzzy navels and tequila shots. Gigging local bars tells you a lot about people's thirst-quenching habits.

"Little help, Doris?" I said.

She saw the unconscious woman dripping blood on the tile and pushed a button that automatically opened two large doors to my right. I carried the woman into the ER and Doris followed, peppering me with questions.

"What happened, Cooper?"

"Don't know."

"How'd she end up bleeding and in your arms?"

"I saw her at the stoplight."

She brushed the hair out of her face and sucked between her teeth. "Did you hit her?"

"No, I didn't hit her."

"What were you doing at the stoplight?"

"Doris, is there someplace I can lay her down?"

She pointed, and I laid the woman on a table.

"Cooper." Doris looked at me over the top of her reading glasses. "You hiding something? You need to call your lawyer?"

"Doris, you been watching too much CSI. Will you just call the doctor?"

Doris didn't really like me because over the years I had repeatedly refused her advances, which increased in frequency and severity as she moved into her third and fourth fuzzy navels. She frowned and tapped her clipboard with a pencil. Her eyes walked up and down me with a mixture of two parts desire and one part disapproval. She scratched her scalp with the tip of her pencil.

"You happen to know her name? Anything is better than 'Jane Doe.' "

"Yeah, actually, I do."

She waited.

"Doris, meet Daley Cross."

Doris leaned in. The skin between her eyes wrinkled. " 'When-I-got-where-I-was-going' Daley Cross?" She raised both her eyebrows.

I nodded. "The very same."

I propped Daley's head gently on a pillow and said good-bye to Doris. I even made it to the seat of the Jeep . . .

But twenty minutes later the doctor found me sitting in the waiting room with a bad cup of vending machine coffee.

"Cooper."

I shook his hand. "Hey, Bill."

"Doris says you know the patient?"

"Long time ago."

"Well, she bumped her noggin pretty good. Slight concussion. Might have a headache for a day or so. A deep contusion in her hand where somebody slammed it in the truck door. Possibly a break in there somewhere, but if so it's a hairline and won't show up on X-ray for a couple weeks. Either way, she'll be sore a few days." He paused. "What have you got to do with all this?"

"I was stopped at the light. She collapsed. Here we are."

"You didn't see whatever happened?"

"No. I saw her hitch a ride back in Leadville, but I didn't recognize her at the time. Or the truck."

He stared out the window. "What color was it?"

"Faded green. Yellow snowplow. Long-bed Ford. Salt rust around the wheel wells."

He pointed to a far corner of the parking lot. "Like that one?"

I looked. "The very same."

"I just put fifteen stitches in the scalp of a long-haired bubba in overalls. Said he fell."

"She had a guitar," I offered.

He turned and looked down a long hallway, then back at me. "I'll take care of him."

"She be here overnight?"

"I can't very well send her home. She's sleeping now. We'll monitor her. Probably discharge tomorrow early."

I turned toward the double doors and flashed my cell phone. "Let me know if that changes."

He glanced over his shoulder. "You really know Daley Cross?"

I shook my head. "Twenty years ago. Another lifetime."

"Wow. What was her big hit called?" He searched his memory. " 'Long Time Coming'?"

I didn't bother to correct him. "Something like that."

"Wow. A one-hit wonder right here in Buena Vista. I've always wondered what happened to people like that."

"Actually, she was a four-hit wonder."

"By the looks of things, her luck has not improved." He looked hesitant to speak. "Judging by the dirt, I think she spent the last few nights along the road somewhere. She's also pretty dehydrated, so I ran an IV. I'll keep it dripping most of the night."

"Thanks. You've got my cell." I headed out to the parking lot, jumped in the Jeep, cranked the engine, and tried not to look in the rearview.

It wasn't easy.

3

The Roastery is the local morning hangout in Buena Vista. The epicenter of town until nearly noon. From there folks mosey across the street to the Trailhead—the local gear shop and farm-to-table lunch venue—where they move from coffee to local IPAs. The Trailhead is also where most of those "currently in transition," aka the unemployed, spend their afternoons sitting at tables with window views of the street, staring at their phones and trying to look like they're doing something important. Most are playing solitaire.

Dinner options include Eddyline—an award-winning microbrewery that cooks up a decent pizza. The Asian Palace serves surprisingly good tempura and sushi, which is a bit of a mystery given its distance from the coast. A strategically parked food truck serves up a mean fish taco, while next door one man's moonshine infatuation has found honest expression in the

Deerhammer Distillery. The local favorite is a drink called a Black Bison. Seems a writer came to town a few years back and made some subtle changes to a Buffalo Negra, and today the Black Bison is the Buena Vista signature and its attraction has spread. It's been added to menus in Steamboat, Vail, and Aspen, and folks come from as far away as Florida just to sip one.

Like much of high-altitude Colorado, BV started out as a drinking town with a mining problem, and little has changed.

I was first in line when the Roastery opened at seven. I ordered two triple-shot Honey Badgers and drove slowly to the hospital, trying to talk myself out of actually walking in. I parked, cut the engine, and continued to argue with myself. Finally I told myself to shut up and walked through the front doors. I rode the elevator to the fourth floor, and the nurse pointed me to room 410.

When I walked in the lights were off, but a soft sunlight washed through the window. Daley was sitting up, staring out the window, her right hand wrapped in an Aircast and resting on her lap. A couple fingers were puffy. The bump on her head was gone, but the purple remained. When she turned and saw me, her jaw dropped. She covered her mouth and her eyes filled.

All she could manage was a whisper. "Coop . . ." Her voice cracked. "Oh my . . ." She lifted her knees to her chest like she'd grown accustomed to hugging herself. I walked over to the edge of the bed, set the coffee cups on the bedside table, and sat with my hands folded in my lap—bringing us eye to eye.

For several minutes she just sat there, shaking her head. Tears puddling. Her eyes had always been golf-ball big and Oreo-round. And big eyes make for big tears. Finally one cracked loose and cascaded down her cheek.

She slid a hand across the sheet. Palm up. An invitation. "How are you?"

I stretched my hands across the side of the bed and cradled hers in mine. She studied the scars on my right hand, tracing the longest with the tip of her index finger. A second tear followed the first. "Nashville?"

I spoke softly. "Yeah."

"Is it okay?"

I shrugged and tried to smile. Making and remaking a fist. "It gets the job done. Tells me when a storm is coming."

She was hesitant to ask. "Do you . . . do you still . . . ?"

I nodded. "Some. When I can."

She reached out and was about to touch her fingertips to my throat, then thought better of it. "Your voice is so different. You sound like the Godfather."

I cleared my throat. "It comes in handy with

people who call and try and sell me something."

She laughed quietly, and the weight sitting on her shoulders rolled to the edges, where it teetered. It would either fall outward and release her, or inward where it would crush what remained of her. She glanced around the room. Confusion on her face. "Do you know how I got here?"

"I pulled up to the stoplight and saw you clinging to a parking meter. I caught you as you fell. Didn't know it was you until I got you in the Jeep and headed here."

She was having a tough time putting the pieces together. "You live here?"

I sipped. "Yep."

She looked confused. "You pick up my guitar?"

"Only pieces remained. Some splinters on the sidewalk. Got your pack, though."

The loss registered. I offered her a coffee. "The Roastery is our local coffee shop. They make a concoction called a Honey Badger that, if you add a triple shot, will start your day off the way God intended it to be started."

She sipped and nodded, but while the coffee began lifting the medication haze, it did little to move the gorilla on her shoulder. We sat there in silence. I handed her a tissue and pointed at her lip. "You got some foam—"

She wiped her mouth and dabbed her eyes and tried to laugh. "I was saving it for later."

I broke the awkwardness. "Where you headed?"

"Biloxi. A casino offered me a stage . . . and a room. I can wait tables too . . ." An embarrassed shrug. She didn't need to say more.

"You have a second guitar stashed someplace?"

She shook her head.

"How're you getting there?"

She smiled and stuck her thumb in the air.

"Got a place to stay meanwhile?"

"Wasn't planning on staying." She pointed at her backpack. "I've got a map of hostels. Some nights I can play at a bar nearby or . . . save a bit to get me to the next town. It's just till I get to Mississippi."

Dr. Bill walked in at this point. "How you feeling this morning?" He lifted the stethoscope out of the pocket of his white jacket and began listening to her heart.

She looked at him with one eye half closed. "Better if the world would stop spinning."

"You took a pretty good thump." He shined a small light in the side of her pupils and then held her wrist, counting her pulse. He inspected her hand. "How's this feeling?"

"Tender."

"Take something for pain. Ice it. Give it a few days. Nothing permanent. You have any questions?"

"I'm okay to leave?"

He looped the stethoscope around his neck and eyed the empty bag of fluids hanging above her.

"Give me a few minutes to process your papers and we'll get you out of here. But you need to lay low. No travel for a few days. No excitement. No bright lights. No computers. No texting. Rest is your friend."

He walked out and I asked, "You hungry?"

Her shoulders tipped farther and the weight fell. Outward. "I could eat a little something."

After the nurse removed the IV and helped Daley dress, we walked down the hall toward the exit, where the sun was burning a hole right through my retinas. I handed Daley my Costas. "These'll help."

She put them on, and when the doors slid open we bumped into the bubba with the stitches in his head. He puffed up and growled in a loud voice, "There's that bi—"

If I thought she'd have trouble taking up for herself, I had another thing coming. He barely got the *bi* out of his mouth when Daley's boot caught him square in the groin. He probably dressed out near three hundred, but her foot lifted him off his heels and set him on his knees, where he began heaving. As he knelt there emptying his breakfast on the floor, she dumped her Honey Badger on his head. "That's for my Hummingbird, you fat, greasy, foulmouthed, bucktoothed jackwagon."

She wobbled a bit, and I caught her where she locked her arm in mine as we walked toward the parking lot. I cracked a smile. "I thought the doc said no excitement."

"I'm not excited."

I helped her up into the Jeep. "I'd hate to see you when you are."

4

We sat in a booth at the Roastery, where Daley sipped her second Honey Badger and nibbled on a piece of quiche. She hovered over her cup. "You're right, this is really good."

"You kind of wasted that last one."

"Sorry." She eyed the menu board above us. "If I'd have known how much it cost—"

"It's no trouble." The circles beneath her eyes told me she hadn't slept in a couple years. "What happened?"

"Well, he was kneeling there on the floor and I thought—"

"No, last night. The green Ford."

She softened. "Just a couple of yahoos being yahoos."

"Where were you coming from?"

"I had a gig last night at this saloon in Leadville. Actually, it started late afternoon. Singing covers for bikers. But"—her face soured—"I got upstaged by two guys on the street. They emptied the bar. One of them was really good.

33

Left me alone with the bartender. So I packed up and hitched a ride here."

I didn't bother to tell her my role in that. "How'd your guitar get mixed up in it?"

"The yahoos wanted more than conversation." She sat back and shrugged. Her eyelids were heavy. "Decided they'd take it." She turned the table. "Have you lived here all this time?"

"I traveled around the first few years. Eventually circled back around. It's home."

She pushed the quiche around her plate. "Cooper—"

I held up a hand. "You don't have to. Long time ago. A lot of water under that bridge. Say, have you thought past the next couple of hours?"

Her top lip was covered with steamed milk froth again. She held up her cup, staring at the contents. "I'm thinking about moving here and applying for a job. They can pay me in these things." She laughed and extended her arm, showing the Band-Aid that covered the hole from her IV. "Let them drip into the same vein." Her laugh was easy and, like her voice, deep with resonation. She looked up and down the street. "What's the name of this town again? Dolce Vita? La Vita Loca?"

I laughed. "Buena Vista."

"Close enough."

"You got a place to stay?"

She shook her head.

"I keep an apartment here in town if you need a place."

"You have a home someplace else?"

"I split time between my mountain home up there beyond the clouds"—I pointed west toward the salt cliffs and the pass that led beyond St. Elmo—"and my apartment down here. Where I lay my head is often a function of the weather."

"Tell me about it." She leaned her head on one hand. "Sleep sounds good. If you don't mind."

The drive west down Main Street took us past the Lariat Bar and Grill. It's a town staple, rooted in the lore that actual cowboys used to belly up and down the dust. Town legend holds that at least one recorded gunfight spilled out into the street. Locals reenact it every year. Some say you can still see bloodstains on the wood floor; others say that dark spot is an oil stain from the time the room served as the garage for the volunteer fire department. Whatever the case, the stains are part of the romance of what is now the town bar and watering hole. And based on the traffic, this is a thirsty town. The bar smells of stale beer, wet cigarettes, and greasy French fries. The waitresses —who were once rodeo darlings and home-coming queens warmed by their boyfriends' letter jackets —sell cold draft beer and will bend an attentive ear, provided your tips are generous. But people with sensible taste will tell you that

35

any use of the word grill in connection with the Lariat is a rather liberal definition. There is a griddle, and they do serve food, but that's about all you can say. The one thing they do really well is live music.

Daley read the sign and asked, "Is that place also known as 'The Rope'?"

"You've heard of it?"

She stared out the Jeep window. Lost in foggy moments that happened years before this one. She chewed on a fingernail. "The manager'll let you play for tips." She was still a second, then suddenly sat up straight and checked her wrist for a watch that wasn't there. "Oh snap! What's today?"

"Saturday."

She palmed her face with her left hand, closed her eyes, and let out a heavy breath. I pulled over to the curb and pushed in the clutch. The Jeep sat idling. I waited.

After a minute she said, "I'm playing there tonight. Or I was. But—" She held up her hand and spoke without looking at me. "I could really use that hundred dollars."

"Frank got you for a hundred?"

"You know him?"

I thought before I answered. "We've met." We were parked on the side of the road next to the railroad tracks. I glanced in the rearview and asked, "How's your voice?"

She shrugged. "Not what it once was."

"No, I mean from yesterday."

"I can sing."

I made a U-turn, drove three blocks east toward the river and Sleeping Indian Mountain, and parked next to the Ptarmigan Theatre. "Wait here a few minutes?"

She nodded. As I hopped up on the sidewalk, she called after me, "Cooper?"

"Yeah?"

"If you're not . . . I mean . . . I don't know that I have the strength to sit here and . . ." She shook her head ever so slightly.

Sometimes it's not what people say but what they don't say that shows how beat down their soul really is. Somebody, or something, had hurt her. A lot. I set the keys on the seat. "Well, if I don't come back, you can keep the Jeep."

She set her feet on the dash and laid her head back, and the wrinkle between her eyes faded.

I keep an apartment in the loft of the Ptarmigan. I use it in the winter when the snow and ice drive me down out of the mountains.

I ran in and grabbed an old Martin D-35 that had become a favorite of mine. Her name was Ella, and she was born in Pennsylvania to German and Brazilian parents sometime in the seventies. She and I met fifteen years ago at a pawnshop in Taos where the chemistry was quick and electric—in an acoustic sort of way. She's throaty, tender, will bark if you dig into her, and yet she'll lift you off your seat if you loosen up on the reins and let her voice speak. I'd named her after a character in a book. This guitar reminded me of Miss Ella and her rich, pure, multilayered, resonating voice. Whenever she opened her mouth to speak you'd do well to listen, because what she said would soon find its way to your heart, where it would peel back the layers and either pierce you or heal you.

I walked back to find Daley sitting at a picnic table beneath an umbrella that spun in the breeze. I unlocked the case, set Ella on my knee, and sat there tuning her.

Daley watched me with amusement. "You know they now have these little electronic thingies that work pretty well."

I smiled without looking up. "You don't say." When I finished, I strummed a few chords and then placed my hand flat across the strings, muting it. Abruptly I turned toward her. "Sing something."

She spoke slowly, raising one eyebrow. "Just. Sing. Something?"

"Anything you want."

Without warming up or making some show of apology, she opened her mouth and poured out a sultry, silky Dusty Springfield tune about Billy Ray being a preacher's son. I nearly melted on the bench.

I've always had a soft spot for the preacher's kid. She knew that. I knew she knew that. And she knew I knew she knew. Which made it that much more fun.

In two seconds I was twenty years younger. The pitch was so perfect and tone so true I almost didn't touch the strings for fear of blurring her beautiful sound. The words rolled off her tongue with a rhythm and cadence pushed by a voice that held a sense of longing. While powerful, it contained a disarming vulnerability. When we were talking, Daley's walls were jagged and Jericho high. Impenetrable. But the moment she opened her mouth and the first note rang out, the gates flung wide. Proving that the music in her was DNA-deep. As much a part of her as her sea-blue eyes. And the only clear window through which she viewed, and understood, the world.

She paused at the end of a line and smiled. "You gonna play or just sit there looking dumb and wonder-struck?" When she sang the part about Billy Ray being the only one to ever reach her, she glanced at me.

Causing me to wonder if she was just singing a song, or talking about us.

5

Describing music is tricky. I'm not convinced that you can describe it like, say, a painting or a novel. While those are both experiences that produce feelings, they do so through the window of the eyes. The image we see—either images or words on a page—enters our eyes, travels through our intellect, where we make some sort of sense of it, and then routes through our emotions. The process is one of intellect and understanding first, emotions and feelings second.

In my experience, music doesn't work that way. Music enters us through the ears, where it makes a beeline to the grid of our emotions. Then it routes through to our intellect where we might "make some sense" of it. Music is felt on one level, and understood or processed on another. This doesn't mean you can't use your intellect to describe it . . . but I question whether the words we use can really do the job. It's like describing the smell of the number 9.

Music is meant to be experienced, not described.

Music has its own language, shared by musicians, and it is just as real a language as Greek or Latin and, if you're new to it, just as complicated. The key to deciphering the language of music is do-re-mi. And yes, it really is Rodgers-and-Hammerstein simple.

For you nonmusical people, this do-re-mi stuff is called "scales."

Scales are the building blocks. The inherent order in music. They are as real as gravity and are hardwired into our DNA. Like preloaded topographical maps. Proof of that hardwiring is seen in our ability to know where a song is going musically the first time we hear it. For a singer or musician, the challenge comes in getting their fingers and hands and voice to make the corresponding sounds. So here is point number two. To really play music, or speak the language, one thing is required. And for it there is no substitute.

Practice.

People can cheat their way to the top in a lot of areas of life. They can steal, bribe, kill the competition, or take steroids to make them stronger and faster. But with music there's no shortcut.

Period.

Fake it and people will throw tomatoes. Listeners can spot a fraud a mile away. That's why standing on a stage or singing on a sidewalk can be such a gutsy proposition. It's why lip-syncers are stripped of their awards and then drawn and quartered on the city gates. Despite this age of tolerance, we will not tolerate a fraud onstage. We value music and we value performance and we expect those who play or sing to do the same.

My ear had always been pretty good. I was one of those folks born with a propensity. My dad used to say that I sang before I talked. So when Daley opened her mouth, the question for me was simple. It wasn't "What song is she singing?" but rather "What key is she singing in?" Said another way, "Where is she in do-re-mi?"

My job was not to compete, not to show her what I knew, not to show her how good I was or had become. My job was to create a shelf, a platform. Scaffolding. To fill the air around her with a structure. Something safe.

Daley smiled. Leaving Dusty Springfield behind, she slapped her right thigh with both hands, creating a chain-gang rhythm, and dropped into a Johnny Cash tune called "God's Gonna Cut You Down." Lower. Deeper. Gravel mixed with soda water.

I smiled and modulated to a new key right along with her. Anytime you start singing Johnny Cash, you're walking on hallowed ground. The thought was not lost on me that the Man in Black most often played a Martin D-35.

She seemed amused. A kid on a playground. Having evidently thought of someplace else she wanted to go, she raised her chin and slipped sideways musically. I softened my touch and listened, wanting to hear where she was going.

So started a rather interesting game of musical cat and mouse.

Her voice became softer, less gravel, more gold. My second-favorite Elvis tune, "In the Ghetto." Anyone who tackles Elvis has got some chutzpah. But not nearly as much as someone who attempts Michael Jackson. I had just caught up with her when she crossed the stratosphere again and lifted out the dross. This time there were no impurities. Mere mortals don't sing "I'll Be There." That's like stepping into the ring with Godzilla. You're about to have your lunch handed to you.

Apparently no one had ever informed Daley of this. With all the care and weight of someone filing their nails with an emery board, she opened her mouth and, so help me, I thought the King of Pop himself had hopped up on the hood of the Jeep. No sooner had she sung the chorus than she reached way back, maybe 1930-something, and belted out Robert Johnson's "Sweet Home Chicago." By the time I had caught up with her, she'd tired of that and jumped trains midtrack to Hank Williams's "I'm So Lonesome I Could Cry." And while she sounded lonesome, I doubted whether a whip-poor-will ever sounded that hauntingly pure.

People passing on the sidewalk stopped to listen as we traveled through the Allman Brothers' "Midnight Rider," Lynyrd Skynyrd's southern anthem, and Bob Marley's "No Woman, No Cry."

By the time she broke into Marvin Gaye's "Ain't No Mountain High Enough," a loose crowd had gathered. No bother. If I thought she was enjoying singing for me, the addition of an audience added another dimension. From John Denver's "Rocky Mountain High" to Ray Charles's "Georgia on My Mind," she finally let loose with CCR's "Fortunate Son."

To say she still had vocal range would be an understatement of biblical proportions. The melody and the medley were magical. The only thing more magical was how she so effortlessly made each song her own. You know you're in the company of someone pretty gifted when the cover they're singing can compete with the original. When she finished, she simply closed her mouth and folded her good hand across the Aircast. She wasn't even breathing hard—and Buena Vista sits at almost eight thousand feet.

In twenty minutes of "play that tune," the trick for me was to be good while not too good. I wanted her to think I could play alongside her in a bar. Nothing more. I throttled back, bringing little attention to myself. Never leading.

She paused a minute, tapping her top lip with her index finger and squinting one eye. I knew she was searching for the next song, and I thought to myself, *This ought to be good.*

A sly smile spread across her face as she sat

back, crossed her arms, and launched into Patsy Cline's "I Fall to Pieces" with the same ease as a kid singing "I Dig Dirt."

At this point a man in a cowboy hat walked over and dropped twenty dollars in my guitar case. Daley stood and hugged him—to which he tipped his hat—and never missed a note or a single inflection.

And while she stood there commanding the attention of most on Main Street, I had two thoughts: her voice, while not what it once was, was still really good. Her vocal control and bravado were probably better. But the thing I just couldn't wrap my head around had nothing to do with her talent and everything to do with her choice of songs. Every song she sang had been made famous by someone now dead. There was not a living artist among them. Also of glaring importance was the fact that she didn't sing a single one of her own songs.

Not one.

As this thought was filtering its way down through me, she turned to me. "Is there anyplace I can go that you can't follow?"

"Probably. But it might take us awhile to get there."

She looked at my hand, then back at me. "When did you start playing again?"

"Few years after I got back."

"But I thought your hand was . . ."

"It was."

"What'd you do?"

"Nine or ten thousand reps of five or six different hand exercises."

"You're better now than you were back when." She had her back to the street now, and folks decided the show was over and started to drift away.

"I don't know." I studied my hand, straightening my fingers, then making a fist. "I felt like I played pretty well back in the day."

A nod. "You did."

"Speaking of guitars," I said, "whatever happened to that McPherson?"

Her chin dropped. Eyes darted. The confident troubadour had been instantly replaced by the almost-made-it or, worse, the has-been. A shrug. "Rent money."

"Loved the sound of that one."

We were poking around the edges of a lot of history. If this conversation went much deeper, we'd rip off a scab that had been twenty years in growing, and I was pretty sure the adhesive in my heart wouldn't hold.

She deflected. "You know, your long hair, gnarled hand, and jacked-up voice really disguise the fact that you're as good as you are. This town has no idea, does it?"

"I play some now and then."

She glanced in the direction of the Lariat a

few blocks away, then back at me. She looked embarrassed. "Fifty-fifty split? But what's-his-name takes 10 percent."

"Keep it." Her tips-only offer told me that Frank was skimming more off the top. "And let me see what I can do about the money."

Her next question totally caught me off guard.

"You ever marry?"

I was looking up into the sun. "What?"

She bristled, as she had with Mr. Overalls in the hospital. A self-protective mechanism that blossomed out of necessity. She pressed me. "Did you ever marry?"

"Why?"

"Because I need to know whether I'm going to turn around and find a Mrs. O'Connor pointing a gun in my face 'cause she thinks I'm an old flame and we have a new spark going."

A fair question. "You have some experience with this sort of thing?"

The hair was still standing up on her neck. "Some."

"No."

"No as in, 'There is no Mrs. O'Connor'? Or no as in, 'She won't think that'?"

"Not married. Never have been."

Her voice and head dropped in unison. "Good." She fussed with her hands. "I don't mean good, you've never married. I just mean good as in I'm too tired to fight today."

Daley's emotional posture was akin to that of a woman with her sleeves rolled up. With no protector and no defender, she'd been forced to fend for herself, and what was once soft and tender had become a thickened, distrusting hide. Sitting on that bench, she was Rosie the Riveter who had made peace with the fact that Joe was never coming home.

Twenty years ago, when I was staring at a hospital ceiling and running through the possibilities in my mind, this one had never occurred to me. I did not like it.

I shot a glance at my watch. "We've got a few hours before we need to be at the Lariat, and I need to be somewhere meanwhile. How about if I drop you—"

"Can I come?"

"It's not the most uplifting of places."

"I won't be any trouble."

"The smell can be a bit . . . overwhelming."

She chuckled. "You should see some of the places I've played."

"It might require a little participation."

"I'm game."

I smiled. "That'd be great. She'd love that."

"She?"

"My girlfriend."

Daley stiffened. "I thought you said you weren't attached."

"No," I said, smiling and lifting one finger in

the air. "I said I'd never been married. Never said I didn't have a girlfriend."

More bristling. Her spine was ramrod straight. "She going to be okay with me?"

I smiled. "I think you can say that." I was climbing into the Jeep, while she had yet to stand.

"What makes you so sure?"

"Just a hunch."

6

Riverview Center is a five-acre, forty-bed assisted living facility set against the granite backdrop of Sleeping Indian Mountain. Picturesque and manicured grounds are both maintained and molested by a healthy herd of flower-eating deer and bordered by the Arkansas River, which produces the constant and tranquil sound of rushing water.

I crossed the short bridge spanning the Arkansas, wound down the drive lined with giant cottonwoods, and parked. It was early afternoon, and most everybody was either napping or in their rooms watching TV. I parked and hopped out, and Daley followed. Her spine was more nimble—less porcupine.

We walked through the lobby, and I wound down the halls until I got to Mary's room. The door was closed. I pushed it open and found her sleeping, so we sat quietly. This was some of my favorite time with Mary. When she slept, she didn't twitch.

Daley surveyed the room and the wall decorations. She whispered, "You should've told me."

"After I started playing again, I was looking for a safe place to wet my toe. Folks here are just grateful for the company, and they aren't too picky if you miss a note here and there or sing off-key. Plus, they're rather captive. Mary was one of the first people I played for. In getting to know her, I realized that we had something in common."

"Like what?"

"We're both Daley Cross fans."

Daley surveyed the walls, which had been plastered with Daley Cross paraphernalia.

"Only she's a groupie," I said. "It's borderline obnoxious."

Mary's dark hair had fallen over her face and drool spilled onto her pillow. I pushed her hair behind her ear and dabbed the corner of her mouth. She blinked and smiled, and immediately the twitch returned.

Mary has severe strabismus—or crossed eyes. When one eye looks at you, the other looks perpendicular, showing you only the white. The focusing eye alternates from left to right and back to left and then back to right. Her right eye zeroed in on me and she lifted her head, allowing me to slide a second pillow beneath it. Her voice was raspy and broken, like Katharine Hepburn's. "I was just dreaming about you."

I scooted the stainless steel stool on wheels closer to the bed and rested my arms next to her. "Yeah, what about?"

"The first time you played for me."

"In truth, I think I played for everyone on the hall."

"Yeah, but you couldn't take your eyes off me."

I laughed. "True." Her right hand was starting to flop around like a fish, so I slid my hand beneath hers and held on to it. She had the softest skin I'd ever known. "Still can't."

Over the years Mary has tried umpteen medications to slow the progression and effects of cerebral palsy. Little has worked. Almost nothing has stifled the twitching.

Except one thing. When I play, she doesn't twitch at all. And she says the ache "washes out" of her.

Mary has been here most of her adult life. She is the darling of the house and seldom has to ask for anything.

A nurse knocked and then let herself in. She waved at me. "Hey, Cooper."

"Hey, Shelly. How's Peter?" I stood and helped roll Mary onto her side, then adjusted the privacy sheet to allow Shelly to change Mary's diaper.

Shelly has done this several thousand times. She could do it in her sleep.

"That little joker switched from tuba to drums. Says he's got more rhythm than the other three percussionists put together and it's about time everybody knew it."

Mary's arm rose up from behind the sheet and interrupted us by pushing my chin away from the bed, thereby averting my eyes. "You better not be looking. I'm still a woman, you know."

I spoke toward the wall. "No more important member of any band than the drummer. Everybody lives and dies on the beat. Don't always get a lot of respect, but they are the tether that holds everybody together."

Shelly rolled Mary onto her back and carried the wet diaper toward the door. "That may be, but if the Energizer Bunny don't get his chemistry grade up, the only rhythm he's liable to hear is my foot kicking him in his—" She mouthed the final word.

"Can't help you there."

Shelly left Mary and me laughing. The laugh brought about a congested cough—something I'd not heard out of Mary in a long time. She coughed some more and broke some stuff loose.

I gave her my stern face. "Has Dr. George heard that?"

"He was in here last week and again this morning." She pointed at a bottle on the table next to her. "Nuclear antibiotics. Supposed to kill the plague." Her focusing eye now switched from right to left. It rolled away from me toward Daley, who was sitting in a chair against the wall. Mary looked surprised to find a third person in the room.

"Oh, hi. Didn't see you." She reached for her coke-bottle glasses, put them on, and pushed them up her nose. Her head tilted sideways as she studied Daley's face. Taking her time, Mary's head reversed direction. Finally it came to rest in the middle. "It's you."

Daley stood and held out her hand. "Hi, I'm Da—"

Mary grabbed Daley's hand with both of hers. "I know who you are." She waved her hand across the walls. "I just can't believe you're standing in my room."

One of my jobs here is entertainment. Actually, that's my only job. As part of that mission, I'd repaired Dad's bus and taken as many residents and their nurses as could fit to concerts around the area. Never an overnight. Just there and back. And Daley Cross was a house favorite. Anytime she sang within a few hours' drive of Buena Vista, I'd hear calls for a road trip. From each of those Mary had kept ticket stubs and programs and marquis posters, and each was now framed and displayed on the walls about us. A living Daley Cross memorial.

Mary looked at me, wiped her hair out of her

face, and reached for the lipstick next to her bed. "You should have told me."

"Would you have believed me?"

"No. But you should've tried."

She pulled off the lipstick cap, but her hand was shaking too bad. She was about to make a mess. Daley sat next to the bed. "May I?"

Mary tried to lie still while Daley applied her lipstick. Mary's body expressed the emotion her face could not. When they'd finished, I laid my guitar case across the foot of Mary's bed, released the brake that stopped the wheels, and began pushing her through the wide door. "You ready, honey?"

"I guess you're not going to tell me what's going on, are you?"

"Nope."

She held Daley's hand as we walked down the hall.

"Cooper O'Connor!"

"Yes, ma'am."

"You owe me."

I laughed. "Then consider this my propitiation."

Her nose curled upward. "Pro-pitchy-what?"

The hallway ended in a large open room where a large black man wearing a suit and black patent leather shoes sat quietly warming up his fingers on an upright piano. He spoke over his shoulder. "Propitiation."

Mary turned. "Not you too."

He began playing louder. "His dad loved that word," he said. "Used it all the time."

Mary spoke above the music, and the space between her eyes narrowed. "You know I can't follow you when you start using fifty-dollar words. What's it mean?"

"It means a payment that satisfies all debts. It also describes a seat on a rather important box, but that's another story."

"Big-Big," I said to him, "this is Daley Cross."

He smiled, his huge hands walking up and down the keys, and made an effort to glance over his shoulder. "Ms. Daley Cross. I knowed that name. How you doing, honey? Welcome to the hymn sing."

The nurses were gathering residents in their beds, wheelchairs, and favorite chairs in a circle around the piano. Ms. Fox sat with her knitting on her knees, mumbling to herself about Renny and when he was going to pick her up. Mr. Barnes was standing in the corner wearing his customary logging boots and gown and that's it. Nothing else. Ms. Phillips was sitting in her wheelchair, taking her teeth out and putting them back in. Ms. Anderson was sleeping in her bed, which the nurses had slid up against the wall. And Mr. Simpson was sitting on a stool looking expectantly at me. The rest were talking quietly amongst themselves. To my knowledge, the only things all these people had in common were that

55

they all lived at Riverview and they had all known my father.

I reached into the closet and pulled out a few extra instruments. I placed three five-gallon buckets upside down in front of Mr. Simpson and a set of sticks in his hands. Then I handed one tambourine to Ms. Fox and laid another beside Ms. Anderson's sleeping hand. Ms. Philips received a single handbell. I started tuning my D-35.

Big-Big didn't wait for an answer from Daley. "Now you just sit down right here next to me," he said, "and let me hear that angel's voice I done hear'd so much about. Let's you and me school this young'un in how a real voice makes music."

Big-Big was still independent enough to live on his own, but a few years ago he'd sold his house in town and I'd helped him move into one of the condos scattered around the Riverview property. Single-unit dwellings with a fabulous view of the Collegiates, they're close enough for a resident to get help if needed. But he could come and go as he liked, and either make his own meals or eat inside with everyone else. It was independent living for the I-don't-know-how-much-longer-I'll-be-independent.

One of the nurses had lit the projector and was sitting at a laptop to scroll the words on the wall. Daley sat down next to me and was about to whisper something when Big-Big rolled into one of my favorites. His voice was custom-made for this one. "When the roll is called up yonder . . ."

I came in behind him, filling in the empty space with my guitar as his peace-filled bellow reached down inside me and made every wrong thing right. Within a few words, Daley came in quietly, singing harmony. Big-Big smiled and swayed his head. After waking everybody up, he transitioned into "I'll Be a Sunbeam" and a perennial house favorite, "In the Garden."

Soon Daley was standing next to Mary, clapping and singing. Mr. Simpson was keeping near perfect time on the bucket-drums, and the percussionists were filling in nicely with tambourine and bell. At one point Ms. Philips dropped her teeth, which skidded across the floor next to the piano. Surprised but not overly grossed out, Daley picked them up and handed them back. Ms. Philips quickly reinstalled them, smiled widely, and continued the timely ringing of her single bell. Impressed with her initiative, Mr. Barnes stepped into the center of the room and extended his hand, asking Daley to dance during the chorus of "Blessed Assurance." She modestly accepted and held her own with a ninety-two-year-old man in an off-tempo do-si-do. Although she almost stopped dancing when he turned and the back of his gown flashed open. She covered her mouth with one hand and pointed with the other. "Oh my!"

I shook my head. "Sometimes he gets the robe turned around."

She laughed and covered her eyes. "Please no."

All this time Mary lay in bed, motionless save her face and neck, given that she was singing at the top of her voice. Big-Big segued into "Come Thou Fount," and I began picking my way through the intro. Doing so brought Ms. Fox to her feet, where she began clapping, staring at the ceiling, and singing harmony alongside Daley. When we reached the fourth verse, Big-Big softened his touch and backed off, making room for Ms. Fox to sing her solo. "Prone to wander, Lord, I feel it . . ."

Upon hearing the sound of a second female voice—Daley singing harmony—the emboldened Ms. Fox carried us through the final verse. The Riverview Center Chorus was in full swing and almost in tune.

After he'd duly recognized her invaluable contribution and Ms. Fox had sat down to the applause of the growing group of nursing staff and residents, Big-Big sang us through "Great Is Thy Faithfulness." Then he glanced over his shoulder at Mary, who sat beaming, waiting on a solo of her own. Big-Big closed out a few chords and then fell quiet, placing his hands in his lap and allowing me to fill in the space with the intro to Mary's solo.

When I'd finished flat-picking the intro, I began

quietly strumming, waiting for Mary's entrance. She timed it perfectly, and her quivering voice managed, "When I survey the wondrous cross, on which the Prince of Glory died . . ." Spontaneous applause brought an even wider smile to Mary's countenance. Daley moved around behind her bed and sang quietly next to her. Mary punched the electronic button on her bed, raising her head and shoulders up past forty-five degrees, and reached for Daley's hand, and the two new best friends finished the song.

Big-Big thanked everyone for coming, made an announcement about the ice cream social tomorrow night, reminded everyone not to feed the deer, and then, when the room fell quiet, began the introduction to the final song. He turned to Daley and said, "Miss Cross, I wonder if you might sit here next to me and sing this one to us?"

She wound her way through the beds and sat on the bench, her back to his left shoulder. She opened her mouth and sang with a purity and resonance I'd not heard in a long, long time.

"O Lord my God, when I in awesome wonder . . ." When she reached the fourth verse, "When Christ shall come with shout of acclamation . . . ," many of the staff were filming with their phones. Everyone else had stopped singing, and Big-Big's eyes were closed. "How great thou art . . . how great thou art." Her last note rang off the tongue-and-groove ceiling, and you could have heard a pin drop. Then Mr. Barnes started clapping and the entire room joined in.

I don't know the song's effect on everyone else, but I know that when Daley stood and kissed Big-Big on the cheek, her shoulders had rounded, the crow's-feet had washed out of the corners of her eyes, and whatever knee-jerk walls she'd carried in here had crumbled and lay in pieces at our feet.

Big-Big stood, bowed to Daley, and said, "Miss Cross, please come back." He pointed at me. "He sounds better with you here."

We pushed Mary down the hall and into her room. Shelly offered to take some pictures of her with Daley, promising to frame them and hang them on the already busy walls. Daley, seizing the moment, climbed onto the bed with Mary, and the two posed like long-lost sisters. Mary was radiant.

As we were walking out, Mary called behind us, "Daley?"

Daley turned.

Mary reached across her bedside table and lifted a CD cover. "Would you sign this?"

The CD was Daley's second album. Now twenty years old, it was the album we'd cut in Nashville just before the fire. Daley signed it and handed it back, lingering next to the bed and studying me. She tapped her fingers on the handrail that kept Mary from falling out and said, "Mary, did Cooper ever tell you about that CD?"

Mary shook her head. "What do you mean?"

"Did he ever tell you he played on that album?"

Mary's eyes grew big. "No!" She looked at me. "He never told me that!"

Daley nodded. "That's what I thought." She slid the stool next to the bed and sat down, then turned the CD over in her hand. "Did he tell you that he wrote eight of these?"

Mary nearly came off the bed. "What?"

Daley moved her finger as she spoke. "He wrote this one, and this one, and this one . . ." As she pointed at each one, Mary's eyes grew larger and rounder. "And that guitar you hear is all him."

Mary looked up at Daley. "That means . . . Coop wrote five number one songs?"

Daley nodded. "Yes."

Mary turned and threw a pillow at me. "Cooper O'Connor! Twenty-five years I been lying here, melting farther and farther into this bed, and you never uttered a peep. Never even offered to play one of your own songs." She threw a second pillow. "I can't believe you never told me."

I shrugged and set both pillows back on the bed—out of reach.

Daley patted her hand. "Just thought maybe you'd want to know."

Mary crossed her arms and smiled. "And I fully intend to take this up with him when you are not here and I don't look like such a fool for screaming at the top of my lungs."

As we were leaving—again—Mary called out, "Cooper?"

I poked my head back in the door. "We're even."

She was laughing at the top of her lungs as I shut the door. "Oh, we're not even close to being ev—"

Daley was quiet until we reached the parking lot. We climbed into the Jeep. I cranked the engine, pulled my Costas down over my eyes, and was about to move the stick into reverse when Daley gently placed her hand on top of mine. She leaned her head back against the headrest and looked at me out of the corners of her eyes. "Thank you."

"For?"

She nodded toward the building we'd just left. "That."

"No, thank *you*. You just made a lot of people's day. And you made Mary's year. Decade, even. You're probably going viral on YouTube right now."

"I didn't give them anything compared to what they gave me." Daley closed her eyes. "It's been a long time since anyone posted any video of me anywhere."

When the sun fell behind Mt. Princeton, the cool crept out of the cracks and shadows. Out here the cold never really leaves. Not even in summer months. It just hides behind the rocks and in the water until the sun goes down. But here on the threshold of October, it crawled out from behind the rocks a little quicker.

Pulling out of the parking lot, I glanced in my rearview. Big-Big was standing on the lawn, watching us drive away.

He was smiling.

7

Though nestled in the bosom of the Collegiate Peaks, Buena Vista is not a winter ski destination like Vail, Aspen, or Steamboat. Winter life here is quiet. Not much outside influence coming in. Summer is a bit different. Given accessibility to the Continental Divide, world-class hiking, four-wheeling, rafting, kayaking, paddleboarding, and mountain biking, the population swells as a couple thousand adventurous college kids bunk here in order to staff raft companies, summer camps, gear shops, and other outdoor adventures. The few thousand locals who call "Bew-nie" home tolerate the ebb and flow of the adventure-seeking tide like snowmelt in the springtime.

Necessary.

The Ptarmigan Theatre was built as a church in the 1860s. Constructed out of granite blocks cut from these very mountains, its walls are four feet thick and rise inside to a vaulted ceiling and balcony that overlook an exquisitely carved stage.

Around 1900, given a dwindling congregation, it was deconsecrated, and a local entrepreneur turned it into a theatre with seating for a couple hundred. It continued that way until it closed in 1929, and sat in dark decay and quiet decline for almost fifty years. A shell of its former self.

By 1990, when my dad bought the building off the courthouse steps for pennies on the dollar, the walls had been graffitied, most of the stained glass had been broken or shot out, the roof poured water, and squatters had dragged in mattresses that soon filled with rats. To keep warm in winter, some of the more determined guests burned a few of the pews and most all of the discarded hymnals and Bibles.

Due to what my father called "a mistake of engineering," however, the acoustics were divine. He didn't know what he wanted to do with it, or if he did he never said, but he couldn't stand the thought of it getting any worse. I remember him standing on the front steps and shaking his head. "How do you deconsecrate a church?" Dad never understood that.

Whatever his plans for the theatre might have been, they never became a reality.

When I first returned to BV, I scratched my head, took a long look at the Ptarmigan, and decided I'd finish what my father had started. If nothing else, it would give my hands something to do while my mind uncoiled. The Ptarmigan was named after a high-altitude, grouse-like bird nicknamed the "snow chicken," which works hard to blend into its environment. It prefers barren, snowy, craggy peaks, and its song sounds like a loud croaking.

Perfect for me.

But attempting to return the Ptarmigan to its former glory presented one immediate problem. Money. When I left Nashville, I had carried little with me. Jimmy in one hand and memories in the other—many of which were painful. Add to that our stabbing good-bye and I just assumed that between the conniving producer and bitter Daley, any monies earned on the songs I'd written had been cut off. Then I called my Nashville bank.

Evidently ours was not the first acrimonious split in Music City. When my banker reported my balance, I nearly dropped the phone. "Excuse me?"

In the five years since I'd been gone, my royalties had stacked up and been earning interest. I wasn't going to buy a jet or a mansion in the Hamptons, but I had options.

Within a few years I'd returned the beautiful jewel of the Collegiates to a quaint theatre with seating for a couple hundred. Further, I had retrofitted the balcony into an apartment where I stayed in winter when the snow and ice kept me out of the cabin. On a whim, I also installed some rather sophisticated recording equipment.

Before long the Ptarmigan became well known

as an unplugged acoustic venue for local acts, school Christmas musicals, "Nutcrackers," and touring choirs.

Having made something of the Ptarmigan, I then turned my attention to the Lariat, aka "the Rope." The Rope plays live music nightly and has made a name for itself on the acoustic singer–songwriter circuit west of the Rockies. They don't pay much, but crowds are decent and, thanks to the summer influx of those thirsty college kids, the word spread. Wanting to keep my involvement quiet, I created an LLC called Timbrel and Pipe and bought the Rope. Other than my attorney, no one around here knows I own it, and I like it that way.

The Rope fills an old brick building with two large, cavernous rooms. The ceilings are more than fifteen feet high—which explains how Volunteer No. 99 used to fit a ladder truck in here in the fifties and sixties. In one room they serve beer and half-truths, and in the other they play music and tell the other half. The acoustics aren't bad, and the more beer Frank serves, the better they get.

Frank Green is the current general manager. I interviewed and hired him over the phone, and to his knowledge he's never met his boss face-to-face. He's a local, and aside from being a liar, a cheat, and a thief who underpays his performers, he's good at his job. He's bald with bushy eyebrows, is growing wider in the middle, seldom takes his eyes off the floor, drives a twenty-year-old truck that blows white smoke out the left bank, and skims three to five hundred a week out of the cash drawer.

Which he uses to pay for his wife's cancer medication and his daughter's speech therapy.

Frank looked up as Daley and I came in. He nodded at me and wiped down the bar, then picked up a mop and began swabbing the floor. His shoulders sloped.

"How's Betty?" I asked.

He dipped the mop in the bucket and then mashed the rinse lever. The smell of Pine Sol filled the air. "Better today."

In all the times I'd asked that question, his eyes had never left the floor and he'd never answered differently. And yet over the years Betty had been in and out of the hospital a dozen times. In and out of ICU. Fighting one infection and then another.

Above him on the wall hung a poster of an idyllic island getaway and ocean vacation. Palm trees, island breeze, little drinks with umbrellas. Frank had never left Colorado. Neither had his wife or daughter. The edges of the poster were curled. It was a visible reminder of the vacation he would never take. I used to catch Frank looking into the picture. Now, not so much.

On more than one occasion—as he sipped too far into a bottle of bourbon—he replayed for me the memories of how his dad, as far back as he could remember, had smacked him on the back of the head and told him with spit puddling in the corner of his drunken mouth, "You're useless. Never amount to nothing. Do us all a favor and just die now."

Frank would stare out the window across the street, swig, swallow, wipe his mouth with the back of his wrist, and slam the shot glass down with a forced smile. "And he was right!" And every time he did that I didn't notice the strength in his Popeye arms or tree-trunk legs, or the bravado in his voice, but the tears in his eyes.

The first few years he worked for me, he was rather fair and honest. That was before his wife got sick.

Frank wears his shame.

I sat in the corner on a stool and plugged Ella into the amplifier. Given the power in Daley's lungs, I needed an instrument with some punch and bellow, and while I'd softened and even muted it in the enclosed room at Riverview, the D-35 had it. Daley stood to my right and slightly in front of me. Mike in front of her. Faded jeans. Button-down oxford. Hair pulled back and up. Her right sleeve was unbuttoned and came down to her knuckles, covering up most of the Aircast. The bling and bedazzle of a once-rising

68

star were gone. She stood there stripped down. No pre-tension. No attempt to be some former version of herself. Daley stood there as Daley.

I tuned while she stood waiting on me. She looked back at me over her shoulder. "I'll buy you an electronic tuner for Christmas," she whispered, and smiled.

I tapped my ear. "Mine's built-in. Like that sharpener in the back of the crayon box."

A question rested on the tip of her tongue. I could practically see it sitting there, see her trying to swallow it.

So I answered, "The surgeon in Nashville must have done a really good job of reconstructing the ruptured membrane, because I can hear like Steve Austin."

"Who?"

I plucked the low E-string on my guitar and tuned it down about two octaves, sending it severely out of tune. "Six Million Dollar Man."

She laughed and the tension rolled off her temples, down onto her shoulders, and out the door where the pain of our past sat smoldering.

Some folks get nervous onstage. Sweat. Stammer. Stumble. Talk too much because the quiet scares them. Others are born to it. One of my favorite things about live music is the joy of playing with someone who, when they step onstage, forgets they're being paid to stand there. Daley's face told me she would have sung for free—in spite of the fact that Frank had quickly apologized and corrected his "mistake," agreeing to pay her the customary three hundred dollars for new live acts.

What made this all the more intriguing was the fact that there were only two people in the bar besides Daley, Frank, and me. She was looking at the promise of playing for an audience of two— who were halfway through their third and fourth beers, respectively. Which meant that in about twenty minutes, they probably wouldn't even hear her.

It promised to be a fun night.

I was warming up my fingers, rolling through some scales, when she glanced over her shoulder again. "Want me to buy you a beer?"

I popped a Tums into my mouth. "I'm good."

She raised both eyebrows. "Acid reflux?"

"Something like that."

She eyed my guitar picking and smirked. "You ready or do you need more time to practice?"

"After you."

She smirked again. "Oh, and we'll be starting in the key of E. You do know where that is, right?"

My fingers rolled through the E scale, traveling up the frets. "Gimme a minute to find it."

Without invite, without pomp, without attempting to calm her nerves with a bunch of excessive talking, Daley opened her mouth, and when she did I thought Janis Joplin herself had walked up onstage. After "Me and Bobby McGee," she jumped straight into "Piece of My Heart." Once she had us good and lathered and her voice warmed, she took a left turn at normal and three flights up toward impossible with Whitney Houston's version of "I Will Always Love You."

I stopped playing, the better to listen to her, prompting her to glance back at me and give me a *What are you doing?* look, but as my fingers touched the neck and the notes came up beneath her voice, I was thinking to myself, *Who in their right mind attempts to sing Whitney Houston?*

Word spread. Or maybe her voice carried down the sidewalk. Whatever the case, six songs in and we were staring at fifty to sixty people who'd been drawn out of neighboring restaurants or off the sidewalk. Many were wide-eyed. All were mesmerized. None were staring at me—which meant I was doing my job. By the time she closed the set with a sultry serenade, the door had been propped open and folks were sipping beers on the sidewalk, fogging up the window from the outside in. Standing room only.

Somewhere in the history of music-making there arose a romantic ideal regarding the life of musicians. How they're somehow more authentic and truthful, more insightful into man's existence and the deep mysteries of the universe if they ring out their song while silently fighting destructive urges and inner demons. This unseen inner conflict adds to the drama. In this whirlwind of soul-sucking angst, anger, and torment, the lone voice fights valiantly, ultimately deriving its power and culminating in a song.

Daley had none of this.

Daley sang out of something else. Something pure. Something she'd protected, despite the fact that no one had protected her. She sang out of a reservoir. No war. No angst. No demons. She simply brought her song to the stage, opened her mouth, and offered it. Because that's what it was.

An offering.

Daley's song spilled out of her like water. And those of us listening had been in the desert a long time.

Midway through the second set, one of the guys who'd been there from the start stood up and staggered toward the makeshift stage, his expression a mix of unbelief and puppy dog adoration. I scooted forward onto the edge of my stool, but Daley held a stop-sign hand behind her back. He reached in his pocket, fumbled through a few crumpled bills, then spilled them onto the ground at her feet. She mouthed, "Thank you," and he returned to his seat—walking backward. Others soon followed. When we closed the second set, Frank brought us an empty gallon pickle jar and placed it at her feet. The bills filled nearly half.

Daley's stage presence was polished like an act

two decades on the road. She made eye contact, conversed with her audience.

—Where you from?

—You two been married long? . . . Let's hear it for fifteen years.

—Thanks for the invite. I'd better pass, but can I sing something for you?

—Hi. Do you have a favorite?

—Oh, it's your birthday. Well, happy birthday.

A couple walking by with a daughter maybe eight or nine had edged into the crowded bar, and the little girl was mouthing along with many of the words.

Daley pointed. "Hey, Mom and Dad? Can she sing with me? Do you mind? Okay, come on."

The girl walked forward through a crowd that parted like the Red Sea. Daley pulled up a stool and helped her climb onto it. Feet dangling. Daley knelt and asked her, "Now what can we sing?" The girl whispered in her ear.

I've never heard a more beautiful version of "Over the Rainbow." Daley had us eating out of her hand. I was as mesmerized as the audience, and eventually I just quit playing and listened. Again she shot me a glance, but I shook my head. Next they sang "On Top of Spaghetti." As the crowd applauded, the girl whispered in Daley's ear, whereupon the two of them brought the house down with "You Are My Sunshine."

Through Ray Charles, Roy Orbison, and two

dozen songs, her voice showered the audience, who drank it in. Drowning in it. When she started into John Denver's "Rocky Mountain High," the entire place joined in, rattling the windows. Once she had them in a foaming lather, she broke into the Righteous Brothers' "You've Lost That Loving Feeling." Followed seamlessly with "Unchained Melody." At this point, every man in the bar wanted to kiss Daley. Including me.

Daley had sung herself into a drenching sweat, which prompted Frank to bring her a towel and open one of the large bay doors, allowing our concert to spill out into the street. Daley wiped her face and arms and made a joke about how while most girls perspire, she sweats. Finally, after nearly three hours, she sat on a stool and said, "I think we've played enough, and while you all have been too kind to me, would you please"— she stepped off to one side—"put your hands together for the finest guitarist I've ever heard, much less played with, Cooper O'Connor."

The crowd—now bordering on a hundred and fifty plus—was not quite ready for Daley to quit. Stomping their feet and pounding glasses on tables, they demanded an encore. Which Daley accommodated with a lush and sultry rendition of "Can't Get Enough of Your Love." The only thing missing was a disco ball and Barry White himself. I thought to myself, *I've seen everything now.*

Watching her perform, I had a thought. I played

a few notes and Daley turned toward me. I said, "Remember this one?"

I began to mimic the thunder and the lightning. Daley turned toward the audience and said, "It's been a long time since I've sung this one. Been a long time since I wanted to."

I whispered, "You think you can remember the words?"

She stood up again, raised her microphone, and with a smirk said, "You think you can remember the chords?"

The audience picked up the tune, and several began holding their phones, videoing. It was some of the most fun I'd had in twenty years. When Daley finished, ringing out that last ascending high note, a pulsating, rose-vine-like vein popped out on her neck. That's when I knew she was all in.

When she finished singing, not a person was seated. The applause ran five minutes. She said, "Since we're all standing, let's end with an old beer-drinking tune. My voice is toast, and those videos you're holding will attest to that. But I need help with this one. Come on, we'll all sing.

"The guy who wrote this spent a lot of time in bars. That's where the tune came from. He wrote these words in the belly of a slave ship when he finally saw the mess he'd made of his life. I like to think he wrote this because he needed it, and if today reminded me of anything, I need it too.

Maybe you sometimes feel the same." She motioned for me to stand next to her and set the mike between us. She touched her neck, shook her head ever so slightly, and then leaned over and whispered, "Help."

Thinking we'd already reached the pinnacle of what she could accomplish that night, I watched in wonder as Daley led a half-drunk chorus of bearded and tattooed sons of miners and truckers and river guides and ski bums and chairlift bunnies in a rousing rendition of "Amazing Grace."

Somewhere in the second verse, she tugged on my arm and pulled me toward the microphone, as if to say, *Why aren't you singing?*

My father was six foot five, deep voice, the wingspan of a Zeppelin, and when he sang hymns he always raised his hands. Didn't matter where he was. Didn't care what others thought. And when he did, everyone knew, because both his voice and his body stood out. I couldn't have been more than four the first time I stood next to him and sang that song. Came up to about the middle of his thigh. Big-Big had played the intro on the piano, and when Dad bellowed the word *A-a-may-zing,* I remember feeling it resonate and rumble through my chest like waves pounding the beach. Afraid and excited, I clutched his leg and held on, knowing something was coming. I remember staring up and watching sweat pour off his face and trickle down his arms.

When I opened my mouth and wiggled a few notes through the scar tissue, Daley turned toward me. She leaned back, stopped singing, and just listened. A tear drained out of her right eye, letting me know that my words had filtered down and in. Everyone else must have shared her amazement, because I sang the last half of the third verse by myself. Just me and the guitar.

It'd been a long time since I'd done that.

Daley and the audience applauded, then joined in again. When they did, the volume grew twice as loud as it had been before, and the night took on an organic melody of its own.

When we finally reached "Bright shining as the sun," everybody raised their voices and their glasses, sloshing beer and foam around the bar. From my vantage point on the stage, I could see out the now-open bay door and onto the street and down three blocks toward Riverview, which sat just across the bridge. Showered in the glow of yellow streetlights, a giant of a man paced back and forth across the bridge. Hands held high.

Evidence that sound carries.

We closed the night to applause and whistles and requests for pictures and Daley's autograph. Frank, who had apparently found religion, bought a round on the house—which the house appreciated. Daley, having just signed a guy's chest and taken a picture with six college kids, turned, hugged me, and whispered in my ear, "I thought they said you'd never sing again?"

I laid Ella in her case and nodded at Daley. "Yes, they said that."

She locked her arm in mine. "I'm glad they were wrong."

I didn't bother to tell her that they weren't . . .

I was twenty years younger. The doctor sat on a rolling stainless steel stool, scooted up next to the bed, and let out a deep breath before he spoke—quietly, as if the tone of his voice would help soften the blow. "You'll never sing again." He paused, then shook his head. "Might not even talk." He glanced at my bandaged hand. "Probably never play an instrument that involves your right hand. You may never hear out of your right ear again. And then there's your liver."

My eyes were having a tough time focusing, and the finality of his words wasn't helping.

"The prognosis isn't . . ."

While his lips moved, and bodies in the hall scurried to and fro past my door, carrying on with their everyday normal lives, I remember thinking to myself, *He can't be talking about me. My songs are on the radio. I'm making a record. Getting married. I have plans.*

He finished speaking, and a pregnant silence followed. It sank in that he was, in fact, talking about me.

My lips were chapped and swollen. I whispered, "Until then?"

"Live your life."

A hoarse whisper. "Like an inmate on death row."

He tilted his head to one side. "That's one way of looking at it."

"How would you look at it . . . if you were lying here?"

He didn't answer.

I stared out the window across a brilliant blue Nashville skyline. "How much time do I have?"

He shrugged. "That's anybody's guess."

8

Midnight had come and gone when we drove west on 306 out of BV, turned south on 321, and wound our way around the Mt. Princeton Hot Springs Resort, past the chalk cliffs onto the gravel road that led to the deserted mining town of St. Elmo.

St. Elmo sits at about twelve thousand feet and thrived during the silver boom. Following the passage of the Silver Act, the price of silver plummeted, and along with it St. Elmo's population. Much like Leadville's. Overnight, 90 percent of its residents packed up, boarded up their houses, and moved out. But when somebody struck the mother lode of ore higher up at the

Mary Murphy Mine, folks returned and St. Elmo thrived. Somebody had to process all that ore, and no mine was more productive than the Mary Murphy. Given their elevation, neither town was all that accessible during winter. A few hard-core locals managed to stick it out, but it took a special breed to survive a winter up there.

Still does.

Daley didn't say much during the drive; she seemed to be enjoying both the quiet and the moonlit view. By the time we rounded the curve and pull-off at the roaring Chalk Creek Falls, she'd turned sideways in the seat, curled up, and dozed off. I did my best to avoid the bumps and not stare at her. I did pretty well with the bumps.

The peroxide was a mystery. She used to have the most beautiful, silky brunette hair. The skin on her hands was cracked, and her fingernails were bitten to the quick. Beneath the hum of the motor and the tires, I could hear her snoring slightly.

We climbed up through the aspens toward St. Elmo, turning onto dirt road 295 that led up to and past the Mary Murphy Mine. The road grows steep there, so I stopped, shifted to four-low, and eased off the clutch.

She woke, palmed the drool off her face, and buckled up her seat belt. "You live up here?"

"Not far now." I downshifted into second. "This was one of my mom's favorite places. My dad used to laugh and tell me that God made me up here beneath the aspens. Took me a few years to figure out what he was talking about. They were in the process of building a cabin when she got sick. We buried her in the spring, and Dad and I moved up here when I was five. Each year the summer got longer, and we'd stay up here until the snow drove us back down. When I . . . when I left Nashville, I wandered west. Spent a year staring at the Pacific while my body healed. Once I was physically able, I started working odd jobs. Whatever would occupy my mind for a few weeks. Then I'd bump into something that would remind me of my rearview mirror, and I'd take off again." Another pause. "A few bumps later and I found myself circling closer to the only home I'd ever known. Been here ever since."

She put a hand on my arm and tried to push the words off the tip of her tongue, but there were too many and she was too tired. And Daley wasn't just tired like she needed a good night's sleep. She needed to sleep for six weeks, wake up, eat, and sleep for six or eight more.

A mile later, we leveled out on the ridgeline and then crossed the creek below the cabin. Mom's aspens lined the road. The breeze filtered through, causing the leaves to clap gently, flashing green and white in the headlights.

I pointed. "Hear that? Dad used to joke and tell me that was all the applause he ever needed."

When she saw the cabin rising up out of the hillside, she pointed. "Your dad built that?"

"He started it when he and mom were dating. After she died, we finished it." I smiled. "All the comforts of home. Electricity. Hot and cold running water. And decent cell phone reception if you stand in the right spot on the porch."

We climbed the steps to the porch, where she stood waiting on me to unlock the door. My hands were full. I spoke over four bags of groceries. "It's unlocked."

I set the groceries in the kitchen, lit a fire to knock the chill off, and then found her on the back porch, staring out across the world. It was a clear night. Moon high. I extended my arm and allowed her to look along the end of my finger. "That peak is about two hundred miles away. Dad would stand right where you are on nights like this and say, 'The veil is thin up here.' "

She whispered, "He was right."

She leaned against me and locked her arm in mine, too tired to talk. I held her hand and led her to the spare bedroom, where I cracked a window, and she slipped off her boots and lay down. I covered her with a blanket, cut the light, and stood at the door.

"Can I ask you something?" I said.

"Anything."

"Why didn't you sing any of your own stuff tonight?"

"With my third album, Sam thought I needed to become more edgy. More"—she raised fingers in the air to form quotation marks—"*relevant*. A few years passed, and I was standing on a stage somewhere in California, or maybe Washington, and I realized the folks in the audience didn't know the songs. Didn't know the words. Didn't sing along. And between the lights, the lasers, the makeup, and the explosions, I didn't blame them." A self-effacing admission. "The songs were no good. Junk. Why should they care? I certainly didn't, and they could tell when I sang them. But I had to make a living, so I began singing what they did know. Covers. Songs they cared about." A pause. "It paid the bills . . . for a while."

"Speaking of Sam, how is he?"

Her eyes dropped. "Haven't talked in a long time. When I call him, he'll call me back, but . . . I don't think he ever forgave himself for shooting you. If he'd known it was you, he'd never have pulled the trigger. He thought it was just two guys . . ."

I let it go. Figured this was not the time to correct her view of history. "What happened between you two?"

I could hear embarrassment in her voice.

"I looked at Sam like an uncle. He looked at me like, well . . . I was young. It took me awhile to realize that a man thirty years older could want something physical from me." A shrug. "A few

83

months after you left, he came to me with some excitement and said he'd put together a collection of really great songs and wanted to make a follow-up record to release on the heels of the successful tour of the album you and I made. So we did. And he was right, it was a great collection of ballads. All right in my sweet spot. Two platinum records. Five number ones. We were all riding the wave. On the surface life was good.

"Then he and Bernadette divorced, and I came home from tour to a candlelight dinner, his shirt unbuttoned to the middle of his chest, and what felt like a date. He put his hand on my thigh, I refused him, told him that wasn't how I saw him. I moved out of the apartment he'd rented for me and handed him the keys. Felt that was best for our relationship. Keep it professional. He was really good about it . . . said he wanted whatever made me happy."

She sat up on the bed and drew up her knees, hugging them to her chest.

"Then I walked into the studio to record my fourth album, and his assistant was driving my Mercedes and the songs I was looking at were nothing like what I'd sung in the past. They were lifeless. Superficial. Pop candy. When I approached Sam, he said the current inventory of available songs was limited. It's just something that happens in the business. Life in Nashville is a function of who writes the best songs. It was the best he could do." She looked up at me. "Then he signed a new girl and she cut a record with some songs that I thought sounded more like me than her. Then two more girls just like her. Several of those songs did really well."

The trajectory of Daley's career had turned sharply downward about this time, so I kept digging. "What happened to the last album?"

She leaned her head back against the headboard. "The industry changed. I was sick for about a year. Fighting an infection in my throat mixed with a weariness I just couldn't shake. I'd had some injections in my vocal cords to help me meet my obligations. That didn't help. All I wanted to do was sleep. Felt like my bones were tired. It was all I could do to open my mouth, but the notes that came out were lifeless."

For so long I'd wanted to know what had happened after I left Nashville. Now I did. For twenty years she'd walked the earth thinking Sam was the benevolent uncle, not holding a grudge, believing she'd simply been the talent who couldn't make it in records. Sam had been the good guy who felt guilty for "mistakenly" shooting me. It's why he brushed the whole thing under the rug. Never pressed charges for a crime he'd claimed was committed. Further, he'd protected Daley and her career—or so she believed.

When she looked in her rearview mirror, she saw a very different history from the one I'd lived. In her mind, I'd rejected and abandoned her. Cut and run. Sam had stuck around to patch up the pieces.

It was the one possible scenario that had never occurred to me.

She smiled as a tear rolled out the corner of her eye and then along the line of her nose. She clutched her legs tighter to her chest. "I used to look for you in the crowds."

I opened the window, pulled the curtain, and laid an extra blanket across her feet. "Up here the mountains sing a sweet song. It'll rock you to sleep."

She was asleep before I shut the door.

I added wood to the fire and then grabbed a towel. Then I walked up to the creek, stripped under the moonlight, waded in up to my ears, and soaked until the frigid cold felt warm.

Given snow runoff, the water temperature in the creeks and streams in and around Buena Vista remains slightly below thirty-two degrees in winter. Add to that the flow of the water, which brings more of that cold across your skin at a faster rate, and it's like packing a body in dry ice. Up here, on the back side of Mt. Antero and Mt. Princeton, where Boulder Mountain, Mt. Mamma, Grizzly Mountain, Cyclone Mountain, and Mt. White all run together, an odd phenomenon occurred. A deep, high-walled bowl developed—what my father affectionately called God's Shaving Basin.

Regardless of the August heat, that bowl held snow year-round and has for as long as anyone can remember. Chances are good there's snow in there from fifty years ago. Whatever the case, the snowmelt from God's Basin feeds into Baldwin Lake and Pomeroy Lake. To get there, it runs through a natural funnel in the rock, creating a waterfall of about ten feet and landing in a second basin just above our cabin. Dad named that one God's Cereal Bowl. I guess he was hungry when he named it. The creek spills out there in a showering spray that's tough to stand under, given the pressure and the cold. It feels like needles piercing your skin. The Cereal Bowl is about the size of an average swimming pool and filled with delicious six-inch trout that dart around the rocks and to my knowledge are found nowhere else in the world. The freezing cold water overflows its edges and then begins its roller-coaster descent into the valley, where it eventually bleeds into the Arkansas River.

The value for me was that God's Basin created a consistent flow of water that was technically colder than ice and just a hundred feet out my back door, no matter how hot the air happened to be in summer.

The first thirty to sixty seconds were the most painful. After that, I never really felt much. Truth is, after five or six minutes, my mind started telling me that I was warm.

9

The first day she slept deeply. Didn't even roll over. On the second day, I checked her for fever, pushed the hair out of her face, then sat next to her on the bed and drank in the smell of her. I stayed there an hour. Maybe two. I thought a lot about what she knew, what she didn't know, and what, if anything, would be gained by telling her the truth.

On day three I lifted her head, fed her some chicken broth, and made her eat some peanut butter toast. When she finished, she laid her head back down, closed her eyes, and slid her hand out from beneath the sheets. Reaching for me. I laid mine in hers and she drifted off. Her hands were rough, and if they told a story, it was not one of tenderness known.

When she woke on the fourth morning, I heard her talking on my landline. I couldn't make out the words, but she sounded apologetic, like the other person was not happy. She hung up and made a second call. Sounded like she was trying to get some information. When she appeared a few moments later, I'd come to little resolution. The truth of our lives would only open Pandora's box, and I wondered if that wouldn't hurt more. She'd already suffered a lot.

When she walked out she was wearing the fog of deep sleep and one of my Melanzana fleece pullovers. She poured herself some coffee and found me on the porch with Jimmy on my lap. I don't know how long she'd been standing there when I saw her leaning against the doorframe.

The clouds hung in the valleys below us. A hundred miles west, dark clouds threatened the year's first snow. When she spoke, her voice was soft but not necessarily peaceful. Worry had returned, as had that self-protective shell. Her tone was apologetic.

"Hey, I . . . I just talked with the folks in Biloxi. They're losing patience. I was supposed to be there two days ago. They said there's some video on the Internet. Me in a bar. Getting lots of views, and people are calling about me. Shows are starting to sell tickets. It might be a chance."

While she talked, I studied her. She'd removed the Aircast. The hand was still a little puffy, but the bruise was turning a darker shade of purple. The circles beneath her eyes, meanwhile, had faded, and a glimmer of light had returned.

"I'm really sorry . . . I checked the bus schedule. Could I trouble you for a ride to the bus station?"

My heart registered a feeling that it had not felt in a long time. The closest word I can use to describe it was *hurt*. I set Jimmy down and slid on my boots. "Sure."

She was staring at Jimmy, and the space

between her eyes had narrowed. When she touched the bullet hole with the tip of her pinkie, I could all but see the question perched on the tip of her tongue. She must have thought better of it, though, because all she said was, "I'm going to take a quick shower."

When she returned from the shower, wet hair and smelling of soap, I slid the Jeep keys into my pocket. "Ready?"

She owned the clothes on her back and a backpack with a lot of room in it. "Yeah."

The thought of her arriving in Mississippi with nothing to play was bugging me. "Have you got three minutes for me to show you something?"

There was a pleading in her face, but I didn't know what to make of it. "Sure."

Just off my kitchen stood a heavy wooden door with three locks. I unlocked all three, clicked on the light, and slid the door open. "You and I met when I couldn't take my hands off your guitar." I laughed. "Not much has changed."

She stepped into the room, and, as it had at the hospital, her jaw went one way while her eyebrows went another. She began counting, her finger bobbing up and down as she pointed along the racks. When she finished she said, "You own sixty-four guitars?"

The number surprised me. Sounded high. "Don't know."

She walked into the room and turned around,

talking to herself. "You own so many you've lost count."

I'd paneled the room in western red cedar and installed a dehumidifier. It would kick on when the humidity rose above 50 percent, but given the arid climate that wasn't often.

Daley walked around touching each guitar. The room was filled with Martins, McPhersons, Gibsons, a few Collingses, Taylors, and others. She looked genuinely impressed. "This is the nicest collection I've ever seen. You are officially a guitar hoarder."

"I've been called a lot of things. That's a new one." I stood off to one side while she continued to walk up and down each row. I'd displayed them in racks—one hanging over the other. Like clothes at a Laundromat.

"If I'm strumming, nothing compares to a McPherson. You know what they say—you can play a chord, go to lunch, and when you return it's still ringing. Harmonic perfection. But sometimes I like a note to die and not keep ringing, so if I'm flat-picking or playing finger-style, the answer varies depending on the day of the week." I shrugged. "It's tough to top a D-28 or D-35."

She turned toward me. "I'm really happy for you."

I waved my hand across the racks. "Pick one."

"What?"

"Any one you like."

She took a step backward. "Peg, I couldn't possibly."

It was the first time she'd called me Peg. It had rolled off her tongue naturally, without thinking. In a heartbeat we were twenty years younger. My voice stopped her retreat.

"What are you going to play when you get where you're going?"

She waved me off, but I could tell the thought bothered her. "Thanks to you, I've got a few dollars. I'll pick up something."

"You're not a very good liar."

She walked down the middle of a row, hands out, fingertips brushing the headstocks. "They said they've got something I can borrow for now."

So she had already approached it with the people in Biloxi. It proved my suspicion; she was worried about it. I picked up a McPherson and handed it to her, bridging the space between us. "This is Rose. Her voice matches yours." I rested the instrument in her hands. "Please."

"She has a name?"

"They all have names."

"But, Cooper—"

"Please," I said again. "For old times."

She turned it over in her hands. "I can't afford—"

"It's a gift. You don't pay for those."

Careful not to hurt her hand, she played a few chords, then turned the guitar over in her hands and said, "It's beautiful." Stepping closer, she kissed me on the cheek. "Thank you." She kissed me a second time. This time not so far back on my cheek. Closer to the corner of my lips. "Really, I don't know what to . . ."

I pulled the hardshell case off the shelf and laid the guitar inside, along with a few extra sets of light strings and several dozen picks, and headed outside to the Jeep. She followed quietly.

Idling down the mountain, she chewed on a fingernail and tried not to look at me. But she didn't do a very good job.

The BV bus station is little more than a spot on the sidewalk where the bus pulls over in its route south from Leadville to Salida. You purchase your ticket in the post office and when you see the bus coming, you wave it down. It's old-school but effective.

I bought her ticket all the way to Mississippi, which she protested, but I did it anyway. Then I drove her to the Roastery and bought her a Honey Badger, and then we walked down the sidewalk and waited. While the milk froth covered her top lip, I opened my wallet and gave her what cash I had. Several hundred dollars. Between that and what she'd made in tips and playing at the Rope, she had close to a thousand. Probably more than she'd had in a long time.

She tried to protest, tried to seem stern. Strong. "Cooper, no. I can't."

I held the folded bills toward her. "I made that money off your voice."

She looked at it. "Then you should teach the rest of us how to save money, because my voice hadn't made anybody money in a long time."

The implication was understated.

I tucked the money into her jacket pocket. She stood, arms crossed, staring into the southbound traffic. We were both quiet.

Finally she broke the silence. "I had fun yesterday. Or whenever it was that we played. Feels like yesterday."

"Me too."

She gazed at the mountains. "I haven't felt this rested in a long time."

My eyes walked the peaks of the Collegiates. "The mountains have that effect." I checked my watch. We had a few minutes.

I'd rehearsed this so many times. Now that my chance had arrived, I couldn't find an opening. I wanted Daley to know the truth. To correct our history. But I needed to stop short of the whole truth. False hope was more damaging than false history.

My voice was a hoarse whisper. "You remember when we first met, I told you how my mom gave a guitar to my dad when they married?"

"Yes."

"And I told you how I grew up playing that guitar, and that when I left here, I stole him from my dad."

She nodded.

"You remember how when I came to Nashville, someone had stolen him from me?"

Another nod.

"You remember that guitar's name?"

She searched her memory. "Frankie? Arlie? Something-ie."

"Jimmy."

"That's it."

"This morning you saw me playing a D-28 with a small hole beneath the sound hole. You stuck your pinkie finger in the hole."

She nodded.

"That's Jimmy."

She looked confused. There were too many pieces and we were too far removed. "Where'd the hole—?" She stopped.

"In the aftermath of the fire, Sam spun two stories. You remember?"

She nodded slightly, suspicious of why I was picking at this scab.

"What if neither one was true?"

"Be tough to prove."

"But what if?"

No response.

"What if there was a third story? The truth, even."

"That would beg the simple question as to why you didn't love me enough to tell me. To fight for me."

I was about to open my mouth when the bus appeared over my shoulder and the piercing sound of the air brakes shattered the thin line of hope stretched across the air between us. Sometimes raising a question as to the possibility of a truth is more effective than actually telling the truth. And my time had run out. "What if I loved you enough not to tell you?"

The bus stopped and the door opened. The driver waited.

Daley shouldered her backpack and picked up the McPherson. Her eyes were watery. The weight had returned to her shoulders. "You ever think about the Ryman?"

I kissed her cheek. "Only when I'm breathing."

She held my hand. Lingered. "You ever think about what might have been? About us?"

"More than the Ryman."

"You think there's still a chance for us?"

"I think your life has been prelude until now. The best is out there waiting for you."

"I stopped believing in me a long time ago."

"I didn't."

She kissed me again, holding her lips to mine. They were soft, warm, moist, inviting, and trembling. She pulled back to look at me, then kissed me again. This time cupping my face in her hands. Finally she turned toward the bus. "You want to come?" she said. "You can stay a week or two. Make it vacation. Or you could stay forever."

Every ounce of me wanted to climb on that bus. To grab her in my arms and never look back.

She was crying now. Embarrassed to be getting on a bus with puffy eyes. I gave her my Costas. "Call me when you get settled. Let me know how you're doing."

I saw her shiver, then hug herself in response. Collecting herself, she nodded, climbed aboard, and when the driver opened the luggage compartment beneath the bus, I handed him the ticket and stowed her bag beneath. As I was sliding her bag in with the rest, I unzipped it and slid in three notebooks. My best stuff. Each written with her in mind. Her voice. In truth, every song I'd written for the past twenty years, I'd written with her in mind.

The driver climbed aboard, the door closed, and I stood on the sidewalk as the bus pulled away. The sight of her face growing smaller as she stared through the glass was one source of pain. And it was poignant. But it was the second source that was piercing: after twenty years, I'd still not told her the truth.

As much as I wanted to run after that bus, to bang on the door and scream for the driver to stop, I could not bring myself to tell her the words she wanted to hear.

I still loved her too much.

10

I made my way home. Slowly. Quietly. I was going to open the windows and doors, but the remnant of both Daley and Coco Chanel was still hanging on the air, so I kept them closed and just walked room to room, breathing. I didn't feel much like eating. Finally I walked into her room, sat next to her bed, laid my head back, and closed my eyes.

The episodes I had experienced the last twenty years were coming more frequently, giving less warning, and lasting longer. Sitting next to the bed, I felt one coming on. I walked quickly up to the creek, stripped my shirt off, and waded in. Over the years, I had developed a habit of leaving my pants on because if things went south, somebody could use my belt to fish my body out of the water.

What comes next happens in waves. The first is the cold. It literally takes your breath away. The next is the pain, which the brain doesn't know how to process because it's getting the same get-me-out-of-here signal from every inch of the body. I try not to focus on it. The third stage is a sludgy sort of paralysis mixed with an odd sensation of prickly heat. After a couple of minutes the pain goes away and you stop feeling cold or hot. You just find yourself shivering in a room where there's light ahead and dark walls on either side. When the walls start closing in, it's time to either get out or head toward the light.

I heard, or maybe sensed, someone coming toward the pool, and then a shadow fell over me. A giant hand hooked beneath my belt and lifted me out of the water like a crane, then set me gently on the bank. I opened my eyes, coughing, sputtering, trying to force movement into my limbs, and saw Big-Big looking down at me.

"I told your dad I'd look out for you, but it's getting tougher."

I had wrapped myself into a fetal ball and spoke through chattering teeth. "How'd you get up here?"

"I'm old. Not dead." He handed me a towel.

He stacked wood for a fire, starting with kindling, then broke a few larger limbs over his knee and made a pyramid. After he lit the pine needles, he knelt down and blew softly on the flame. When it caught, he slowly added more sticks, feeding it. Within minutes it was roaring and popping and cracking. I inched closer. His tone of voice told me he wasn't too happy. "You gonna just sit there? Watch her leave?"

I didn't respond.

"You think it's just some giant cosmic mistake that she ended up broke and busted in your town, on your street corner, in front of your Jeep?"

Still nothing.

He shook his head. "Your father would be chasing after that girl. Running full speed."

"My father's dead. And I will be shortly."

He spat. "Whether you live or die isn't the point. And you don't know squat about your father." Big-Big was getting animated. "That girl deserves to know the truth. To know that all this ain't got nothing to do with her. That she ain't the reason."

I shook my head. "I can't ask her to fall in love with a dying man."

"You been dying since you drove back up this mountain twenty years ago. You want to lose twenty more? Living like a hermit up these hills. Love was made to be given away. Why you holding on to yours?"

"The truth of me will only hurt her."

"I used to think the same thing. Thought that by keeping it to myself, I was protecting you. Truth is—" He shook his head and spat again. "The truth is the only thing that doesn't hurt. The truth is a giant hand. It both cuts us free and holds us tight."

"You make that up?"

"No. Your father did." He rubbed his hands together, searching for words. "I need to tell you something."

His tone had changed. Hurt was bubbling up. I waited.

He sucked through his teeth. "Your father died in that water. Drowned right there."

I sat up. This was a different story. "I thought you said he died in the house from a heart attack."

He nodded. "His heart quit working all right, but why it quit working is another thing."

"Okay . . . why'd it quit working?"

Big-Big stared at me. "Complications."

"Complications from what?"

Big-Big's eyes darted left and right and then stopped, piercing through me. "It jes' be broke." He looked like he had more to say but let it go. Instead, he pulled the weathered letter from his vest pocket and set it gently on the ground next to me. At one time, I'd read it with greasy hands. At another, I'd spilled some coffee on it. Yet another, I'd torn the pages in two. Tape now held the pieces together. Most every other time, I'd stained it with tears.

Big-Big spoke over me. "Your turn."

My father had written the letter the night I'd left. Big-Big had found it lying faceup on his desk after his death—like he wanted it to be found. This much I knew. Big-Big had given it to me upon my return. For a long time I had treasured it, memorized it. My father's last words to me. A few years in and Big-Big asked to read it again. I saw how he held it. How his shoulders rounded as he held it. Saw the glassy reflection in his eyes. So we began taking turns holding on to it. Passing it back and forth every year or so. One year the tenderness wore off and I got mad.

Hence, the tape. By now I didn't need the letter to know what it said. I'd read it so many times I could recite it backward. And while it answered most of the questions of my heart, it did not answer the one that remained.

Big-Big turned and rested his hand gently on my shoulder. His voice was a warm whisper. "Cooper?"

I knew what he was going to say. He'd said it before. I rested my hand on his.

"You can't tell a dead man you're sorry."

I unfolded the letter, and for the ten thousandth time washed myself in the sound of my father's voice.

Dear Son,

You left tonight. Drove out of the Falls. I stood on the stage and watched the truck's red taillights get smaller and smaller. I'm sitting here wondering whether I should've let you go. Wondering if I should've gone about all this the way I did. Maybe I was wrong. I don't know. I know my heart hurts. I imagine yours does too . . .

The handwritten letter continued for three pages. I knew it by heart. Water in the desert.

Dad had signed his name five times. Two in blue ink. Three black. The date at the top had been scratched through five times, and a new date written in its place. All of which occurred on the anniversary of my leaving. That meant Dad had pulled the letter out every year, reread it, and then changed the date and signed his name afresh.

Maybe that image comforted me most.

I folded the letter and inserted it back into the envelope. After twenty-five years my father's voice still echoed. His last words to me. And when they settled in the middle of me and I once again realized that the words I had long wanted to speak, the words I came home to offer, would never get spoken, but lay silent and sour, where they cut my soul like slivers of stained glass, I cried like a baby.

PART II

11

When I was growing up, Dad never talked much about my mom. It wasn't that he didn't want to. I think it just hurt too much. He told me they met in a bar where he was playing and she was waiting tables. Over the weeks she quit serving him beer because she fell in love with his voice and said it was too pure to be poisoning with so much alcohol.

What she didn't know was that he was ordering the beer to get her to come around. Problem was, he didn't like the taste, so whenever she walked away he poured the beer between the slats of the deck beneath his feet. Dad said he was glad when she put her foot down because he preferred coffee, and given that refills were free, he saw more of her that way.

Finally, one night she set down the coffeepot. "Why don't you just ask me out? No person on earth drinks this much coffee."

He said that was good too, 'cause he was peeing every five minutes.

He said when they got pregnant with me, he used to sing to my mom's stomach at night. Press his lips to her skin. Sing "Jesus Loves Me" or any number of old hymns. I'd be lying if I said I could remember it, but I do have a vague awareness that I heard singing before I heard language. I think that's why I sang before I talked. I carried a tune before I said *Momma* or *Dada* or *truck*. When I did speak, to my father's great delight my first word was *Jimmy*.

Jimmy was a wedding present given to my father by my mother. It cost her a year's worth of tips. A Martin D-28. If you're a guitar person, you don't need an explanation. If you're not, it's simple. The D-28 is the guitar by which all others are judged. Period. Whether you know it or not, when you think *guitar,* you're thinking of a D-28. Given both its history and its pedigree, Jimmy was always the most valuable thing in our house.

As a result, I grew up in a house where music and singing were as natural as breathing. Asking me to imagine life without music was like asking a fish to consider life without water. When I was not quite a year old, my father would sit me on his knee and teach me licks. Baby food in one hand, pick in the other. No, I don't remember it, nor did I really understand it, but something in my brain did. Like his singing to Mom's stomach, those early lessons formed a pathway in my brain where I began to perceive and ingest the world, my surroundings, what I felt, through music. Dad says I was making chords on a ukulele before I could walk. I don't have very many memories of my mom, and I can't see her face except in pictures, but sometimes I can hear her singing. Dad said her voice just melted him, and the closest thing to it that he ever heard was my voice as a kid.

Our cabin sat at almost thirteen thousand feet. Perched on a shoulder near the top of a mountain. At times that made it difficult both to get to and get out of. Few folks had ever been up this high. Even the old silver and ore miners didn't think the land was worth the hassle. Given that nobody else wanted it, Mom and Dad were able to buy it.

This wouldn't mean much until years later. While it was true that the land wasn't valuable, it turned out that the water rights were. And water we had aplenty. That might not sound like much of a benefit, but in Colorado people kill each other over water rights. And given that we owned the mountain, including the top and any source or spring inside, no one had rights to that water other than us.

One of the things that attracted my mother to my father was his occupation. He was a tent preacher. He dabbled with prospecting when we were home, but the thing he "did" was preach. His revival show was popular in and around Colorado, so we traveled a lot. It wasn't that he didn't believe in brick-and-mortar churches, he just felt more at home in a church without walls. His style brought folks from every kind of background, including many who wouldn't feel comfortable in a steeple-church, under one tent.

Tattooed bikers sitting next to hippies who hadn't bathed in a year next to a man in a ten-gallon hat next to a man singing Motown next to a woman with her dress to her ankles and her hair up in a beehive. They saw it all. I grew up in it, so it seemed normal to me then. Now I think we must have looked more like a circus than a church.

When I turned three, Dad started getting calls from churches in nearby states, Texas or New Mexico, so we would load up on Wednesday or Thursday and drive all night en route to a Friday night through Sunday morning revival. Sometimes Sunday morning would stretch into Sunday afternoon or evening, so by the time he got the tents torn down and chairs stacked and piano loaded up, we'd get home on Tuesday only to leave again on Thursday. Dad was a big man, but doing all this loading and unloading by himself was more than he could handle. Then he happened upon Big Ivory Johnson.

Because revivals occur mostly at night, Dad spent a lot of daytime hours in the small towns where he preached, drumming up interest. He'd eat in the local diner, hamming it up with the waitresses; he'd get a shave in the local barbershop; he'd do a load of laundry at the Laundromat; and, given that the residents were a rather captive audience, he'd take his message to local prisons. That's where he met Big Ivory, who was serving a five-year sentence for assault—which, given his size, must have been easy to do. Big Ivory was about six feet six inches tall, probably weighed close to two hundred and eighty pounds, and while his teeth were the color of ivory, his skin was coffee black. He said when he got out, Dad was the only guy of any color who offered him a job.

Dad had been waiting on Big-Big when he walked out of prison. The way Big-Big tells it, Dad rolled down the window of his bus and said, "You hungry?"

Big-Big said, "I looked at this white man and thought, *He crazy*. But my stomach be growling." Their friendship started at breakfast.

I had trouble saying *Ivory,* so I just called him Big-Big. From that day on, I don't remember the bus leaving without Big-Big either driving or navigating.

I was four when Mom died. All I remember is that she got sick and then she was gone. Big-Big had worked for my dad almost a year by then. Folks came from all over for the funeral, and the procession was more than a mile long. They buried her beneath the aspens because she loved to hear the wind through the leaves, and Big-Big helped lower her casket down into the earth.

If my father ever had a crisis of faith, it was as he kept watch by the fever-riddled, emaciated body of my sweating, delirious mother. Big-Big told me later that her dying really shook him. Said he'd never seen a man cry like that. Said Dad was a tent peg for a lot of people, but she was his. As was I. Which explained my nickname. Peg. Like Big-Big, it stuck. Folks been calling me Peg ever since.

After the funeral Dad took me by the hand, tears draining out his eyes, and said, "Would you mind not singing for a little while?" It took me some time to understand why. During the next year, Dad didn't talk much. We moved up into the mountains and he walked the aspens with Jimmy, playing. He would try to sing, but most times the words wouldn't come or when they did, only in fits. Sometimes he'd pan the creek for gold. Just stare for hours into the plate for any sign of color. I think he was looking less for gold and more for Mom's reflection.

Since I had a good bit of free time, my playground became the mountain. Dad would cut me loose after chores. "Don't get beyond the sound of my whistle." That gave me a lot of room to roam.

Late in the evening, when the breeze picked up, he'd walk through the aspens with his hands raised. Then he'd come back with red, puffy eyes. One evening he waved his hands across the aspen grove, brilliant with crimson red and yellow. He said, "We see hundreds of trees. Thousands, even. But underground their roots are connected, making all this one giant organism." He paused. "If one tree gets sick, the whole grove gets sick."

The following year we returned to the revival circuit, and by the age of six I was spending more nights in the back of the flatbed than at home. Dad preached. Big-Big played piano. The older I got, the more I realized that while my dad was a big man, Big-Big was Dad times two. Given the size of both men and the striking difference in the color of their skin, I began to guess that some people came just to see what all the fuss was about.

One of the perks of a large stature was a barrel chest and booming baritone with enough volume to carry between mountain ranges. Dad seldom used a microphone. Big-Big had bear paws for hands and his fingers were the size of sausages, but he could light up a piano. I still don't understand how he made the chords without double-punching every other key. I used to sit and watch his fingers glide across the keyboard. Often the church we were visiting would lend their choir to fill in where Mom had left off and add a much-needed female voice.

Whenever we returned home, Dad would unload and then hike up through the aspens. After several minutes, his voice would echo back to me. Always the same song. While my ears may have heard the melody and my mind may have understood the words, it was my heart that got pulled on. It was a lament. A song of loss. I guess Dad could sing it with such emotive clarity because he'd known such emotional pain.

One night when he returned, eyes red and wet, I asked him, "Dad, what's that song?"

He poured himself some coffee and we sat on the porch, where he propped his feet up on the railing. Colorado stretched out before us. I could see west for nearly two hundred miles.

Dad was quiet several minutes. "Somewhere in the sixteenth or seventeenth century," he began, "a blind harpist named O'Cahan wrote that tune. It survived two hundred years until an itinerant fiddler played it one night on the streets of England. History does not record the fiddler's name, but a music collector named Jane Ross heard and transcribed the tune and published it. Called it 'O'Cahan's Lament.' The tune lay dormant awhile until some folks named Weatherly came from England to these very mountains looking for silver." Dad waved his hand across the landscape.

"Most, if not all, of the silver rush occurred within eyesight of where you now sit, so I like to think that what happened next had something to do with these hills. Your mom certainly thought so." Dad sipped his coffee. "Things get a bit complicated here, but an Irish-American woman named Jess Weatherly played the tune for her brother-in-law Fred, who was something of a songwriter. Turns out that over the course of his life he wrote and published some fifteen hundred songs. He'd written a song some years prior but had never attached the right melody to the words. Somewhere around 1911 or 1912, Jess played that tune for Fred. He reshaped the lyrics he'd written to fit the tune and published the song you hear me singing."

We watched in silence as clouds filtered through the mountaintops.

"In my limited education, it's probably the best ballad ever written. There's something that happens in the rise and fall of the melody that speaks to us on a level that's deeper than our thinking. It was sung at President Kennedy's funeral and has been recorded by everyone from Judy Garland and Bing Crosby to the Man in Black." Dad smiled. "Elvis said he thought it'd been written by angels and asked for it to be played at his funeral. You probably don't remember this, but the night your mom died, she asked me to lay you next to her in the hospital bed. She wrapped her arm around you and sang it to you while you went to sleep in her arms." Dad stopped. He was quiet a long while. "I sat next to the bed and tried to listen." He motioned to the aspens. "So sometimes . . . I go there to remember."

I waited a minute or two before I asked, "Will you teach it to me?"

Dad nodded slowly.

"You want me to get Jimmy?"

"Jimmy stays quiet on this one." Dad set down his cup, cleared his throat, and tried to sing, but something choked out the words. "This might be tougher than I thought." He tried again, and this time the words came.

"O Danny boy, the pipes, the pipes are calling . . ."

Over the years, we sang that song together a hundred times. It was ours. We made it so. It was our way of honoring Mom and of sharing a memory without ever having to talk about it. It was how we acknowledged and waded through the pain without being crippled by it. "Danny Boy" was the song that taught me what songs can do. That music heals us from the inside out.

That night he finished the story as he sat on my bed, tucking me in. "No credit was ever given to Jess Weatherly. She died penniless in 1939, while Fred enjoyed both fame and wealth."

I couldn't understand why someone would do that, and Dad picked up on my distress. "Songs outlive us," he said. "They're supposed to. We write them in order to give them away, but"—he smiled and tapped me in the chest—"just be careful who you give them to."

Dad said he and Jimmy could lead folks most anywhere. Sometimes he would start in the back, winding his way forward. Never even strumming a chord. He would just start tapping out a slow rhythm on the spruce top. Using the guitar like a drum. Dad knew every kind of music known to man and he could play most of it, but when it came to people who were hurting inside, he played old hymns. The simpler the better. Despite his common appearance, Dad was classically trained. He knew Bach and Mozart and Pachelbel, and while he loved their music and he had lightning in his fingers and he could fill the air with more notes than most could comprehend, he said when it came to people, less was more. Fewer notes. Less noise. Just a simple lead. He said, "You play too much, too busy, and people will sit back and observe. Marvel in your talent. Play simple, and people will join in. Sing along. Which, by the way, is the goal. Our job is to put a song in their mouths and let them sing it back to us. That's all that really matters." Then he added, "The great players aren't great because of all the notes they can play, but because of the ones they don't play."

One day we passed a gas station with a bunch of velvet Elvises hanging over clotheslines. He nodded once. "Pop stars may set the world afire, but they come and go. They're a flash in the pan. So are their songs. But good hymns? They live past the people who wrote them. Hymns never die." He looked down at me. "How many Grammys did Elvis win?"

I shrugged.

"Two." He palmed the sweat off his face. "For what song?"

Another shrug.

Dad loved the history of music. And he loved to share it.

"In the mid-1880s," he began, "a Swedish preacher named Boberg wrote and published a poem. No music. Just words. A few years later he attended a meeting and heard his poem sung back to him, attached to an old Swedish melody. Nobody really knows how or who put the two together. Then in the 1920s, a missionary named Hine had climbed into the Carpathian Mountains to minister when he heard—get this—a Russian translation of Boberg's Swedish poem attached to the Swedish melody. Hine was standing in the street preaching on John chapter 3 when a nasty storm blew in, so a local schoolteacher housed him for the night. As Hine watched the storm roll through those mountains, he added what we now call the first verse. Next he crossed over into Romania and Bukovina, and somewhere beneath the trees and birds, he added the second verse. He finished the third verse after spending time with the Carpathian mountain dwellers and, finally, the fourth verse when he returned to Britain. The song as we know it ended up in the States at a youth camp in California in the early 1950s, where crusade team member George Beverly Shea handed it to a man named Billy Graham. Then in 1967, a fellow by the name of Presley recorded 'How Great Thou Art,' and the album went platinum." Dad held up two fingers. "Twice."

A couple minutes passed, and rain started pelting the windshield. The wipers tapped out a delayed rhythm. Dad started singing quietly. More for himself than anyone. "O Lord my God, when I in awesome wonder . . ." Words like those sang me to sleep more often than not.

I never did understand why Dad did the tent thing. The brick-and-mortar thing would have been a lot easier. A lot less work too. To make matters worse, he never took an offering. That doesn't mean people didn't give. They did. But Dad never asked. He wanted folks to give out of conviction, not manipulation. Given the piles of crutches that stacked up over the years and the empty wheelchairs, he could have made a pile of money had he wanted to and probably flown to and fro in his own plane, but I never once saw my dad pass a plate.

When it came to music, Dad said his job was to remind people of the words and let them sing. He was musically talented enough that he could have played lead or rhythm for just about anybody, but he always said he was just background. "Spotlight the song and give it back to people. Put it in their mouths. Songs don't belong to us.

A song is a light we shine on others, not a light we shine on us."

We'd been setting up the stage one day, and it was hot. We were resting. I'd gotten curious and realized that my father was unlike every other father I knew. "Dad, why do you do what you do? I mean, are you ever going to get a real job like other dads?"

He laughed. "I sincerely hope not." He pointed to the front where people walked in. You could see the parking lot in the distance. "My job is to lead people from there to here. To walk them up and set them down in the presence of the One who can help them. Thenay."

"Why?" I said.

"'Cause He's got what they need. Not me. People want to dress me up in a fancy suit and put me on TV." He shook his head and pointed at the lights. "Those things have an odd effect on a man." He sucked between his teeth. "But remember, diamonds are only brilliant when they reflect."

I'd only recently become aware of money and success and how others seemed to have it and we didn't. "Dad, can I ask you something?"

"Sure."

"Do I have an inheritance?"

He laughed. "Who you been listening to?"

"Well, I mean, will I have money one day?"

Dad took his time answering. "Yes, son, you have an inheritance."

I smiled. I knew it. We were rich. Dad had been hiding it all along. He'd struck a silver vein somewhere on the mountain and he was just keeping it quiet until I got older and we could build a big house and buy a Cadillac.

Then he said, "I'm not leaving something *for* you. I'm leaving something *in* you."

I didn't like the way that sounded.

12

My first significant memory of the impact of my father on other people and what he was actually doing with his life came when I was eight. Word about Dad had spread. People were driving from California to hear him, and he began looking for bigger venues. We hired four guys just to park all the cars, and we'd grown from one tent to five—tied in the shape of a cross with the center being the stage. Each tent could seat over two hundred, and on most nights every chair was full. Not only that, but folks who couldn't find a seat were standing four and five deep along the edges. Crowding in. Kids sitting on their fathers' shoulders. Moms nursing babies. Old folks in wheelchairs.

Evidently fire and brimstone are more palatable than most folks let on. So with growing need, Dad needed room to grow.

He used to go on long hikes by himself. A quiet time to think. A few miles south of BV, Dad found a high-walled canyon set against the base of Mt. Princeton that had piqued his interest. He pulled out a topo map and showed it to me. From the air it looked like someone had cut a piece of pie out of the side of the mountain. The thirty- to forty-acre section of flat ground, shaped like a funnel, extended out from rock walls that rose several hundred vertical feet. To someone like Dad, who communicated to hundreds, if not thousands, at a time, it created a perfect venue.

There was just one problem. Somebody else owned it. Wanting to show it to me, he hiked me past the umpteen No Trespassing signs and we slipped up through the evergreens, through the national park that bordered our property, and to the ledge that overlooked the ranch below. A bird's-eye view. He pointed. "We'll put the stage back there where it narrows." Another direction. "All the tents out here, parking over there, bring in the portable bathrooms over there." He wiped his hands together like he was dusting them off. "Piece of cake."

I scratched my head. "But, Dad, we don't own any of this."

He waved me off. "Somebody does."

That next week Dad approached the land-owner, Mr. Tom Slocumb—a cattleman whose land had been in his family a hundred-plus years.

Dad, Big-Big, and I drove across the cattle guard and parked out in front of the man's ranch house. Dad spoke to both of us. "Come on. If Mr. Slocumb doesn't like me, maybe he'll like you two."

Dad knocked on the door, and a small, wiry man wearing a hat and spurs and a belt buckle the size of his head answered the door. He sized each of us up, spending considerable time studying Big-Big. He looked like he was not in the mood for door-to-door solicitation. "He'p you?"

Dad shook the man's hand and explained who he was and what he wanted. Mr. Slocumb listened while pushing a toothpick around his mouth with amazing dexterity. Every few seconds he'd flip the toothpick end over end and then shove it in either corner of his mouth, where it would sit motionless for a few seconds until his tongue started the whole process over again. Halfway through Dad's story, the man reached in his back pocket and pulled out a pouch of chewing tobacco. He opened it and began digging his fingers into it like he was tossing a salad. This was about the time I noticed he was missing the index finger on his right hand. Once he had the salad good and mixed like he wanted it, he raised a goodly sized wad of brown leaf tobacco into his mouth and packed it into his cheek. When he was finished, it looked like he was sucking on a golf ball. As he listened to Dad talk, one part of his mouth was flipping the toothpick end over end while the other chewed voraciously on the tobacco. I kept waiting for him to spit, but he never did.

When Dad finished, Mr. Slocumb looked at me, then back at Dad, then at Big-Big, then back at me, and finally back at Dad. He tipped his hat back slightly and hung his thumbs in his belt loops.

"Let me get this straight. You happened to be trespassing one day on my land, where I've posted more than two hundred No Trespassing signs, and you happened upon my pretty little meadow up yonder. And you thought to yourself, this'd make a great site for a preaching tent revival where you're gonna have a stage and some tents that will just magically appear. And this man here"— he thumbed at Big-Big—"who's bigger than any human I ever seen, is gonna play pianer while you—" He glanced at me, flipped the toothpick, and then stared back at Dad. "While you preach fire and brimstone to several hundred, maybe even a few thousand self-proclaimed and attentive sinners who are gonna miraculously appear with cars and picnics and umbrellers. And every one of them people, in order to get to your little revival, is gonna parade across my pasture here and then park on the grass that I intend to feed to my cattle before it snows this winter."

He paused and swallowed. "And to top it all

124

off, you're gonna do all this without passing no plate, without taking nothing from nobody and without talking once't about money or giving or how if they don't they's stealing from"—he pointed up—"the Lord." He nodded. "That right?"

Dad nodded. "That pretty much sums it up."

The man laughed. "Mister, you got bigger—" He glanced at me again. "Than my bull out yonder." He rolled his eyes and turned to Big-Big. "Fella, what size shoe you wear?"

Big-Big never hesitated. "Fi'teen."

The man sucked through his teeth. "I believe it." Then he pointed at the drive toward the highway nearly a mile in the distance. "You see that sign in the distance? The one that's nearly as big as a drive-in theatre screen that you drove by to get to my house?"

Dad nodded.

"Well, in case you didn't read it, it says that this property, which been in my family now for three generations, is being sold along with all my cows 'cause we ain't got no water."

That didn't make sense to me, because winding through the man's property looked to be a rather large and very dry riverbed. I spoke out of turn. I said, "What happened to your river?"

"That's a good question. And I've asked the same thing many times myself." He pointed to the riverbed snaking around and through his property. "That used to flow with the most pure water. Adolph Coors himself ain't got better water than that right there, and I reckon it's been flowing in that river since God squeezed it out of the mountain. But then some city slicker with a law degree done some digging in some law books somewhere and bought the land to the north of me." He pointed. "And as it turns out, his water rights predate mine, so—" Another flip of the toothpick. "I'm screwed. And so are my cows."

I scratched my head. "Where'd the water go?"

He waved his hand across the land toward the north. "Through his fields." He turned toward the highway. "It joins the river 'bout a mile that way."

My dad finished his sentence. "Leaving you high and dry."

"Yep. So now my riverbed is dry and my cows is drinking mud and there ain't no hay in sight nor any hope of any. So I tell you what, Mr. Preacher Man. If you can fill up that dry riverbed and get my cows a drink of water, you can use my little medder up yonder for as long as you've got breath to preach. If not"—he held out his hand, palm up—"I need ten thousand dollars." He smiled, revealing a mouthful of stained teeth. "Otherwise, you're SOL."

A wrinkle appeared between my eyes. I looked at my dad. "What's SOL?"

He thought for a minute. "Sorta-outta-luck."

The rancher nodded. "That too."

Dad craned his neck, studying the back of the man's property where the riverbed wound toward the vertical cliffs. "You got a bulldozer?"

The man shrugged. "It's wore slap out, but I got one."

"Can I borrow it?"

The man didn't even offer a response. He just looked at Dad and sucked on his tobacco.

Dad continued, "If I can get you some water, you'll forgo the ten thousand and let us use your meadow?"

"Mister, you gonna just snap your fingers and water's gonna all of a sudden appear?"

Dad shrugged. "That's one way of looking at it."

The man's disbelief was palpable. "You gonna do what three years' worth of appeals and sixty thousand dollars' worth of attorney's fees couldn't do?"

Dad didn't respond.

The man considered Dad. "I tell you what, Preacher Man, you get my cows some water and I'll help you park the da—" He glanced down at me. "The cars. Otherwise—" He held out his hand again, palm up. "Ten thousand."

Dad shook the man's hand. "Deal."

The man raised a single eyebrow. "You gonna get me ten thousand dollars?"

"No." Dad was staring at the mountain. "I'm gonna get you some water."

Big-Big and me drove out of the driveway in the

truck while Dad piloted the dozer. We followed him for two miles on the highway with our hazard lights flashing, 'cause he was bouncing down the road like a drunk snake while trying to get used to the steering.

Big-Big spoke through a smile. "I seen it all now."

When we got to the T in the road, Dad sent us to town to fill up every five-gallon can we could find with diesel while he drove up to the cabin. When we got there two hours later, he was in full-on creek-construction mode. By evening on the third night he'd burned through a lot of diesel and had carved a four-foot-deep trench spiraling around our side of the mountain. Would have made a great creek, had there been any water in it. When I asked Dad where he was going to get the water, he said, "I'm going to try and poke a hole in God's Cereal Bowl."

On the fourth morning Dad and I walked back up to the rancher's front door and knocked. He met us in much the same way as he had before. Flipping a toothpick end over end.

Dad said, "Wonder if we might go for a drive?"

The rancher did not look impressed, but he obliged us, and so Dad drove us to the back side of the man's property where the dried-up riverbed of his once-flowing river met the granite cliffs of Princeton. As a crow flies, our property was only about a mile from the rancher's, but it took nearly thirty minutes on the road. As Dad said, you had to go around your elbow to get to your thumb.

Dad got out of the truck and started looking at his watch. Then he started walking the riverbed with his arms raised. The rancher leaned against the truck, crossed his arms, and eyed Dad with a bit of amusement. At 10:30 a.m., Dad counted off ten paces from the side of the cliffs to what happened to be the middle of the dusty riverbed, where he set down a small round stone. He was purposeful in setting it down and made sure the rancher saw it. Then he too leaned against the hood of the truck and crossed his arms. Casually, he said to the man, "How much you spend on your legal battle?"

Mr. Slocumb didn't even blink. "Sixty-three thousand, eight hundred and fourteen dollars."

Dad nodded and kept staring up at the cliff.

When 10:35 came and left, the man waved his hand toward the river stones. "Maybe you should walk out there and dance. Sing a tune or something."

Dad just kept staring at the cliff.

At 10:40, Mr. Slocumb said, "Mister, are you on the level?"

Dad shook his head. "Probably not, but—" He stared up at the cliff and smiled. "I know where to find water."

As he was speaking, a rumbling sound occurred

above us, followed by a roar that sounded like a coming storm. I was standing in the back of the truck and I could hear it getting closer, so I moved around behind the truck, hiding behind the tailgate.

Seconds later a stream of water as big around as the front end of the truck shot like a cannon off the edge of the cliff, extending some eight to ten feet out from the rock wall, where it then landed directly on top of the rock Dad had set in place. The initial explosion carved out a pool in the sandy bottom, which, as the flow increased from up above, filled the riverbed to its banks.

As the water fell from above us, the man's mouth dropped open, chewed tobacco leaves spilled out, and his eyes grew big as half-dollars. He walked to the bank, stared up, then down at the water, then back up as tiny spray droplets landed on his face and shoulders. He did this several seconds as the roar of the now-raging waterfall landed on our ears.

When the water had reached the defined edges of the bank, it did what all rivers do. It began flowing downhill, following its natural course through the rancher's pasture and directly past his more than two thousand thirsty cattle. He stared in absolute disbelief at the cliff, the water, and then back up at the sixty-foot waterfall shooting onto his property. He stared for a minute, then two, as if he were waiting for it to stop as suddenly as it had started.

When it did not, he said, "Is it gonna keep doing that?"

Dad nodded.

Mr. Slocumb took off his hat, wiped his brow, and threw his hat down. "Well, I'll be a suck-egg mule! Preacher Man, you did it! You actually did it!" He started laughing and charged into the water, which rose to midthigh. He then walked against the current into the waterfall, opened his mouth, and held out his arms. The weight of the water on the man's back and shoulders pushed him down into the pool, where he rolled and frolicked like a dolphin.

Finally he stood up, splashing, laughing, and spitting. "There's enough water here to fill fifty thousand head, let alone two." He raised both hands to his mouth, drank several large gulps of water, spat with great delight, and then started dancing a jig.

I wanted to ask what happened to the rest of his tobacco, but never did. Given that the water temperature was subfreezing, he didn't stay there long. He walked to the bank, stepped out, picked up his crushed hat, and pulled it down tight over his head. Then, without warning, he grabbed my dad in a great big bear hug, which struck me as funny 'cause Dad was nearly half again as big as the rancher. Once he'd finished hugging him, he began shaking my father's hand with both of his.

Dad laughed. "We start parking cars at four Friday."

The man laughed. "Mister, I'll he'p you park ever' last one."

13

One unintended outcome was that the resulting waterfall could be seen from the highway more than a mile away, creating an easily recognizable landmark. Word spread, the name caught, and our first weekend at "The Falls" was sold out—and memorable.

We started setting up tents on Thursday, the stage on Friday morning. When Friday noon rolled around, there was already a line of cars trailing out the gate. Dad loved parking cars. Said it was like putting his finger on the pulse of the congregation without their knowing that he was the doctor. He'd open a door, give them a hand, and ask folks how they were doing. By six o'clock he and Mr. Slocumb had parked several hundred cars.

In the lull before the service, Mr. Slocumb wiped his sweating face with a towel and said, "You like doing this, don't you, Preacher Man?"

Dad shrugged. "Years back I learned how to ask one question, and people will spill fifteen years' worth of pain in three minutes. Even the quiet ones will open the door to what hurts. And when they do . . . I try to listen." He paused. "With the ears of my heart." He borrowed Mr. Slocumb's towel, wiped off his face, and then waved his hand across the rancher's pasture. "People don't drive out here to the middle of nowhere to be enter-tained. There's better entertainment elsewhere. No, they make the drive because they're hurting. Broken."

He pointed at the tent. "You think this is some strange circus tent show, and I'm just some quack snake-oil salesman." He shook his head. "This is triage." A long silence followed. "It's where we stop the bleeding."

I'd never seen so many cars or so many people. Big-Big started to play the piano. The choir was swaying, humming. Several lights were flickering over the stage, swaying in rhythm with the wind—which had, oddly enough, picked up all of a sudden. A bunch of the women were waving fans. Cooling themselves. Everyone was waiting. I don't know what they were expecting, but I doubt it's what they got.

Dad's booming voice rose up out of the back. From my seat on the edge of the stage I could see my dad, his face shining with sweat. Had a white sweat towel draped around his neck. Muddy shoes. No suit. No flashy tie. No gold rings. Just Jimmy hanging around his neck. I think Dad did that on purpose. Because when folks saw him, they immediately knew he was one of them.

Dad took his time making his way forward, slowly tapping out a rhythm on the body of the guitar. Making him both percussionist and guitar player. We never handed out song sheets because they were expensive to print, most ended up in the mud after the service, and if you played songs folks already knew, they didn't need them anyway.

Dad wound his way toward the stage like a corkscrew. By the time he reached the stage, everybody was standing and singing so loud they didn't even need him. He had started a wave with enough kinetic energy to carry itself to shore. A lot of the kids were standing on the chairs or sitting on their daddies' shoulders. Amidst a raucous chorus, Dad set Jimmy down and sat next to me, toweling his forehead. Big-Big kept playing at the piano. The volume beneath that tent was so loud it hurt my ears.

Near us, a lady pressed a baby to her bosom. Couldn't have been but a few weeks old. The mother rocked slowly, covering herself with a cloth diaper. A group of kids had come up front and were holding hands and singing and dancing in a circle. Dad and I sat on the edge of the stage, blanketed in song. Big-Big softened his touch on the keys, and the choir quietly hummed. Soon the entire place was just humming along. Dad put his arm around my shoulder and spoke, looking out across more than a thousand people—all looking at him. Dad was smiling at the kids. "Out of the mouths of infants and nursing babes . . ."

Sometimes I felt like my dad spoke in riddles. Half the words were his. The other half he found in Scripture. This was one of those riddles I didn't understand for years to come. He saw the look on my face and he touched my vocal cords with the tip of his finger. He whispered, "God gave us pipes for a reason."

I was too young to follow him. "What's the reason?"

He gently touched my chest with his index finger. "Music cuts people free." A pause. "It silences the thing that's trying to kill us."

The echo of his words had yet to fade when the wind suddenly changed direction. It was blowing right to left. As the words left his mouth, it changed from left to right. Like somebody had shut one door and opened another. That meant it was swirling. Which meant just one thing.

A storm.

In late fall, storms come on fast and they come on strong, with little warning. I saw a man's comb-over stand straight up like a rooster, and then the temperature dropped about fifteen degrees. The space between Dad's eyes narrowed and his forehead wrinkled. In the time it took to sing a single song, the sky had turned the color of India ink and lightning spider-webbed sideways across the mountain peaks. While I was asking myself, *I wonder what Dad's going to do,* the rain came. In sheets. In seconds, the rain was blowing sideways under the tent, stinging my face. The wind lifted the canvas like a sail and stretched the ropes attached to the pegs. A couple of the ropes snapped with a loud pop, and one corner of the tent ripped off and sailed out through the night sky like a giant Frisbee.

It was my first angry storm.

Lightning flashed above us, and a single bolt traveled down a dead evergreen tree that had grown up against the cliffs. The tree lit like a candle dipped in gasoline, and sparks jumped from the tree to the tents, lighting the canvas on fire. As the canvas ceiling became a wall of fire, people scattered like cockroaches. Pandemonium. Folks were fighting, scrambling over each other to get to their cars. Slipping. Shoving each other out of the way. It was ugly.

And the rain was unlike anything I'd ever seen. Several inches in just a few minutes. And yet it seemed to have no effect on the fire. Then hail the size of golf balls began to fall, denting hoods and rooftops and driving everyone back underneath the tents. Folks were bleeding. One man ran back into the tent, blood dripping down his face and the front of his white dress shirt as he screamed something about the 'pocalypse and the end of the world.

I crawled beneath the piano bench, which had been vacated by Big-Big as he was trying to secure the tent corners. The only part of the tent not torn was covering the piano. Somehow the wind had cut the power to every light save one. A single bulb, powered by the batteries in the bus, swayed above the piano. I was witness to the second coming of Noah's flood, and the only two things dry within five square miles were Jimmy and that piano.

With the storm raging, wind ripping, rain stinging, hail cracking windshields, I remember lying there, wrapped up in a fetal ball, shaking and covering my ears with both hands to shut out the shrill whistle of the swirling wind.

For a moment I lost track of my dad. When I opened my eyes again, I found him kneeling, staring at me—his face inches from mine. Water dripping from his eyes, hair, and nose. Darkness and fire created the backdrop beyond him. His right arm reached in like a giant excavator, wrapped around me, and lifted me out. I wanted to cling to him, but he set me on the piano bench and then sat next to me. The wind was blowing so hard I had to lean into it to sit up straight. Dad brushed the wet hair out of his face, nodded at the piano, and spoke just three words. "Let it out."

I tried to scream above the whistling wind. "What?"

He leaned in and spoke slowly so I could read his lips. "Let it out."

I looked around at all those people. All those terrified faces. All that anger. That fear. I felt helpless. I'd wrapped one foot around the leg of the piano bench so the wind couldn't rip me off the face of the earth. I tried to touch the keys, but my hands were shaking.

Dad looked down at me. "Peg?"

I didn't answer. I was too scared. I wanted to run like everybody else.

He leaned in closer. His nose almost touching mine. "Son?"

"Yes, sir."

He placed my hands gently on the keys. "Let it out."

I looked down at my chest and shouted back, "Let what out?"

He smiled. "The part that makes the song."

So I did.

My shaking fingers hit the keys, made the chords, and I played with every ounce of terrified strength within me. The harder that wind blew, the higher the flames climbed, the more the tent whipped in the air above me, the tighter I wrapped my foot around the leg of the bench and the louder I played. That dark storm had covered the sky, stretching ten miles in either direction, coming to rest in Mr. Slocumb's cattle field just beyond us.

We were next. Out on the prairie, five miles distant, lightning struck the ground and hit a propane tank the size of a semitrailer. The ignition caused a white flash that lit the darkness and rolled it back like a scroll. Followed by a sonic boom that nearly ripped me off the bench. Whatever emotion had filled me exploded out my fingers. As much a protective mechanism as an artistic expression, I played as loud and as hard as I could.

What I didn't realize was that while the storm had my attention, something else inside the tent had everyone else's. They weren't screaming. Weren't fighting. Weren't swinging chairs. In fact, they were just standing. Watching. And most of them were looking in my general direction. I looked at Big-Big, wondering what song he'd started, but Big-Big was just standing there staring at me. He wasn't singing a lick. I looked up at Dad, but he wasn't singing either. He was just sitting there with his hands in his lap. Then I looked back at all those people, and while the storm raged around us, it had quit raining inside the metal framing of the tent. I say metal framing because most all the canvas had been ripped off. The rain streaked down my face, but when it hit my lips it tasted salty. My fingers were slinging water, but the piano was dry and everything around me was dry. That meant the water wasn't rain.

Somewhere in there I heard a sound. A beautiful sound. And I thought maybe I'd heard it before but maybe only in my dreams. It was like an echo around a corner. A siren in the distance. Something higher up. Only when I shut my eyes did I realize that the sound was me. I was singing. Singing at the top of my lungs. "O Lord my God . . ."

The sound of me surprised me.

Dad stood up, dug a pick from his pocket, hung Jimmy over his shoulder, and came up underneath me—his deep baritone filling in the space below my prepubescent voice. Big-Big reassembled the choir, which had voluntarily dispersed, and I don't really know what all happened next. In the thirty-six years since, I've tried to make sense of it, but I cannot. It does not make sense to my rational mind. But that's the thing about music. It doesn't enter through the mind. It enters through the heart.

There's a lot I don't know, but this is what I know for certain: the storm retreated before our very eyes and the torrent left as quickly as it had come. The night cleared, ten billion stars stared down on us, and the air took on that pungent, crisp earthiness known only after the rain. The people returned, righted their chairs, sat down, and acted civil. I don't know how long I played, but I know in the years to come Dad used to joke, "First song that boy ever played in public was an Elvis tune."

My dad loved the King.

Dad followed the storm with his "We Are Not Alone" sermon. Which made good sense, given that we all just witnessed round one of the coming Apocalypse. But while Dad was talking about how "some have entertained angels" and "therefore since we are surrounded by so great a host of witnesses," my attention was focused on a man sitting on my piano. He had climbed up there during the storm. When Dad got to talking about Revelation chapter 4 and how it's a picture of the throne room of God and how all the heavenly host are singing "Holy, Holy, Holy" 24/7, I wanted to raise my hand and say, "No, sir, they're not." But I was pretty sure if I did, everyone, including my dad, would think I was crazy. So I kept my mouth shut, but I never took my eyes off the man on the piano.

Hours later, after everyone had gone and Dad and Mr. Slocumb had unstuck several cars and trucks with his tractor, Dad found me still sitting on that piano bench, where my feet didn't touch either the ground or the pedals. Dad put his arm around me. "Time for bed, big guy."

"But what about—" I pointed.

Dad looked puzzled. He scratched his chin and sat next to me. "What about what?"

I was tired. Eyes heavy. I waved my hand. "What do we do about him?"

"Who?"

The guy was sitting just a few feet away. He smelled like rosemary. Long blond hair. Muscular. Green eyes. Smiling. For the last hour or so, he'd been dancing and shaking a tambourine, so his shirt was soaked through. Every now and then he'd glance over his shoulder at me.

I pointed. "Him."

Dad pressed his palm to my forehead. "What's he look like?"

I pointed, somewhat irritated. "He looks like that guy right there."

"Okay, but describe him for me."

"You can't see him?"

"I just want to make sure we're talking about the same guy."

"Blue jeans. Flip-flops. White shirt. Blond hair. Ponytail. Ring on his finger."

Dad said, "How big is he?"

I sized him up. "Bigger than Big-Big."

"Does he scare you?"

"Yes."

"Does he look like he wants to hurt you?"

"No."

"When did he get here?"

"He walked in during the storm. Soon as I started playing."

"What's he do when you stop playing?"

"Sits down."

"What's he doing right this second?"

"He's whittling with his pocketknife, letting the shavings fall at his feet."

Dad smiled, picked me up off the bench, and carried me to the truck. It was almost two a.m. I put my head on his shoulder and spoke through closed eyes. "But, Dad, we can't just leave him."

Dad laughed. "Son, he's not going anywhere. Guys like him . . . they never leave."

Over time, Mr. Slocumb's cows grew fat and healthy, his hay grew tall and green, and with some encouragement from my dad, he turned the Falls into a public outdoor venue. With the help of an architect and engineer out of Colorado Springs and a loan from a Denver bank, Mr. Slocumb built Colorado's finest outdoor amphitheater, with seating for five thousand. The stage backed up against the cliffs, using the acoustics of the stone walls to project outward—which it did with relative perfection. He brought in sound engineers from LA and New York who captured and broadcast performers' voices while not blasting out those in attendance. He constructed bathrooms to serve the masses, a restaurant and concession to feed the hungry, and he learned how to drain his fields and pour enough asphalt so parking was never muddy.

Word spread, and when finished, Mr. Slocumb had created a venue sought after by performers and producers because of what they called the purity of the sound. Add to that a private airport ten minutes south that allowed performers to jet in and out, and an audience willing to drive from Fort Collins, Denver, Aspen, Vail, Breckenridge, Steamboat, Salida, Littleton, Telluride, Ouray, the

Springs, Silverton, and Montrose, and Mr. Slocumb found himself in the center of a world where music was valued.

He had just one problem—not enough seating. Shows were routinely sold out. By the time I turned eighteen, we'd held over a hundred services at the Falls, and Mr. Slocumb had helped park cars at every single one. And each summer, Dad and Big-Big baptized hundreds of people in the pool beneath the waterfall.

Including Mr. Slocumb.

14

In the weeks that followed the storm, I heard several nicknames aimed at me. "The kid who stopped the storm." "The kid who played in the rain." "The boy with the girl's voice." I had become something of an onstage oddity. People started coming to see me, and that meant I had both admirers and critics.

One evening after a service, I was cleaning up trash when five kids surrounded me. Started poking at me. Shoving me around. Next thing I knew, the ringleader, who was a head taller and wore a nose ring, jumped me from behind and was doing a pretty good job of feeding me a mud pie. I was having trouble breathing with all that mud in my nose and mouth. I was also having trouble calling for help. They were all laughing and taking turns kicking my legs and side while nose-ring boy controlled my head by my hair.

Next thing I knew a shadow appeared, and nose-ring boy suddenly levitated off the ground. I rolled over as the other four kids scattered like bees while my bullying friend hung suspended from the crane that was Big-Big's arm. A blood vessel had popped out on Big-Big's temple and was throbbing in rhythm with his heart. I sat up, spat the mud and blood out of my mouth, and wiped my face with my shirtsleeve.

Big-Big looked down at me. "You okay?"

"Yes, sir."

Big-Big raised the boy higher. "You sure?"

I nodded. He turned, set the boy down, and said, "Git!"

The boy disappeared out among the cars where his friends were cackling and calling Big-Big names. Big-Big lifted me and dusted me off. The vein was still pulsating on his temple.

"I tol' your dad I'd look out for you." He wiped my face with his handkerchief. "Looks like I'm not doing too good at my job."

Dad appeared over my shoulder, and we three stood there quietly. Big-Big's face took on a dull, muted complexion, like someone who'd known the darker side of people.

He said, "Peg, that boy ain't gon' leave you alone. Bullies never do. They don' fight fair.

That's why he brought his friends." He knelt and looked across at me. "Prison be the same way. Nex' time he approach you, you bes' punch him hard as you can right in the teeth 'fore he ever say a word. Jes' close his mouth. And don' jes' punch him once. You punch him 'til you can't punch no mo'. That be the only way to shut all five of them up." Big-Big looked at Dad, then back at me.

Dad nodded.

I pointed at the stage. "What about all that 'turn the other cheek' stuff?"

Dad's eyes narrowed. "When someone's trying to control you, you come out swinging. And keep swinging. Bible never said be a doormat." He looked down at me. "I'm not telling you to look for it. I'm telling you not to run. Stand your ground."

The following week Dad pulled me aside. He extended his hand, and in his palm he held a man's silver ring. Chunky. Had an oak tree engraved on it. He'd wrapped a pipe cleaner around the shank to make it fit a smaller finger. He said, "Put it on. Right hand."

I slid it on.

Dad looked at me square. "Now don't take it off."

"Yes, sir."

That week at school, nose-ring boy cornered me in the cafeteria. He pushed me down, stole my lunch money, and started cackling like a hyena as his buddies surrounded him and cheered. Then he started dancing around in a circle and kicking me.

Big-Big and my father were nowhere to be found. I climbed up off the floor, and the boys pushed me around like a pinball. Finally I squared up to nose-ring, who outweighed me by about fifty pounds. He opened his mouth to say something, but I never gave him a chance to get the words out. I hit him as quick and as hard as I could. And because I was scared, I didn't hit him just once.

When the cafeteria attendant pulled me off him, the other hyenas had vamoosed, and the boy's nose was sitting sideways on his face where it looked like a red balloon had exploded. The cafeteria attendant gripped my arm real tight, digging in her fingernails, and shook me. She was screaming pretty loud. "What do you think you're doing!"

I didn't bother answering her, but reached across the space between us and ripped the nose ring out of the boy's nose, tearing the skin between his nostrils. She jerked me around by my collar and marched me to the principal's office, where they called my dad.

I sat in that office, staring at the bloody ring on my right hand, wondering. Shortly, the bully who had pushed me down appeared with his dad. He was pressing a bag of ice to his face, whining, "It hurts!"

My dad appeared a few minutes later, and the principal took us all back. He said, "Mr. O'Connor, I'm suspending your boy three days for fighting. He'll get zeroes in all his classes. I figured you'd want to know so you could discipline him as well."

Dad smiled. "Thank you." He turned to me. "What happened?"

I looked at the kid. "He pushed me down, took my lunch money, and started kicking me. His buddies helped."

The kid spoke around the bag of ice. "Thash not true."

I pointed at his right front pocket. "Two dollars."

The principal said, "Is that true? Did you take his two dollars?"

The kid's voice rose. "No."

The principal motioned. "You mind emptying your pocket, son?"

The kid's father interrupted. "You can't expect . . ."

The principal waited while the kid emptied two crumpled dollar bills onto his desk. Then he said, "I'm suspending both of you. I won't have this kind of behavior. Do I make myself clear?"

Dad put his hand gently around my neck, resting it on my shoulders. He turned to the kid's father. "Let me make it clear for you. I fully expect that if this ever happens again, my son is going to jump up on your boy like a spider monkey. Further, he has my permission."

The principal started to protest, but Dad raised his hand. "Now, since he's got a few days off school, we're going to eat a cheeseburger, then we're going to get some ice cream, then we're going fishing. Might even take in a movie. Do I make myself clear?" He guided me toward the door.

The principal called after us, "And you call yourself a God-fearing man! A preacher!"

Dad turned and nodded. "I do. And I've never used the word *doormat* in conjunction with that description."

Halfway through my second cheeseburger I said, "Dad?"

He looked at me over his burger. "Yep."

"Is today why you gave me this ring?"

He stacked a pickle onto his cheeseburger. "Yes."

I nodded and eyed the ring. "Dad?"

Dad sipped his root beer. "Yes?"

"Thank you."

By the time I turned nine I'd gotten used to the blond guy and his friends showing up at Dad's services. I didn't know if other people saw them or not, but no one else mentioned them, and I didn't want to open my mouth and act the fool. I decided they were sort of like a rainbow. Not something you saw every day and you could only see from just the right angle.

One day when Dad and I were closing up after a service, he found me sitting at the piano. He said, "Time for bed, big guy."

I pointed. "What do I do about Blondie?"

"Back again, huh?"

I shook my head. "Never leaves."

He tapped his ear. "He's come to hear you."

"But, Dad . . ."

Blondie had started bringing friends. At first, it was just one or two. But lately the numbers had grown. More like a crowd.

"They're everywhere."

He laughed. "They must really like the way you sing."

I wasn't quite sure Dad was getting the picture. What I was seeing wasn't puppy dogs and lollipops. And to me they were as real as the piano. "Dad, this guy could turn Big-Big inside out. He's no joke."

"Is he angry?"

I considered this. "I don't think he's angry, but I do think he's at war."

"Do the others look like him?"

"Pretty close."

"Can you hear anything?"

I nodded.

"What do you hear?"

"I hear . . . singing."

"Can you hear the words?"

I nodded and spoke quietly, knowing they could hear me. "Yes, sir."

Dad laughed, reached into his satchel, and handed me a little black notebook and a pen. He said, "Then maybe you should write down their songs."

I've been writing them down ever since.

15

Dad was rather intense about my musical training. While he took care of the bluegrass, Big-Big schooled me on the blues. Big-Big grew up in Memphis, literally walking up and down Beale Street, so he knew a thing or two about Delta blues. One of the highlights of his younger life was that he'd actually heard Robert Johnson, and he vehemently maintained that Mr. Johnson did not sell his soul to the devil. "Couldn't have. Anybody that plays like that ain't owned by no devil."

But Dad felt one primary piece was missing. And that piece was the dreaded classical. Mozart. Bach. Beethoven. I hated it. And I hated all those white-wigged paintings.

For my tenth birthday, he gave me two presents. The first one I didn't want: Miss Vermetha Hagle. Miss Hagle was a BV local who had played thirty years with the philharmonic something-or-other. Dad paid her to give me lessons for four excruciating hours every Wednesday.

Having a cavity filled was more appealing. She was horrible. Her lessons were horrible. Her bedside manner was horrible. Her breath was horrible. And she sat like there was a pole shoved six feet up her backside. She'd never married and I could understand why.

But no matter how I pleaded, no matter how I feigned sickness, no matter what manner of excuse I dreamed up, Dad wouldn't budge. Gibraltar. He said, "You can't break the rules until you learn what they are."

"But why can't I just learn from you and Big-Big?"

" 'Cause you already know more than me and Big put together. Now, I don't expect you to like it, but I do expect you to learn it. And I expect you to learn it really well."

I suffered nearly eight years under that horrible woman with her yellow teeth, beady little eyes, and ruler, with which she constantly smacked the backs of my hands. But those lessons were one of the best things my dad ever did for me. And if I bumped into that woman on the street today, I'd kiss her on the mouth.

The second thing my dad gave me for my tenth birthday was a guitar of my own. Given the amount of time I was spending playing his guitar, he knew I'd caught the bug. Playing guitar was no passing fancy. The problem he bumped into was that for me, Jimmy had become the guitar by which all others were judged.

The guitar Dad gave me had nylon strings, so when he handed it to me, I think my face betrayed my concern. He quickly explained, "Guitars have voices. Like people. A nylon string guitar, if played right, can be more expressive than a steel string. More emotive. I know you love Jimmy, but you have more range than Jimmy can keep up with. This one can keep up."

I studied it. The body was smaller, which made it easier to play, but the neck was wider and strings thicker. A bit of a trade-off. I ran my fingers across the strings and tried to hide the fact that my heart was hurt that he'd not given me Jimmy. But playing that guitar, I understood what he was talking about. I didn't have to push as hard to get as much sound out of it, which helped given my smaller hands and fingers. I named him Half Pint.

Puberty brought some changes to my voice. Most were good. I grew in volume, power, control, yet oddly enough retained the ability to reach high notes while also extending the ability to sing lower. Note I said *lower,* not low. Dad sang low. I sang above him. Over the next couple of years, Dad and Big-Big turned the music over to me, and as I came into my own, the crowds grew. A lot. Pretty soon, more people were coming to see me than to hear him. Though Dad tried to protect me from that knowledge, I knew it.

And that wasn't always good.

Our schedule never changed. Depending on the distance, we were out on Thursday or Friday morning, back Sunday night or Monday. About once every two months, we were gone a whole week to ten days. I grew used to the road, and there were few parts of Utah, Wyoming, Nebraska, Kansas, Texas, New Mexico, and Colorado that I'd not seen. While Dad knew where he was going and could get there with his eyes closed, he left a lot of the navigation to me.

This meant that I learned to read a map, and with so much highway time I read a lot of them. I found them rather interesting. This drove my ninth-grade geography teacher nuts, as I missed most of the first quarter but still made straight As. She was further incensed when I didn't miss a single question on the final, including both extra credit questions.

Dad worked with my teachers, who were more than mildly irritated by my constant absences, but they couldn't argue with my work or work ethic. Dad cracked the whip, and while he and Big-Big shared the driving, I studied.

Sort of.

While Dad and Big-Big sat up front, Jimmy

and I stretched across the backseat of the truck cab. There were twelve-hour days when I played nonstop. There were four-day weekends when I played for forty hours. Dad and Big-Big would find old gospel or bluegrass stations on the AM radio, and I'd play along. As the months and years ticked by, I got to where I could hear the first few notes of a song and know what key it was in and usually where it was going. My ear grew so in tune that I could play back music in my mind, slow it down, and hear individual notes and chords on a guitar. Dad would hear me in the backseat picking out a rather complicated tune, and he'd say, "Okay, now play it on Half Pint." So I'd switch guitars and play the same song on nylon strings. I didn't know it at the time, but Dad was challenging me to express and emphasize different emotions with the same tune. He was teaching me to speak a new language. The language of guitar.

As my musical ability grew, so did my interest in and imitation of those who played it. Dad was careful to steer me away from rock-and-roll, declaring that everything I needed to know could be gleaned from bluegrass, blues, and classical. And, of course, hymns. He said, "You learn those four, and everybody in rock-and-roll will want to be you, and not the other way around."

I would not describe my dad as rigid about much of anything save one thing: listening to the

Grand Ole Opry on the AM radio stations that broadcast at night as we drove cross-country. If he was driving, and they were broadcasting, he was listening. I heard a lot of country music. Many of the best guitar players the world knew came out of bluegrass, and most of them played the Opry. This meant I was introduced to some of the best and most well-known licks on a nightly basis. The songs were not difficult to learn. Ninety-nine percent of them were just three or four chords, a bridge, and a chorus. I could hear a tune, and my fingers would dig it out—match the notes. Dad and Big-Big would shake their heads and just look at each other.

One would comment, "That ain't fair."

The other would respond, "No, it is not, but it sure is fun to watch."

Thursday nights were Dad's favorite because they showcased their best. Dad never missed. Like, never. We set our drive-time schedule around what he called Ryman Radio. Some of the biggest names in the business came out to play on Thurs-days, and some shows were two or even three hours long. When a particularly great player would light up the stage singing some harmony or playing something only a few can play, Dad would turn up the volume and slap the dashboard.

"Think of all the greats who have stood where that boy is standing. Monroe. Scruggs. Williams.

Cash. The King." Several times, after a particularly good show, he would click off the radio, nod knowingly, and glance in the rearview. "You'll play the Ryman one day."

Big-Big would nod in agreement. "That's right."

I'd never dreamed that high. "You think?"

A long pause. Another glance. "And that'll only be the beginning."

In between my sophomore and junior years, we were driving back from a weekend outside Taos, and Big-Big was teaching me a Robert Johnson lick. He said something about Johnson being one of the first recorded members of the 27 Club.

"The 27 Club? What's that?"

"Musicians, singers, and songwriters who all died at the age of twenty-seven."

I thought he was talking about some type of disease. "What'd they die from?"

"Some were freak accidents, but most died from drugs or suicide."

Dad scratched his head. "I've never understood that. Why would you leave a show to get high or drunk? Just what did these folks need to escape from? They're playing music. Where's the hard part in that?"

Dad's fame continued to grow. His face graced the cover of several regional magazines and newspapers. One headline read: "Sham or Surety? Barroom Picker Turns Tent Revivalist. Do the

Blind See and Lame Walk, or Is It Smoke and Mirrors?"

Whatever people's opinion, whether skeptic or believer, attendance grew. A lot. Packed venues and standing room only became the norm. We received invites from churches and pastors from all over. Many just wanted to profit off my father, but Dad had two rules, which he never broke. First, he never sold tickets, because he didn't view himself as entertainment. "Just what exactly would we charge people? Why would I charge for what I have been freely given?" Second, he never took an offering. Never passed the plate or the hat or whatever. That raised a lot of eyebrows among critics, but Dad figured if you want to give, you will. He didn't need to twist your arm. As a result, folks didn't feel manipulated, and they trusted my dad.

And despite his no-offering policy, people did give. They'd seek Dad out and put a check or cash in his hand, and Dad would accept it. Gas cost money.

As it turned out, a lot of people did this. Dad bought two things with the influx of cash: a tour bus for us and an eighteen-wheeler that carried all the tents and chairs and piano and sound equipment. Then he began hiring drivers and crews to set up and take down the tents. They'd drive ahead, set up, and we'd arrive in time for the first service. This meant Dad and Big-Big were more rested, and as a result, their sermons were a bit longer.

As attendance grew, and the growing number of unexplainable happenings happened, what some newspapers called miracles and others called sleight of hand, so did the number of critics. Naysayers. Picketers would hold signs and shout, and a few even slashed tires. More often than not, we were labeled as a traveling medicine show and Dad the lead snake-oil salesman. Reporters and investigative journalists would plant crippled or blind folks. Dad could spot them a mile off.

But controversy brought attention, and that brought radio and television crews with trucks and tall antennas that broadcast across the West.

I asked him one day, "Doesn't that bother you?"

He laughed. "Not in the least bit."

It was not uncommon for Dad to preach five times over a weekend, and by the time word spread among the locals, more than five thousand people would attend his final Sunday service. That meant that by my senior year in high school I was routinely playing before more than fifteen thou-sand people in a weekend. Sometimes more. I didn't realize it at the time, but that was a larger number than many of the big names in the record business.

My talent brought with it increased notoriety on many levels. One level, for which I was grateful, was with members of the opposite sex.

In short, chicks dig guitar players. Girls would find me before a show, make small talk, or give me their number. "Call me."

My dad was not overly protective, but he did shield me from the record companies that came calling. One night he could sense the growing tension in me, so he sat next to me on my bunk.

"Coop, there are going to be a lot of people who tell you how great you are, and how they can make you greater. Put you on some pedestal from which you can never come down. Truth is they don't care a thing about you, they just want what you got. All they care about is what they can make off you. They look at you like a jumping chicken, and they're going to offer you lots of money to jump on their stage.

"Nothing wrong with making lots of money, and if ever a boy was born to stand on a stage, it may well be you. But if you start making money at the expense of why you do what you do, or why you were given this gift in the first place, then you need to ask yourself how badly you want that money. In the end, the cost might be more than you can pay." He tapped me gently in the chest. "Robert Johnson wasn't the only man with a guitar to stand at a crossroad and talk with the devil. Every man with a guitar crosses that same street, and the conversation is always the same. So are the promises."

16

There was a bubbling inside me I could not describe. A rumbling, even. I could not tell you what motivated it or where it was coming from, why or how it got there, but I felt like Dad was holding me back. Crushing me under the weight of his thumb. And I was getting more than a little irritated. "Dad, are you saying I can't ever make a record?"

"No. I hope you make fifty records. I'll buy every one. But what you do with an instrument is only half of the gift that is in you." He pointed to the black notebook that he'd given me, which I'd started carrying between my belt and the small of my back. "I've seen how people respond to you when you sing what's yours. The words you write reach deep. When a man in a shiny suit with a lot of money comes along and wants to cut a record with you singing your own songs the way you want to sing them, the way you want to play them, more power to you. Have at it. Big-Big and me will be in the front row cheering. Until then, guard your gift and guard that notebook. Day may come when you find it's priceless."

One salesman or recruiter after another sought me out. They'd heard about my instrumentals, and the rumor of the hummingbird-blur of my fingers moving across the neck of the guitar and keys of the piano, and since they'd never heard anything like it from someone my age, they wanted to see for themselves.

But given that I was seventeen, they knew Dad was the gatekeeper. So they'd approach him. Shake his hand. Try to reason with him. Problem was, they had their box, and since I wasn't a very good fit in my present form, they wanted to take the parts of me that they liked, run them through their music grinder, and then stuff what remained of my soulless body into their prepackaged form.

While I did not want to admit it, even I could see this. They wanted to completely eradicate any scent of the whole gospel, hymn-singing, Sunday-morning-music thing and saturate me in the cheap cologne of whatever they were selling. Make a rock-and-roll star out of me. Long hair. Mohawk and mascara. Tight leather pants.

Eventually they started sending midlevel execs in suits with cash. And over time, the wads got bigger. Dad would listen, figure out their angle, and when they wouldn't take no for an answer, he'd close the door.

One day a persistent man found us in a dried-up mining town in northern Colorado. He wore a funny-looking hat and carried a thick wad, and he decided to bypass Dad. He snooped around until he found me tying down tent corners. He never said a word. He just licked his thumb and started counting out the money. I wanted an electric guitar so badly I could taste it, so the sight of fifty hundred-dollar bills had a drug-like effect on me.

He said, "Can you read music?"

Thanks to Miss Hagle, I could read music about as well as I could read English. I nodded.

He spread some sheets in front of me. "Can you play this?"

It was about as complicated as "Happy Birthday to You." So I signed some papers, took the money, and agreed to meet the man in town in a few hours. I found him in an abandoned gas station with a Fender Telecaster hooked up to an amp and what looked like an expensive tape recording machine. The man was savvy. He'd painted my name on the guitar. I spent a few minutes getting comfortable with it, and then he spread out the music in front of me. I'd play a number through the way it was scripted once, sometimes twice, and then he'd cut me loose and say, "How would you play it?" It was at that point that I saw the perfect intersection of the three corners of my musical training. When I cut loose, that's when he really started smiling.

This continued for an hour or so. And I will admit, it was a lot of fun. Addicting. At one point he excused himself, walked to a pay phone, and made an animated call to somebody who sounded equally animated. The two talked a few minutes while my new friend sipped from a stainless flask. When he hung up he returned to me, offering the flask and smiling. "Nip?"

What could it hurt? I took the flask, turned it up, and pretended to be as cool as he. I would learn shortly that it was not real cool.

We played another hour. He'd sip. I'd play. Then I'd sip. And play some more. I'd gotten pretty relaxed too. Finally, after I'd played everything the man could dish out, he smiled, packed everything into the trunk of his car, slammed it shut, and tipped his hat at me. "Stay close to the radio. I'll be in touch."

The world was spinning pretty good, but I still had it by the reins—or so I thought. I nodded coolly, and the man climbed into his car and turned the ignition, only to discover that he had a problem. That problem was about six feet four inches tall, dressed out at about two hundred and forty pounds, and was standing in front of his car with a disapproving look painted across his face. I'd seen that look before.

The man sank down in his seat and stared beneath the top of his steering wheel and over the top of the dash and began to laugh uncomfortably. I was a little foggy, but I heard little humor in it. Nervously, he lit a cigar.

Dad looked at the man but pointed at me. "Did you ask his age?"

The guy talked around the cigar. "I don't give a rat's derriere how old he is." As he spoke, he let out a cloud of smoke and slurred his way through *derry-air*.

Dad spoke softly. "Try seventeen."

The man knew he was toast. But he wasn't about to go out without a fight, so he floored it, flipping Dad over the hood and burning rubber out of the parking lot—whereby he ran directly into a roadblock of four patrol cars.

As our venues had grown, Dad had employed the local police to help keep order. Doing so had endeared him to the local deputies, who could make good overtime money just by wearing sunglasses and looking official. So when he'd told them that some salesman had hoodwinked me, they were more than a little protective. As the man was sitting there considering his options, Dad all but pulled him out of the window of his car and slid my "signed contract" from his coat pocket. He then dragged the man around the back of the car, retrieved the recording tape out of the trunk, and shook the guy like a rag doll. His shiny flask clanked on the pavement below.

"This all?"

The policemen all smiled. The man, now angry, began to spit venom. "I ain't telling you sh—"

The man sounded like he wanted to say *sugar,* but Dad applied enough sufficient pressure around his throat to choke off the rest, so I was never really certain.

Dad lifted the man off the ground and waited as he began kicking his feet and his face turned the color of a blueberry. Finally he nodded, and Dad let go. Dad dropped the tape onto the ground and stomped on it. Then he took the guy's cigar and lit the paper. The man was not too pleased, and began telling Dad how he would soon hear from his high-priced Los Angeles attorney.

Dad put him back in his car, smashed his hat down tight over his face, crumpled his cigar in his lap, and then held out his hand to me. Palm up. I put the five thousand dollars in his hand, whereby Dad quickly shoved it in the man's mouth and sent him on his way. Then he did the one thing I was dreading.

He looked at me.

And said nothing.

I wanted the earth to open up and swallow me whole. It was one of those rare self-aware moments when I saw the whole of my life in a quick and clear slide show. Despite some real hardship, starting with the death of my mom, my dad had been nothing but good to me. He'd given unselfishly. I'd never lacked for anything. I'd had a better musical training than kids coming out of Berklee. I'd seen more of the country than any of my friends, most of whom had at one time or another traveled with us, prompting responses like, "You get to do this every weekend? This is the coolest thing I've ever done."

The only thing Dad had not given me was Jimmy, and that was because Mom had given it to him.

After a painful and angry gaze that lasted several years and bored a hole through my soul, Dad stepped into one of the patrol cars with a deputy and returned to the revival. It wasn't until both the man and Dad had driven off that I realized I was still standing there with that stupid Telecaster hanging around my neck. When I looked down, I saw my reflection in the mirrored surface of the flask at my feet.

I stuck my thumb in the air, and it wasn't long till an older woman stopped. "You need a ride, honey?"

"Yes, ma'am."

A mile later her front right tire blew. I changed it for her, but not being much of a mechanic, I was soon covered in grease from fingertip to forearm. She grimaced a bit when I tried to get back into her car. I didn't blame her. I turned and started putting one foot in front of the other. Five miles is a long time to think.

The walk back sobered me. In every way. I returned to the revival at sundown just in time to hear Dad's "Dirty Hands" sermon. I won't bore you with the details. You can probably figure it out. In a nutshell, he talked about how sin stains your hands and how, because they're always in front of you where you can see them, they stand as a constant reminder of what you've been dipping them into. Lastly, he talked about how it's difficult to raise dirty hands to a holy God and how the only way to get them clean was to dip them in the blood. It made for some eye-opening illustrations. I wanted to puke just listening to him. And given the amount of rotgut alcohol I'd consumed, I was on the verge anyway.

His voice echoed out of the tents and found me on the highway. "Now, look at your hands. Palms up."

The slide show of Dad's movements played in my mind.

"Take a long, hard look. Take your time. I want you to look back into the stuff you don't want to look at. You know what I'm talking about. The dark places. The closets you've shut. Be honest with yourself. What've you been dipping your hands into?" A long pause. "You got it? Picture clear?"

In my mind's eye I could clearly see him turning his hands over and back.

"Now ask yourself, what have you gained?"

He always asked that question twice. I mouthed the next words as he spoke them: "And what have you lost?"

For me, the answer to the first question was

nothing but a mess. The answer to the second started and ended with a huge crack down the foundation of my father's trust in me.

The sinking feeling in me did not improve as the sound of his voice grew closer.

The sermon always ended with several thousand people sticking their hands straight up. Sometimes I'd squint my eyes from the piano bench, and all those hands looked like amber waves of grain.

I'd heard it all before. In the twenty-five years since, I've thought about it a good bit, and it's not rocket science. The problem was me. Despite my father's best wise counsel, his constant sacrifice, his warnings to the contrary, his five thousand sermons, and a deep knowingness in my gut that I needed to stay as far away from that serpent as humanly possible, there was something in me that couldn't stand the thought of my dad being right or of him telling me what to do. Said more simply: I wanted what I wanted, when I wanted it, the way I wanted it, because I wanted it. Period.

The older I got, the more I felt like I was under his thumb. Not that he was doing anything different. He was the same dad he'd always been. If anything, he'd become more lenient and I had more freedom. That meant the change had occurred in me, and that made it even worse. Something in me hated my dad's "rightness," and that he held me to some plumb line while most of my friends could do whatever they pleased.

The anger swirled, bitterness took root, and I began listening to whispers of what I could become if he weren't holding me back in some stupid traveling circus. I had more musical ability in my pinkie than he'd ever had and he was just jealous. Where the throngs once thanked him for his sermons and his prayers, they were now thanking me for my music. People were coming to hear me. Not him. He was riding my coattails, and he was beginning to feel like deadweight.

Even now, when I hear myself repeat those things, it stings.

Life at seventeen seemed so clear.

I stood on the highway, out in front of the packed parking lot, and just shook my head. It was evident that I'd not thought this through. I couldn't fight my dad. I knew he was right. I also knew I hated the fact that he was right. I'd had all I could stand. Next to me was a bridge crossing a roaring river. I walked to the railing and threw that Fender as far as I could out into the water. The bubbles swallowed it and the current flipped it, turned it, and then smashed it on a boulder, snapping the neck off the body. *Fitting,* I thought. Then I unscrewed the cap on the flask, turned it upside down, and emptied the remainder of the whiskey into the river.

Then I walked the five million miles back to my father.

That night, after we'd straightened the chairs, swept up, and emptied the trash, I found myself staring at the piano. Sitting in the dark. Fingers touching the keys but making no sound. The piano bench was the only place where the argument inside my head fell silent. Where I knew which voice was lying and which was telling the truth.

Dad found me there. Neither of us said anything. He was hurting. I was hurting. I knew I'd betrayed him. This was on me.

He started. "I ever tell you about the time your mom found me drinking?"

This was not where I thought this conversation was headed. "What?"

He stared up at the mountains beyond us. "We were up at the cabin, we'd just found out we were going to have you, and for reasons that are still a little foggy, I'd gotten pretty far down into a Mason jar of moonshine. There was a cigar in there somewhere, but that too is foggy. Given that I don't really drink or smoke, I was drunk as a skunk. The world was spinning like a top. Your mom found me out on the ridgeline walking around in my birthday suit. Stumbling like a pinball from tree to boulder. Naked as the day I was born."

"So that old rumor really is true?"

"Every word." He nodded several times. "The way your mom told it, I was actually howling at the moon."

The thought of my enormous, naked, drunk father howling at the moon lifted a chuckle up and out of me.

"If you ever needed proof that your father actually did let his hair down at one time in his life, that would be Exhibit A before the jury." He shook his head. "I woke the next morning with a sledgehammer cracking open the top of my head. It took me an hour to roll over. Your mom finally pried one eye open and said, 'You alive?' I think I grunted something, stood up, fell down, stood up again, and finally made my way to the creek, where I just fell in. After the shock of thirty-four-degree water shook some sense into me, I put together the fact that I had to preach in a few hours. She wrapped me in a towel, fed me some coffee, and told me to brush my teeth." He laughed at the memory. "She kissed my fore-head and said, 'Cigars are not your friend.' "

"You had to preach?"

"And to make matters worse, it was Easter." He palmed his face. "I'm still sorry about that."

I looked out across the empty seats. "What'd you say?"

"The truth. It was written across my face, and I couldn't have hidden it had I tried. So I told them what happened." We were quiet awhile. Then he sat next to me. "Sing me something."

I folded my hands in my lap. "Don't much feel like singing."

"Trust me, that's usually when you need to."

I played a few chords. Tried to make light of it. "Any requests?"

Dad rested Jimmy on his knee and said, "You lead, I'll follow."

I knew he was hurting. I was too. The tone of our voices spoke the pain in our hearts. But between Dad and me, we always had music. It was the concrete bridge no fire could burn. I played the intro and then started quietly singing. He joined in at "Tune my heart . . ." I held it together for a couple of verses, finally choking up at "Bind my wandering . . ." When I got to "Take and seal it . . ." I quit singing altogether.

That was the night I learned the value of an old hymn. How something so old and "out-of-date" could say words my heart needed to hear and didn't know how to say.

I wiped my face with my forearm and then slid that empty flask out of my pocket and laid it on the top of the piano. We both stared at it.

Dad's tone was soft, as were the notes he was quietly picking. "And then there's that."

"Dad?" I extended my hands, palms up. The recording and the drinking were minor. We'd get over that. The trust thing ran much deeper. "How do I raise dirty hands?"

"I asked your mother that same question on Easter morning as the sun was boring a hole through my pupils. I'll tell you the same thing she told me." He set Jimmy down, stood, raised his hands as high in the air as he could reach, and said, "Both at once."

Several hours later, as the first rays of sunlight cracked the mountaintops, I was still playing. When the words "sung by flaming tongues above," came out of my mouth for the umpteenth time, I actually heard what I was singing. Flaming tongues. The words painted a picture, and the picture got me to thinking. If someone had written that, then they'd thought that. Seen it in their mind's eye.

Which was good. It meant I wasn't crazy after all.

17

I would like to tell you that the conversation with my dad solved all our problems. It did not. A year passed. I turned eighteen, grew another two inches, which brought us nearly eye to eye, and my head swelled due to constant comparison of my talent with others in a relatively small talent pool. The record companies kept calling, and pretty soon I was letting the same anti-dad voices live rent-free in my mind. Fueling my discontent. Wanting what they were offering, which was money and the promise of adoration. I silently grew angry and bitter. I wanted my own stage.

That stuff circled around in me, creating a tornado that had only one eventual place to go—out my mouth. Ezekiel 28 was the story of my life.

I don't like talking about what happened next.

It was a Wednesday. We'd been in New Mexico. Dad had driven through the night to get me home for my four-hour lesson with Miss Hagle. I was working on a Bach piece, and it was important to him that I finish it. Miss Hagle worked days, so my lessons ran six to ten, and then I hung out with a few buddies. I'd get in between midnight and one, and Dad was usually asleep. I figured I'd see him the next day.

Wrong.

I got to the light at Main and Highway 24. Miss Hagle's house sat a few blocks east through the center of town. But when the light turned green, I turned right and drove like a bat out of Hades to Salida, where my band was tuning up for a show. I hadn't been to Miss Hagle's in three months, and while I knew the Bach piece forward and back, I had little interest in playing it. Ever.

I skidded to a stop outside Pedro's Mexican Restaurant and Bar, burst through the back door, grabbed my Fender—which I'd bought at a pawnshop with the money Dad had itemized for Miss Hagle, along with another thousand that I'd skimmed out of the cash box over the last year— jumped up onstage, and played two and a half hours of some really good rock-and-roll.

About a year before, some guys from high school had formed a rock-and-roll/country band and asked me to play lead. We'd been playing at Pedro's for about six months and crowds were growing. Tonight the place was packed, standing room only, an hour wait at the door, and Pedro was smiling like a Cheshire cat.

Three months earlier, some music critic happened to be on vacation around here when he and his family stopped in for Mexican food. Turns out he was a columnist for several popular guitar magazines. When the article came out, he compared the speed of my fingers on the neck to hummingbird wings. My face had graced the cover and the headline had simply read: "Peg— The Next Great One." The good news was twofold: my name was getting out there, and the magazine was such that my dad would never see it. At least not until such time as I returned the conquering artist and proved him wrong with awards and accolades draped around my neck. I could not have scripted this any better.

We played three hours. Pedro was ecstatic. The room was stuffed way past the fire marshal's regulation, and the crowd chanted for three encores. When the show finally ended, I was nervously studying my watch and calculating how much time it would take me to drive home plus stop for a roadside bath to get the smell of smoke off me. I handed my guitar to my drummer for

176

safekeeping, told the fellows I'd see them next week, and spun gravel out the parking lot. Just outside of Salida, I pulled off and bathed in the moonlight in a shallow pool. I stuffed the smoky clothes in a trash bag, put on the stuff I'd left the house in, and redlined the truck, getting home about twelve thirty. I shut the door and walked up the steps to the porch. There were no lights on. The only thing out of place was the smell. There was something different in the air.

I pulled on the screen door, and Dad spoke to me from a chair in the corner of the porch. The dark corner. "Some dinner in there for you. It's hot."

"Oh, hey." I paused and let my eyes adjust. He was sitting there with a plate on his lap. A napkin tucked in his collar. I tried to speak calmly. "What're you doing up?"

He took a bite of something, then spoke with his mouth full. "How's Miss Hagle?"

I managed a fake laugh. "Still slapping me with the ruler."

"How's Bach?"

More laughter, hoping Dad didn't detect the nervousness. "Dead."

He pointed the fork toward town. "You pay her?"

"Yep." The weight of the bald-faced lie wrapped around my neck like a millstone.

This time his fork motioned toward the kitchen. "Can you eat?"

I was famished. I could have eaten a cow. I also needed an exit from the conversation. "I can eat a little something."

He took another bite. "It's in there waiting on you."

I walked into the kitchen and turned on a light, and my stomach jumped into my throat. I nearly threw up. Dinner was takeout. Takeout from Pedro's.

I experienced several emotions at once: a searing pain in my heart, embarrassment, shame, and rage.

I stood in the kitchen wondering what I was going to say when I heard the screen door open behind me. Dad walked into the kitchen, pulled the napkin from his shirt collar, wiped his mouth, and leaned against one countertop while I shoved my hands in my pockets and leaned against the other. The two of us stood there awhile.

I couldn't look at him. After several minutes he said softly, "Anything you want to talk about?"

I didn't respond. Just walked into my room and shut the door. On the bed was a copy of that stupid magazine that stupid writer had sent to the house. My stupid-looking face was staring up at me. My goose was cooked, and no sweet little singsong with my dad would ease the pain of this betrayal.

I didn't sleep much that night.

• • •

Dad was gone by the time I got up the next day. We were slated to hold a service at the Falls that night, and he was no doubt setting up. Churches were busing in kids from all over Colorado. Many were coming to see me. I arrived late to standing room only. Must have been a couple thousand cars and fifty buses. I parked the truck and meandered toward the side of the stage, where Dad was in the middle of his "Why Are You Here?" sermon. That just ticked me off even more, because I knew he was speaking it directly to me.

I leaned against the back wall with my arms crossed. I'd heard it all before.

He waved his hand across the audience. "Why are you here?" He paused. He loved to throw "book learning" around from time to time, and I knew what was coming next. He said, "What is your *ray-son-day-trah?*" He chuckled. "That's French for 'reason for being.'" He set his Bible down on the stool and paced across the stage. "Think about it." He pointed to his throat. "Vocal cords. You ever wondered why the Bible calls them 'pipes'?"

He paced across the stage, clapped his hands once. Then he clapped again, louder. Then a third time. "Now you do it."

The audience clapped once in response.

"Why do you think God made your hands to do that? Seriously. Of all the things to do with your

179

hands, why add that to the possibility?" He then turned, shot both arms straight up in the air, and walked to and fro across the stage. "What's this remind you of? Football game? A rock concert where your favorite big-hair band is playing?" Laughter rippled through the audience. He picked up his Bible. "I've read this thing a few times through, and I can find no place in here where it talks about worship that does not include a movement of the body."

He waved his hand across the audience. "What is it you're looking for? What's your dream? To make some money? Own a nice home? Drive a nice car?" He paused. "I'm not against any of those things, but I don't think they're your reason for being." Dad walked to the edge of the stage and picked up a huge framed collage of magazine covers showing entertainers and public figures.

He held it up to the audience. "Is this why you're here? To see your name in lights?" Then he walked back a second time and picked up a large framed mirror. He paced back and forth along the edge of the stage, showing the audience their own reflection. "What if this is your reason?" he said.

Dad paused long enough to let the question settle. It was also at this time that he saw me. Or rather, he let me see that he'd seen me.

Then he turned, slung Jimmy over his shoulder, and said, "I'm not the best player, and I know others with far better voices, but let's you and me do something. Let's sing something together." Dad began strumming, the audience recognized the tune, and five thousand voices joined in. "Come Thou Fount . . ."

I wanted to vomit.

After the first verse, Dad stopped strumming. "Okay, that was good. But be honest with yourself. If the One who made the moon and stars, this mountain behind me, the One who gave your eyes their color and made your fingerprint unique, who gave you your own specific voice unlike that of any of the other several billion people on the planet . . . if He were right here . . ." Dad pointed at the stage. "Standing here. What would you be doing?" He knelt, raised both hands, and bent slightly. "Probably something like this." He slung Jimmy around behind him and lay facedown on the stage. "Or this." Dad stood. "Right?

He resumed strumming lightly. "What if this were a rock concert?" he asked. "What would you be doing? You'd be hopping around like a dancing chicken. Music is its own dimension and it reaches people at a level that is beneath their DNA. Nothing else brings about a corporate reaction like music. It exposes what and who we worship."

Dad pointed at the audience, making a wide sweep with his finger. "Every one of you is a custom-designed instrument with one singular purpose." When Dad's arm finished his arc, his hand was pointed my direction and his eyes were drilling a hole in me. "Worship." His voice rumbled out of his belly and his eyes were a crystal sea. "It's your *ray-son-day-trah*." Dad set Jimmy in his stand and then stood looking at the two framed pictures. "Question is, what and who do you worship?"

I was done listening.

I marched down the aisle, climbed the steps, and strode across the stage. I grabbed Half Pint out of his stand, walked to the center of the stage, and slammed him like an ax into the center of the mirror. Then I swung him into the framed collage of magazine covers. And then I walked up to my dad and struck him as hard as I could across his face, and my oak ring split his lip. As the blood trickled down his chin, I spoke through gritted teeth.

"I'm done with you and I'm done with your traveling circus."

I slid the ring off my finger and threw it as far as I could, over the trees and toward the river alongside the cliffs. I then grabbed Jimmy, hopped off the stage, and walked toward the truck, the audience parting like a wave as I passed.

Behind me, I could hear Dad speaking. There was no anger in his voice. Only sorrow. "Sing with me," he said. Big-Big began playing, and five thousand voices joined in with Dad's. "When peace like a river . . ."

When I got to the parking lot I kicked open the bus door, grabbed the cash box, slammed it open on the floor, and took the zippered leather case that held all the money Dad used to pay our expenses from weekend to weekend. Usually about two thousand dollars. I climbed into the truck, cranked the engine, dropped the stick into drive, and floored it, leaving two ruts in Mr. Slocumb's pasture. When I glanced in the rearview, Dad was still standing on the stage. Watching me leave. Blondie was still sitting on top of the piano.

I didn't care if I ever saw either of them again.

Five hours south, I pulled over and stared at a sign lit by my dim headlights. Literally, the road forked. The road to the right would take me to Los Angeles. I didn't care too much about the big-hair bands and giant pyrotechnic shows coming out of LA or the makeup most of the guys wore. Some had talent that impressed me, but most of it sounded angry, and I couldn't understand half of what they were saying anyway. The road to the left would take me to Nashville. And while I wasn't a die-hard country music fan, I felt like the music I wanted to make was more closely akin to what was coming out of Tennessee than from California or New York.

Sometimes I wonder how my life would have

turned out had I turned right. Or better yet, made a U-turn.

Twenty-one hours and one thousand, two hundred and thirty-four miles later, I pulled into Nashville. Eighteen years old, dumb, wet behind the ears, naïve, and ignorant. Not the best combination. At a downtown motel I sat on the bed, hung my head in my hands, and stared at the sparseness of my life. Next to me sat the leather money purse. I unzipped it, and when the money spilled on the bed, my jaw fell open.

The cash was wrapped in a map and held together with a green rubber band. I'd never seen that much money in my life. I counted it. Twice. Twelve thousand eight hundred dollars. I glanced at the motel door to make sure it was locked, bolted, and chained.

Then I looked at the map. It showed the state of Colorado. A hand-drawn star covered the spot in the mountains where our cabin sat. Next to it Dad had written:

No matter where you go, no matter what happens, what you become, what you gain, what you lose, no matter whether you succeed or fail, stand or fall, no matter what you dip your hands into . . . no gone is too far gone. Son, you can always come home.

I stared at my dad's words. They did not comfort me.

18

It took me about twenty-four hours in Nashville to learn what most everyone else there already knew. The talent pool in Music City is more dense than most anywhere else on earth. And while I might have been something standing on the stage at Pedro's, in Nashville I was just one more dumb kid with six strings and a dream.

After a week I'd gotten nowhere. Fast. Learning the hard way that it's not what you know or how good you are, but who you know—and I didn't know anybody. Given so much life on the road, I did know how to stretch a dollar. My motel cost twelve bucks a night if I rented it by the week. Eating ramen noodles and canned beans, I figured I could last a couple of years—though I might lose a few pounds.

At the end of another discouraging day I opened the door of my motel.

Whenever I left I took Jimmy with me, but the cash I had stashed inside the back panel of the air conditioner. I thought I'd get settled before I went through the hassle of opening an account. You know, choose my bank carefully. I was further emboldened in that the panel of the air conditioner had to be removed with a specific screwdriver, one of those weird six-sided heads that required a trip to the hardware store for the right fit. *Nobody just carries that bit around in their pocket,* I thought. *My money will be safe. Right?*

Wrong.

When I walked in, I saw at once that I'd not been the first to think of the whole hide-the-money-behind-the-air-conditioner thing. The panel door had been unscrewed and was lying on the floor. The screws were lined up in a row.

That night the manager, a petite lady who wore an apron and pulled her hair back, came knocking, asking for next week's rent. She found me sitting on the edge of the bed, my head sunk in my hands.

The reality of my life hit me like a train that night as I sat in the cab of my truck, unloaded my pocket, and counted out every penny to my name—seven dollars and forty-nine cents. And while that sight was painful, it was not nearly as painful as the deeper reality: it would be a long time before I could go home.

I spent that night, and many more just like it, in the cab of the truck with my arms wrapped around Jimmy, thinking about what I'd had with my dad, how I had taken it for granted, and how everything my father ever told me was absolutely true.

After two weeks of trying to sell my soul to anyone who would listen and trying *not* to think about what I would give to be back on the bus with my dad in any town other than this one, I got a gig at a Laundromat. That's right, ten bucks plus tips at the Spin and Twirl. One night a week. Plus they'd let me wash my clothes for free, and it sat two miles from a truck stop where I could take a shower for a dollar.

Within a few weeks my reputation had spread and I got a second gig at the Fluff and Fold. After three weeks someone actually came looking for me: Dietrich Messerschmidt, owner of a car wash called the Sudsy Schnitzel. And no, I didn't make that up.

He drove a giant green Cadillac, wore a terrible comb-over toupee, and even had one of those little wiener dogs, named Sweet, or "Sveet" as he said, that made all his commercials with him. Most irritating and meanest dog on the planet. I guess if I had to live with that man I'd be angry too.

Dietrich had a virtual monopoly on Bavarian Alps–style car wash/hot dog places in Nashville. German name or not, he apparently didn't know what Wiener schnitzel actually was, and I didn't correct his mistake. It seemed to be working for him. If you bought a deluxe or platinum wash, he'd throw in a free drink and foot-long dog at half price while you waited.

Between these three jobs I made about fifty bucks a week. At least I wouldn't starve. Or if I did, I would do so slowly, and my clothes and my truck would be clean, and I wouldn't be any more of an embarrassment to my father than I already was when he came to identify the body.

One night I looked down from the little stage at the Schnitzel and recognized a man I'd seen the previous three weeks in a row. He was neatly dressed, but he definitely had his own style: Sansabelt slacks, white shoes, green socks, hat, golf shirt, and enough eyebrow, nose, and ear hair to cover half his head. Each week he bought two "schnitzels" and then spent several minutes preparing them: one with onions, peppers, and spicy mustard, and a second with cabbage, onions, and this strange cheese that smelled like the nasty stuff you pick out of your belly button. He would arrange these on two plates, with two napkins and two drinks, and then he'd sit quietly and eat one of them. Occasionally he would mumble quietly to the other schnitzel.

When he was finished he'd stand, run his hands along the inside waistband of his slacks, wipe the corners of his mouth, fold his napkin neatly, and wrap everything—including the uneaten dog—in the aluminum foil in which it had been served, then drop it in the trash can. I thought to myself, *This is where the lonely come to die.*

This week the sight of the old man talking to somebody who wasn't there, and clearly hadn't been in a long time, got to me, and I said, "Sir, can I play you a song?"

He wiped his mouth, folded his napkin, and

turned slowly, rotating on the axis of his backside. He cleared his throat and spoke with a bit of an accent. "Do you know 'Danny Boy'?"

I swallowed. "Yes, sir."

The old man took off his hat and shot a glance at the uneaten dog. "That was one of her favorites."

Sitting there on a stool in Dietrich's combination hot dog and car wash joint, I sang "Danny Boy."

I sang it with all my might. When I looked up, the car wash had stopped, literally. Someone had pulled the lever and stopped the mechanical tracks from pulling the cars through, and everyone was staring at me.

When I reached the last verse and sang, "And I shall sleep in peace until you come to me . . . ," the old man stood, set a hundred-dollar bill on the floor at my feet, and cracked a quivering smile as the tears puddled in the corners of his quivering lips. Then he tipped his hat and walked out. I never saw him again.

When he'd driven out of the parking lot, I stared at the trash can, wondering if it would dishonor his wife if I were to eat her untouched dinner. Dis-respectful or not, I dug through the foil and devoured that uneaten dog. Given that I lived like a vagrant in the cab of my truck, the resulting wind and odor were a small price to pay.

At night I would walk Broadway listening to the bands. Lower Broad is maybe a half-mile

189

long, incorporating a couple square blocks, and all the bars and honky-tonks are packed in there like sardines. At any given time more than forty bands or singers, songwriters, and musicians are playing. They play four-hour shifts, there are three shifts in a day, and most everybody plays for tips. Some bars are three and four stories, and they'll stage a different act on every floor.

Two of my favorites were Tootsie's Orchid Lounge and Robert's Western World. Both were world renowned for the talent they would put on the stage, and a virtual breeding ground for some of the greatest performers ever. I couldn't afford to eat or drink in either, so I'd stand outside and listen.

One night some guy walked out of Robert's and dropped some papers. I picked them up and handed them to him. "Excuse me, sir?"

He was too drunk to care. "You can have 'em, kid. Them's the keys to the kingdom."

He staggered away, and I looked at the papers in my hand. They were song sheets, but unlike any song sheets I'd ever seen. I stood there studying a page like a monkey holding a Rubik's Cube and realized it must be the Nashville Number System. I'd heard of it, but never seen it. No reason to. But I knew enough to know that if this was the language musicians spoke in this town, I needed to learn it.

The next day I dug through some books at the public library and figured out that it wasn't as complicated as it looked. Actually, it made good sense. In the 1950s many of the Nashville studio musicians couldn't read or understand formal musical scores. They were phenomenal musicians, but formally transcribed music was as Greek to them as Nashville notation was to me.

It wasn't uncommon for them to play for four or five artists in a single day, and often an artist would come in and want a piece of music played in a different key than scripted. The studio musicians needed a quick way to change the key without spending hours rewriting a score. So some guy devised a musical number system, and Nashville notation was born. Given its simplicity and the way in which it solved a problem before it became one, fellow musicians adapted the system and developed it into a complete method of writing chord charts and melodies—combining Nashville shorthand with formal notation standards. The NNS uses whole numbers in place of chord names, parentheses, hash marks, circles, up and down arrows, underlining, positive and negative signs, fractions, colons, semicolons, and a host of other punctuation marks. It looks more like a math problem than music.

Soon my nightly trips to Lower Broad included sketching out a song's structure in my notebook using the system. But the books had only taught me so much. I needed to see some real song sheets with comments in the margins.

Standing on Broadway, listening to music, and attempting to write the NNS in my head, I had a thought: Certainly not everyone took their music home. Some of it had to end up in the trash.

I was right. The trash cans behind the bars were gold mines for discarded sheet music. At first I just picked from the edges, but soon I was knee-deep in nastiness, digging my hands through leftover nachos and chicken bones.

It did not escape me how far I'd fallen. From the spotless ivory keys onstage with Dad and Big-Big, playing before fifteen or twenty thousand, doing something I was pretty good at, to standing in muck and mire at the bottom of a Dumpster, my hands draped in melted cheese and sour beer. Every time I threw my leg over the side and climbed down into a bin, I heard the echo of my dad's "Dirty Hands" sermon.

Bouncers would throw me out, thinking I was just some drunk, but one night the bouncer at Tootsie's saw me holding rolled-up sheets of paper covered in ketchup. The guy looked like he'd been born in a weight room.

I hopped down. "I know, I know, I'm gone."

"Pal, I've thrown you out of here every night this week. You're either the most persistent drunk on Broadway or real hungry."

I dusted myself off. "I am hungry. I could

probably eat most of a cow right now, hoofs, horns, and all. But to be honest, I'm looking for these." I held out the sheets.

"You're digging through that . . . looking for those?"

"Yes."

"That's a first." He considered me. "You from around here?"

I shook my head. "Colorado."

"You play?"

The smell of me was wafting up and starting to make me gag. "Yes."

"You any good?"

Funny how so simple a question can get right to the heart of the matter. I could have told him about my history, the thousands of times I'd performed, the hundreds of thousands of people I'd performed for, my training, my knowledge, my mastery of piano and guitar, and how I was so confident in myself and my abilities that I'd thumbed my nose at my dad, stolen everything he held dear, broken his heart, and shattered his trust, then driven twelve hundred miles because I believed I was as good as anyone. I could have told him about my home and how I now knew I could never go back there until I had become what I believed I could become. That my life was riding on the wager that I was as good as anyone. And not only that, but that when I opened my mouth to sing, I could melt hardened defenses and make people believe that what I was singing was true.

But I have a simple rule about musicians. Don't tell me what you know. Don't tell me how good you are. Just play. And since I couldn't do that standing in a Dumpster in the alley behind Broadway, and since I didn't feel like blabbing out a sob story I was sure he'd heard a hundred times before, and since I didn't like leaving my truck unoccupied past midnight, I just said, "Yes."

His eyes walked up and down me. Then he held up a finger. "Wait here." He disappeared inside and returned three minutes later with a stack of clean, white, neatly stacked papers. "When you want more, come see me."

"Thanks." I turned to go.

He stopped me. "And, pal, take a shower, 'cause you'll never find a girl in this town smelling like that."

"Tell me about it."

I reached the river, walked a few blocks, and turned the corner to where I had parked the truck in a dollar-a-day grass lot. If you paid a month in advance, it was half that.

No truck.

I walked to the spot where I'd parked it, and nothing but grass stared up at me. I turned, scanning the lot. Making sure I was in the right place. I stared at the number on the fence. R07. Pulled the receipt from my pocket. R07. I wanted to scream, cuss, and shake my fist, but at who?

Nobody had made me come here.

I was too tired to protest. I found a gravel spot next to the fence, lay down, wrapped my arms and one leg around Jimmy, and slept in fits over the next few hours. When the sunlight cracked I couldn't stand myself anymore. I had to be at the Schnitzel after lunch, so I had a few hours. I walked down Second Avenue toward Church, where I found a thrift store. I bought jeans, a T-shirt, a towel, and some slightly used running shoes for three dollars. Then I went next door to the dollar store and bought some deodorant, a toothbrush, and a three-pack of underwear. Call me weird, but I have a thing about wearing somebody else's underwear.

With my new clothes stuffed in a plastic grocery bag, I turned down Commerce to the Cumberland River and a park commemorating Fort Nashborough. Alongside some beautifully manicured grass, the city had built a dog park alongside the river. Complete with an animal bath. I stripped down to my underwear and used the free flea and tick shampoo and accompanying fountain to eradicate the memory of the Dumpster. I was soaping up my pits when a lady in high heels walked by with three high-maintenance yap dogs and gave me the evil eye.

"Morning!" I hollered. "Send those pups over here. I'll wash 'em." Something about the whole picture did not comfort her, and she did not take me up on my offer.

19

The next couple of weeks didn't see much improvement. That stack of song sheets the bouncer had given me kept me busy for a few weeks. I knew the songs because I'd heard them played and could replay them in my mind. The tough part was figuring out what the symbols meant, or better yet, what they instructed me to do musically. To figure that out, I'd play the song and study the symbols, giving my mind time to add meaning to the symbols on the page. Thanks to Miss Hagle, that transaction took place relatively quickly.

The only benefit to not owning a truck was not having to put gas in it. But now I was without a place to sleep, and that became a rolling nightly question. I slept in parks, commercial warehouses, an area of woods where I found a soggy mattress beneath a rotten tarp, even beneath an overpass. I didn't like shelters or "homes," and if you really want to know why, it's because I didn't want to have to admit that I'd fallen that far. Those guys had reached the bottom. I had not. Or at least, I wouldn't admit I had.

My singular need was simple: I needed to get noticed. And I had my doubts about that happening at one of two Laundromats or a greasy hot dog and car wash joint. What kind of self-respecting record executive or producer frequents either? For me, Broadway was key.

During my brief time in Nashville, I'd noticed that guys like me who didn't have a stage would perform on street corners. At any given time on Broadway, there'd be musicians at the intersection of every Hope Circle North and Hungry Street South singing for their supper.

Desperation is a great teacher, so at eight p.m. one Wednesday I chose Second and Broadway. Why there? Because it was empty. Across the street was a three-story honky-tonk packed to the gills with people wearing hats and cowboy boots. The band currently rocking the house was a three-piece country act led by some guy with a big hat and a bad voice. To his credit, he had great stage presence and was pretty good at making you forget how badly he played. I looked through the windows and saw all those people with their beers raised high and I thought, *They have to leave sometime, and chances are pretty good they'll leave through that door.*

So I set up shop and started playing. In about twenty minutes I had a crowd of ten to fifteen. After thirty minutes, forty to fifty people were standing in front of me, dropping tens and twenties in my case.

I'd hit the jackpot. I could feel my star on the rise.

An old boy with a black eye and a scab on his forehead walked by and pointed at the cash in my case. "Better tuck that away," he said. "Take my word for it." I did too.

By ten p.m. there were a hundred people packed in a tight circle around me, and while I was having fun and taking requests, I was starting to get a bit worried. I was actually pulling people out of the bars, which, I had a feeling, wouldn't make the bar owners or the performers inside them all that happy. 'Course, if they were all that torqued, they could invite me in to play, so I kept at it.

Eventually I saw a police car stopped in the street just west of me, and a cop routing traffic around the crowd that had spilled over into the street. The officer seemed happy enough, which let me know this was not his first rodeo, but I couldn't shake an uneasy tickle on the back of my neck. And when the big-hat-and-bad-voice cowboy walked out of the bar and made a beeline toward me, pointed at Jimmy, and said, "Nice guitar. It's a shame they don't make them like that anymore," and then disappeared into the crowd, the hair stood straight up on my neck.

At eleven o'clock I thanked everyone, closed the case, and hurried up First Avenue, looking over my shoulder. Problem was, that's not the direction I should have been looking. I remember stopping at Bank Street and looking both ways, taking one step out into the street, and then I remember feeling a real bad pain in the back of my head and somebody turning out the lights.

The next time my eyes opened it was morning, and a police officer was shaking me with his toe. "Hey, fellow, you alive?"

The blood had caked on the back of my head and neck, and everything from my shoulders up was in a lot of pain. I tried to open my eyes, but one was swollen shut. The only thing I saw were six empty pistachio shells scattered on the street next to me. Like someone had tossed them down with the same indifference and disdain with which they'd handled me.

Then I reached for Jimmy.

But Jimmy wasn't there.

The paramedics doctored my head and offered me a ride to the hospital, but I turned them down, knowing I couldn't pay my bill. Plus, they had no remedy for the pain inside me.

I wandered the streets for weeks. Without a guitar, I had to give up my car wash and Laundromat gigs. One night I found myself standing at the apex of a tall bridge that crossed the Cumberland, staring down at the water. The only thing that kept me from jumping was the knowledge that when they found my body, *if* they found my body, somebody would call my dad. Given everything I'd taken from him, I couldn't stand the thought of him receiving that call. So I walked back down the bridge.

The next morning I found myself in Printer's Alley eyeing the Dumpsters. While the bars all faced outward toward Broadway, a single shop faced the alley—a guitar repair shop. Based on the looks of things, it'd been there awhile. As I stood there with my stomach growling, a guy walked by me, raised the roll-up door, and began turning on all the lights. In the window hung a sign. Help Wanted.

I knew I couldn't apply for a job in my present condition, so I bathed in the dog fountain, and once my clothes had mostly dried I pulled my hair back in a ponytail, knocked on the door, and pointed at the sign.

The owner said, "You know anything about guitars?"

"Only how to play them."

"Ever worked on them?"

"No, sir."

"How's your ear?"

"It's okay."

He handed me a guitar. "What's wrong with the B string?"

I plucked it and let it ring. "It's flat." Then I tuned it by ear and handed it back to him.

He pulled another off the rack. "And this one?"

I ran my fingers across the strings, then tuned it. "Strings are old. Need to be changed. Whoever played it last has real acidic sweat. And I think that half the strings are lights while the other half are mediums."

The man smiled and handed me a third guitar. "One more."

This one was a little different. It was mostly in tune, but when I tried to tune it, something was off. I played it briefly and discovered the problem. "This one has a warped neck. Can't help you with that."

"Would you like to learn?"

"Yes, sir."

He extended his hand. "Riggs Graves. Welcome to Graves's Guitars."

"Peg."

"Peg your real name?"

"Does it matter?"

He laughed. "Only if you want me to pay you."

Riggs handed me an apron, and thus began my education into the fascinating world of guitar repair. Twenty-five years earlier Riggs had come to Nashville with dreams, like most everyone else. When those didn't come true, he fell back on the only thing he knew to do. Repair guitars. He'd been doing it ever since and had a pretty solid reputation, as evidenced by who walked in and out of his door day in and day out.

While working for him solved my income problem, it didn't solve my housing dilemma. After a week Riggs picked up on the fact that I wasn't one to clock out early. He also noticed I wasn't one to shower often. He said, "You live nearby?"

I pointed in a northerly direction. "Couple miles that way."

I'm not a very good liar.

He pointed toward the river. "You got to walk over that bridge to get there?"

I nodded.

He looked right at me. "Long way down, isn't it?"

I didn't respond.

He was adjusting the truss rod, lowering the action on a Gibson. "Back when I was about your age," he said, continuing to work, "I was trying my best to play all the famous places up and down this street. When my level of play proved that I would no longer be able to do that, the guys at the bar next door offered to sell me this space. Somehow I got a mortgage and set up shop. Had no other place to sleep, so I rolled out a foam mattress right there on the floor. That turned out to be a stroke of good luck, 'cause the headliners at the Ryman would knock on my door at all hours of the night. I got to know some of the greats. And little by little, I built an apartment on the second floor. It's not much, but it's empty. It's dry. It'sgot a hot shower." He smiled. "And if you listen closely, you'll never miss a show at the Ryman. It's yours if you like."

When Riggs walked me up the narrow stairway and showed me the single-room apartment with a bed, a shower, a sink, and a window that overlooked the Ryman, I could have kissed that man on the mouth.

20

Whoever had stolen Jimmy had stolen more than my father's guitar. He'd stolen my desire. Making music was too much of a reminder of my own idiocy. So I tuned guitars and mandolins and banjos, but I didn't even think about performing. For several months I lived my life within a few city blocks. I spent my days and many evenings working with Riggs. When I clocked out, I'd climb up to the roof, sit in a chair, and eat my dinner while listening to the sounds of Broadway. None were better than those coming out of the Ryman. One story up, I lived above the horns and business and cutthroat world below me. If I wanted peace, I climbed to the roof. From my perch I didn't see many people, and I'm pretty sure no one really saw me. There was a tall hotel a block away, and occasionally I'd see someone standing on the balcony, but for the most part that world above the street was mine alone.

Six months into my new job, Riggs was watching me play scales on a guitar as I tried to figure out what was wrong with the sound. As I grew more comfortable with him, I loosened up and would allow myself to dig into a guitar every now and then to see what kind of sound it put out.

One day he nodded toward the Ryman. "You been to a show?"

"No."

"Never?"

"Never been."

"One of the acts there tonight is an old customer. Gave me a couple of tickets. You want to go?"

I didn't have a lot in the way of clothes.

He was leaning over his workbench straightening his tools. "I've got to run to the store this afternoon to pick up a few shirts. Why don't we close up early, and I'll buy you a new shirt or something. You can't very well go to the Mother Church of Country Music dressed like that."

"I'd like that. I'd like that a lot."

While he drove, Riggs asked, "You ever listen to the Opry?"

"Growing up, I listened with my dad thousands of hours."

Riggs was always reading biographies. Loved history. He and my dad would have gotten along fabulously. "You know the history?" he asked.

"Looks like an old church."

He switched hands on the steering wheel. "Around 1890 a fire-and-brimstone preacher named Sam Jones was holding Holy Ghost tent revivals along the river for the rough-and-tumble riverboat crowd. Fellow by the name of Ryman owned about thirty-five steamboats, and he, like everyone else in town, had heard about the charismatic Jones. Ryman was a total skeptic, but he ambled down the docks one night to see what the fuss was about. Something happened, and he walked away different.

"He leveraged his fortune to build what he called a 'tabernacle' for Jones, and in 1892 the Union Gospel Tabernacle was completed. Aside from being a popular church, it hosted musical acts. It had excellent acoustics, and pretty soon everybody wanted to play there. Folks called it the Carnegie Hall of the South. Wasn't just musicians. They had ballet. Political debates. Broadway musicals.

"Then in 1943, when the world needed a shot in the arm, the Ryman rented out its venue on Saturday nights to a local radio show. The Opry played there for thirty years. Hank Williams, Patsy Cline, Johnny Cash . . . even Elvis. All of them played right here." He tapped the dash with his index finger. "By '74 the Opry had outgrown the Tabernacle, so they up and left— of course Sam Jones was long gone by then too.

"For twenty years the Tabernacle sat locked up, leaking and rotting. I used to sneak in through the backstage entrance and walk through her, smelling damp mildew and rotting wood and trying to listen for an echo of the greats, but the only sound was pigeons. I'd creep up on that hallowed stage and look out across all those empty seats and wonder just what in the world had gone so wrong as to uproot something so good. So right." He paused.

"Finally the performers raised the money and reopened the Ryman. Today all kinds of people play there. Some deserve to. Some don't. But there was a day, not too very long ago, when folks would stand on that stage and sing out a song that was not about them. It was something beautiful that blanketed the people. I'd like to think that there are still folks around who can do that, because that kind of song is something special. Folks like that don't come around all that often."

That night I sat in the balcony with Riggs and tried to hide my tears. *My dad would love this.*

After the show, as we were walking out, Riggs introduced me to a lady.

"Jen, this is Cooper O'Connor. Goes by the name Coop, and if you really get to know him he'll let you call him Peg, for reasons I've never quite understood."

She shook my hand while Riggs continued. "He works with me and lives atop my store. He's pretty handy with most anything, is honest as the day is long, and might be a good guy to know if you need someone close by."

The following week, on my nineteenth birthday, I started working nights at the Ryman.

I started in the stage crew. We'd tear down one set only to set up another for the next night's show, often long into the night. Many times I got only an hour or two of sleep before I heard Riggs roll up his security door.

Working with Riggs brought with it another benefit. He was well known, had a thriving business, and as a result had a constant stream of some of the world's greatest guitars coming through his door. All of which I got to play. Martin, Gibson, Taylor, Collings.

I really fell in love with a handmade guitar called a McPherson, but given that they started at about seven thousand dollars, I just enjoyed those from afar. The McPherson was designed and built by an engineering genius who offset the sound hole. Most guitars have a sound hole right in the middle beneath the strings. McPherson argued that center-hole placement removed much of the resonance, so he positioned it off to the side, giving the top more resonating surface.

He also made one other change that was fundamentally different from every other guitar; he cantilevered the neck. Most guitar necks joined the body in a dovetail joint, but McPherson argued that had a way of deadening the sound. Why not cantilever the neck above the body to allow more sound travel and resonation? It worked. It was one of the most melodious, ringing, bell-like guitars I'd ever played. Almost had a voice-like quality. A lot of the bluegrass guys didn't care too much for it, because it had too much resonation. Bluegrass guys like to play a note and then let it die so they can get on to the next. But fingerpickers or singer-songwriters or rhythm folks or studio guys who needed something to fill in, who strummed to create a blanket of sound, loved McPhersons.

Playing so many guitars made me think of Jimmy a good bit. Every time I strummed a guitar, I compared the sound to Jimmy. I wondered where he was. Was somebody taking good care of him? Did they play him? Had they pawned him? Thrown him over the bridge? Stuffed him in a corner? Of all the things I'd done to my father—striking him in the face, stealing his money, stealing his truck—the deepest pain in me had to do with Jimmy and my failure to take care of him.

I could never go home without him.

Working with Riggs in the daylight and at the Ryman at night became my life. I got to know some of the regulars at the Ryman, and before I turned twenty I'd seen maybe a hundred shows and begun to appreciate music from the audience side of the stage. Which was good. It taught me a lot that experience from the stage had never taught me. How to interact with an audience. What draws them in. What turns them off.

Most of all, I learned one thing that my father had told me early but I'd never quite appreciated: "Great music, the kind that moves people, is an offering. Anything less is a counterfeit, and those who hear it know it best."

I also confirmed for myself another of Dad's truths—the great players aren't great because they can dazzle you with hummingbird wings for fingers. They dazzle by knowing what notes to leave in and what notes to leave out. And more often than not, it's the leaving out that makes them great.

Almost three years had passed since I left home. Riggs fed me dinner every Sunday and introduced me to his family. His wife. His son. His house outside of town. His midlife-crisis Harley, which his wife wouldn't let him ride. During those years I tried to put thoughts of Colorado behind me. Dad. Big-Big. The tents. The sound of the highway beneath the tires of the bus. The sun coming up over the mountains. My dad's voice in the aspens. Snow on my face. Jimmy.

It was a lonely time.

That does not mean its education was lost on me. I kept my eyes and ears open and became a pretty quick study of people.

Either through experience or condition, we think of a bar as a good-time hangout. It's primarily a function of flashing neon signs and media bombardment, but think about the names we give them. Lounge. Speakeasy. Watering hole. Club. Do any of those sound like someplace you don't want to go? 'Course not.

Think about every advertisement you've ever seen for wine, beer, or spirits. Very intelligent and well-paid executives have spent hundreds of millions of dollars to cause you, Pavlov's dog, to salivate at the sight or sound of their ad. Television shows with catchy theme songs do the same. Who doesn't want to go someplace where everybody knows your name? Where you can pull up a chair and laugh with your friends. Take a load off with total strangers. Turn your back on the outside world, even if just for an hour.

But the longer I lived on Broadway, the clearer it became to me. Truth is, folks frequent bars to medicate something. That something is one thing when they walk in. It's another after a few drinks. Usually less shrouded. Alcohol is the great unveiler. The backstage tour. The thing that pulls back the curtain on Oz. Most who walk in that door drink to drown. Or drown out.

The second major lesson I learned is that an entertainer lives three lives. They occur in descending order. And like gravity, no on escapes the inevitability. The first is the best. It's the ascendancy. The rocket shot. Where they feed daily on the all-you-can-eat buffet of hope and promise. That's the one everybody talks about and likes to remember.

The brilliance of the flame varies, but for a star to be made, a rocket must take off. Some possess the blast of a bottle rocket. Some the *Endeavor*. Stars vary in their brilliance, and some shine longer than others. Whether a long, slow burn, a trip to Mars, or a self-inflicted flash-in-the-pan, they all eventually run out of gas. It's the nature of being the rocket. And as their sustainability fades, the has-been entertainers are left orbiting the casinos, which are filled with broken people who have hung their hope on the lever, the wheel, the dice, or the cards, praying, "Please, dear God . . ." And because casinos are really good at taking people's money and making them feel worse than they did when they walked in, they offer live entertainment to medicate the malaise. Or lessen the blow.

No matter how bright the marquees, the casino stage is the entertainer's second life. And while there are exceptions, casinos are cemeteries for entertainers. Where stars go to flame out. From Biloxi to Atlantic City to Vegas, casinos pay the has-beens to be, once again, what they once were. Which they never are. Fading stars take the money—which they swore they'd never do when they were riding high—and gig to thinning crowds and tired memories, in clothes that are too tight, with voices that don't carry. Because some applause is better than no applause.

The casino circuit lasts longer for some than

others, but it too must come to an end. Those who can no longer play casinos, play bars. Life number three. Where an entire stage has been replaced with a single stool. Where sound crews have been replaced with a pedal at your feet. Where pyrotechnics and lasers have been replaced with a sixty-watt bulb hanging from a frayed cord above your head.

Whatever the case, no matter how it's spun, bars are the bottom. The last stop before the black hole. While many launch a career from honky-tonks and roadside speakeasies, nobody rebirths a career from a bar. Those who return to play bars are played out. Done. For the singer, song-writer, musician, entertainer, pop star, once-was-has-been-never-will-be-again clinging to life support, the bar scene is hospice, and the drunken, muted applause all the morphine they're going to get.

The third and possibly most valuable bit of information I gleaned from my life in these years was this: a lot of contemporary thought and criticism is given to gauging and critiquing voices. Comparing one to another so we know where their pedestal ranks in relation to others. Inside us, there is an incessant need to segment and compare. The experts who joust in this field use words like *vocal quality. Timbre. Nasality. Range. Head notes. Neutral larynx. Chest register. Vibrato. Tone. A list. B list. C list. Star.* When the critics are done tearing apart a single set of vocal cords, trying to understand what makes it sound the way it does and what its limitations are, the voice they were cutting on is left a twitching corpse on the sidewalk. Disconnected parts with little resemblance to the whole. Roadkill. Not enough left to sing "Ring around the Rosie."

I don't understand half the language used by critics. What I do understand is how music makes us feel. Watch any group of Southern boys when they hear the first riff of "Sweet Home Alabama." What do they do? Jump to their feet, remove their hats, cross their hearts with one hand, and raise their beer cups with the other. No discussion. No collaboration. They are tied to a tether and the music tugs at it.

Music reaches people at a level that is beneath their DNA. Dad was right. Again. Music exposes what and who we worship.

In my mind, the single highest compliment an audience can pay a musician is this: the last note rings out and is dangling from the rafters of heaven, where it echoes and resonates before fading. The audience responds with pin-drop silence. That's right. Crickets. With head-shaking disbelief and awe. Followed by rising, ear-piercing applause that lasts long after the performer has left the stage.

That's when you know that the music wasn't about you. In truth, it never was.

21

One Wednesday night about midnight I found myself in a small area backstage next to a phone hanging on the wall. I stood there, twirling the knotted cord between my fingers. I danced around it, trying to act like it didn't have my undivided attention. After an hour, I dialed the number.

A voice answered, "Hello?"

There was a lot I wanted to say. To explain. But more than that, I wanted to hear his voice. I stood there quietly. Silence settled over the line. Twenty seconds passed. Then thirty. When he finally spoke again, his voice was soft. "Are you safe?"

I'd been discovered, so I reached to hang up the phone, then stopped short. I returned the phone to my ear. Stood there. After a while I managed a broken whisper. "Yes, sir."

I heard him sit down in the creaky chair in the kitchen. I could see him sitting with his elbows resting on the kitchen table, staring west out across the mountains. I could smell coffee from the percolator.

He cleared his throat. His gentle words wrapped around me like velvet arms. "You find the map?"

The picture in my mind's eye was of the motel room where the air conditioner cover had been left open on the floor, the screws all lined up in a row, and the memory of how I'd lost my dad's life savings pierced me. "Yes, sir."

He paused, and I could hear his palm brush over the whiskers on an unshaven face. "Good. That's good."

I returned the phone to the cradle and slid down the wall, leaning my head against peeling wallpaper. A calendar on the wall caught my attention. It was my twenty-first birthday.

While I had very little desire to play publicly, that did not mean I didn't want to play. To write music. I was seldom without my small black notebook. I'd become so good with the Nashville Number System that I could write a song with verses and complete music in just a couple minutes.

Riggs used to watch me with muted amusement. He wasn't nosy but he was interested, so every now and then I'd ask him a question. Turns out he had been a studio musician for a few years, and what I lacked in some of the specifics, he knew.

One day he handed me a Martin he'd been tweaking for a customer and then tapped the notebook at my back. "Play me something?"

I hammered out a few licks and sang a verse and chorus. Not too much.

He walked away and said nothing. Couple hours later we were locking up, and he put his hand on my shoulder. "Don't keep all that to yourself." He mussed up my hair. "I don't dig at you. I reckon you'll talk when you feel like it. But there are two types of people in Nashville. Those who want to get something. And those who want to give something."

He pointed at a Martin hanging on the wall. "That thing is only beautiful when it's making the sound it was meant to make. Otherwise, why's it hanging there?"

I walked upstairs, stood on the roof, and cried. Everything in me wanted to go home. To fall on my dad, tell him about Jimmy, and tell him "I'm sorry." But there was another part of me that would not let me do that. And that part needed to make something of the mess that was me. To walk home with something more than scars and empty hands. To be something other than a failure. I was caught in the middle of that tug-of-war.

I didn't know what to do with the ache in me, so I developed a rhythm. Riggs trusted me. He would take vacations and leave me a week in the store. Sometimes two. My boss at the Ryman gave me my own set of keys. Trusted me with lockup. I kept to myself, did my work, arrived early, stayed late, did more than I was asked, and kept my ear pointed at the stage. I was learning on multiple levels. This endeared me to what I learned were, though admired and adored, mostly lonely people.

I got to know the acts, the performers, managers,

producers, agents, everybody who came through the door. I got them what they needed when they needed it. I became known as the jack-of-all-trades. I hemmed shirts, tuned and strung guitars, bought new boots when a pair didn't arrive in time, gave a guy my shirt, called babysitters to tell them so-and-so would be late, reserved rooms at hotels, gave directions, ordered takeout. Many nights I solved problems before they became problems. Some of the biggest names in the business began trusting me. Phone numbers. Home addresses. Drives across town. Safe-keeping. They trusted me with their secrets. Their confidence.

While I could have leveraged this time with the stars to advance myself, I did not. I didn't care. Or at least I told myself I didn't. Riggs had grown increasingly suspicious that I'd once been more than I let on, that I could have been more than hired help earning a little better than minimum wage, that I once had dreams. To his credit, he didn't probe. He could see that I needed a place to mend. To heal. I kept my nose to the grindstone and worked with a singular purpose— to save up enough money to pay my father back what I owed him. Which was a lot.

At a fair price, the truck was $7,500. I'd stolen $12,800. On today's market, Jimmy was worth between 17 and 25K. At a low end, I needed $37,300. I told myself that when I had that I could walk home, face my father, and buy myself out from underneath the weight on my shoulders and the stone in my gut.

I'd not told Riggs my story, but he saw my affection for Martin guitars every time my hands touched one. I had told him I'd once owned a Brazilian D-28 named Jimmy. When he asked what happened to it, I didn't answer. I think he thought I pawned it or something. He asked me if I'd know Jimmy if I ever saw him again. I told him that when my mom gave Jimmy to my dad, she'd had Ruth 1:16–17 engraved into the back of the headstock. Only way to remove that was carve it out or remove the neck—both of which were unlikely.

Life in Nashville was not all hardship and pain. One part was better than anything I'd ever known.

Life at the Ryman.

When the crowds left, when they turned out all the lights, when the floors had been swept and mopped and the bathrooms cleaned, when power to the soundboards had been cut and echoes faded, I was left locked inside. Alone with my voice and one of the most hallowed stages in all of music. While some around Music City thought that understanding the Nashville Number System was the key to the kingdom, in reality it was the Ryman. Every night, right or wrong, I strapped on a borrowed guitar from Riggs's shop and played my heart out for an empty auditorium.

For two years I "performed" there six or seven nights a week. I looked for Blondie, but he never showed. Not once. Only the rats knew.

Then Daley Cross came to town. And took the world by storm.

And fire.

22

Daley Cross had been discovered in a California talent show. Malibu looks matched to an angelic, pitch-perfect voice. A one-in-a-million combination. Her people touted her as a country voice with crossover star potential. Meaning she could make money in several markets. Including world tours and multiple endorsement opportunities. Her stage presence endeared her to young and old and belied her twenty-one years. The buzz backstage was that her Ryman performance could be the ignition to her rocket shot. All she needed was a hit. A song that distinguished her from the rest of the dime-a-dozen pop star crowd.

For the last year I'd heard the rumblings. They'd have been tough to miss. Her first single had climbed into the top ten. An easy-to-sing pop jingle that got a lot of airplay and showcased a bit of her range. The conversation around her included words like, *It's only a matter of time.* Over the last several months she'd begun making the rounds of second-tier talk shows and drive-time radio shows. Her sound and picture were becoming more heard and seen. Her brand was growing. She was on her way.

Whenever I heard her, I couldn't understand what all the fuss was about. Don't get me wrong, whatever "it" was, she had it, but whenever I heard her voice or saw her glittery picture gracing some magazine cover or television screen, I always thought that whoever was in charge of her was trying to make her fit into a box she wasn't made for. Someone had taken the sum of her, chopped her into little pieces, and was trying to reassemble those pieces into some formula that had worked elsewhere. I sensed in her a resident sadness that no light show, electric guitar solo, or eyeliner could disguise.

Evidently I was alone in this analysis, as everyone else was head over heels for her.

With much media buzz, her show had come to the Ryman. Several black tour buses and just as many semitrailers logjammed the streets. Her rehearsal began early afternoon, ran late into the evening, and included a lot of people yelling, "Again!" or "Daley, that won't cut it. Not in this business."

One guy in particular liked to throw down his earphones and clipboard whenever he wanted to emphasize his immense dissatisfaction. To me, she seemed little more than a pinball, and somebody without her best interest in mind had his hands on the flippers. As she sang the same stupid song for the umpteenth time, I kept wondering why she let them try to make her into someone she wasn't. She could sing that song fifty times, but she'd never find her voice in it.

But nobody was asking me, so I kept my nose down, mouth shut, and hands on the mop.

By one a.m. the frantic crowds and people trying to make themselves look busy had left and I was alone. The Ryman was dark save a single light on the stage, which the sound engineers left on every night in honor of those who'd stood there. I checked off my "final" list, double-checked the doors, and wandered to the stage. Daley Cross's band had left their instruments onstage, and given the multiple security guards posted around the block, they weren't going anywhere.

Next to Daley's microphone stood her guitar. A McPherson. It was really difficult for me not to put my hands on a McPherson. So I picked it up, slid the strap over my neck, and began running my fingers up and down the neck and strumming out a few chords. It was both aesthetically and acoustically beautiful. Melodious. Rang like a bell and filled the air with a sonic tapestry. It sounded so good and leant itself to a finger-picking style . . . so I dug back in my memory and began playing a song I'd written years ago about the storm that threatened to rip the tents apart and how Dad had lifted me out from underneath the bench and told me to "let it out."

Though I'd initially written it on a piano, I'd transposed it. It sounded especially good on a guitar because over the years I'd learned how to simultaneously flat-pick and strum the strings while also tapping the body of the guitar in a percussive, drumlike rhythm that created the feeling of a coming violent storm. The style I'd developed allowed the listener to both hear and feel the music through the use of contradicting major and minor chords.

Minor chords are sad, anxious, heavy. They grab your attention in that by their very nature they are uncomfortable. Disconcerting. They make you want to run for your life. Major chords are happy, warm, full, light, and triumphant. They make you want to do the impossible. The first would lead us to the second. But to get to triumphant and resolute, we had to endure anxious and fearful.

The second way I accomplished this style was to use an actual sound from the storm. A shrill whistle that I'd learned from Dad. In an odd mixture of physics and sheer volume, he could curl his tongue and press his lips tight to his front teeth and blow. Actually, *shrill* doesn't even come close to describing the sound. As a kid I'd spent countless dizzying hours mastering it.

If I played it right you could hear the thunder rumble, lightning crack, tent rip; then a rising crescendo replaced that uncertainty, lifting you and erasing the memory. Then before you knew it, the storm had faded and you were galloping atop notes that reached out from the stage, wrapping you in their arms and shaking off the fear.

It's a song about promise. Gifting. Calling. About identity. And, I guess, it's a song about how music is sometimes the only thing that will silence the raging storm in us. My dad had always loved that song.

Three verses, a bridge, and a chorus later, I finished playing, retuned the low E string to a drop-D tuning, the way I'd found it, and was about to set the guitar back in its stand when I heard the sound of someone clapping quietly.

The hair rose on my neck. "Hello?"

The clapping quieted.

"Somebody there?"

A woman's voice responded. Her two words betrayed a weariness. "Just me."

I began retracing my steps in my mind. Had I locked all the doors? Had she been here the entire time? Who was she? I considered dropping the guitar and running. I tried to sound like I had some authority. "Ma'am, this building is closed for rehearsal."

A chuckle. "Thank goodness."

While I tried to sound in charge, I'm afraid my voice took on a hand-caught-in-the-cookie-jar tone. "I'm going to have to ask you to leave."

I could hear the smile on her face as she spoke. "Sure, just as soon as you put down my guitar."

Ouch. I really had been caught with my hand in the cookie jar. I placed it quietly in its stand. "I was afraid you were going to say that."

She rose from her seat in the back of the auditorium and began making her way toward me. "Don't worry. You play it a lot better than I do."

I had not watched her evening sound tests because I'd had my head buried in replacing some lightbulbs, but her voice was unmistakable. Daley Cross was a good five inches shorter than me, but she did not seem to know this. She made her way across the stage, hands behind her back, and looked up at me. I waved my hand across her guitar. "I'm sorry. I didn't hurt it. You can—"

"That's a beautiful song."

I figured I'd try the play-dumb approach—which was extraordinarily stupid given that I was standing on a stage and had been holding her guitar while my echo faded off the walls. "Song?"

She smiled and circled me, singing the chorus back to me. " 'Let it out . . .' " She quit singing as abruptly as she began. "Where'd you hear that?"

I chewed on my lip a second, asking myself just how honest I wanted to be with her. "In my head."

She looked up at me. Surprised. "You wrote it?"

I wasn't sure where this was going or how my answer might contribute to me losing my job.

If my boss knew I'd been rather cavalier with what had been entrusted to me for safekeeping, I was pretty sure she'd fire me on the spot. My instructions had been pretty clear: "Clean up, lock up, touch nothing. Whatever you do, don't, under any circumstances, mess with the musicians' instruments. Don't even breathe on them. Ever."

And Riggs had vouched for me, which made it even more troublesome. I could lose both jobs.

I waved my hand across the stage. "Nothing's missing. You can check. I was just locking up and—"

"Where'd you get the music?"

"I can't afford to lose this job." I scratched my head. "So if you could just forget—"

"Where'd you learn to play like that?"

I rubbed my hands together. "Listen, Miss, um—"

She held out her hand. "Daley. I'm playing here tomorrow night." She looked at her watch. "Or tonight."

Our conversations were walking in circles around each other. I said, "I feel like I'm talking about one thing and you're talking about another."

She pointed behind her. "I couldn't find an unlocked door, so the rent-a-cops let me in."

That explained it. Sucker punched by security. "Oh."

"Don't worry. Your secret's safe with me. Provided—" She stood across from me, motioning for me to pick up her guitar. "Please." She smiled, walked off the stage, sat in the front pew, and pulled her knees up into her chest. "You play that again. Just like last time."

"You're not mad about me playing your McPherson?"

She waved me off. "My producer gave me that. Said he thought it matched my voice."

I turned the guitar in my hands. "Nice producer."

"Why do you say that?"

"It's a ten-thousand-dollar guitar."

"He can afford it."

"How long have you been sitting there?"

"Long enough."

I sat on a stool and folded my hands in my lap. "Couldn't we both go home and forget this? I'll walk you back to your—"

A single shake of her head. "Can't sleep." She wrapped her arms tighter around her knees and waited, warding off a cold wind I couldn't feel. She looked both bone-tired and soul-weary.

"So all I have to do is sing this one time and we can both go home and you'll forget we ever met?"

She smiled.

My fingers rolled quietly across the strings. "That's not an answer."

"We can go home, but I doubt I'll forget."

"So, you *are* mad?"

She rested her chin on her knees. "In the last

six months I've listened to hundreds of demos. Maybe more. None of them touched me as deeply as your song."

I muted the strings. "Can I ask you one question?"

"Sure."

I eyed the photoshopped glamour posters along the wall. The one where the unseen fan at her feet pushed back her glistening hair. "Is *she* listening? Or are you?" I looked back at the front row, my fingers tapping the strings.

She let out a breath, and the square edge of her shoulders melted into a relaxed round. "I'm listening as me."

So at two a.m. in the Ryman, with nothing but air between us, I lifted my voice and played for an audience of one—offering my song out across the world that lay before me—and the well-constructed walls of two broken strangers came tumbling down.

When I finished, she shook her head and wiped her face on her sleeve. She sat there a minute, slouching in the seat, closing her eyes, resting her head against the back of the pew. For almost a minute she said nothing while one toe tapped unconsciously.

Finally she stood. "Thank you." She crossed her arms again like the cold wind had returned. She half turned and spoke over her shoulder. "Very much."

She had made it to the exit when I hollered after her, "Hey, would you—"

She turned.

"Would you sing it with me?"

She took a step back toward me. "Really? You wouldn't mind?"

I stepped to the side, out of the direct rays of the single light shining down. "No."

She nodded. "I'd like that." She came back and climbed the steps leading onto the stage. "You teach me the words?"

I slid the notebook from behind my back and opened to the page.

She pointed to the Nashville Number System. "You understand this?"

"I can get by."

"The guys in my band are always telling me I need to learn it, but it's Greek to me." She read through the words again, finally brushing the pen strokes on the page with her fingertips. "Beautiful." She looked up. "Where's it come from?"

"My dad was . . . is a tent preacher. I was just a kid. A bad storm rolled in. Lightning caught the tent on fire. Thunder everywhere. I hid under the piano bench. Sideways rain stinging my face. People scattering like ants. My dad reached down and lifted me up with one arm, set me on the bench, pointed to my heart, and whispered in my ear—"

She finished the sentence by singing, "Let it out."

"It was the first time I played before a group of any size."

"I think I would like your dad."

I worked my way through the intro and nodded for her to come in. She started quietly, breathing in the guitar, breathing out my song. Her voice was custom-made for it. She had the range and the volume to toy with the verses, which she refrained from doing, I suspected, for fear of hurting my feelings. By the time I started playing the second verse, she'd opened up her lungs and sung my song back to me.

When the last note faded, we sat quietly. One minute. Then two. Finally she raised an eyebrow. "How'd that sound? Was that okay?"

She'd had a rough go lately. Too many negative responses. Like a dog that's been on a leash so long that even when you take it off it won't walk beyond the length of the chain.

Her singing my song was one of the more beautiful things I'd ever heard. I tried to figure out how to tell her that without sounding like her growing and adoring fan base.

"I've always thought that the best voice is not the one that can sing the most octaves, or the loudest, longest, whatever . . . but the one who makes us believe that what he or she is singing is true."

She relaxed a notch. "Well, did you? Believe?"

I laughed. "Yes."

She smiled like she too had been caught with her hand in the cookie jar. She eyed the doors and spoke softly. "Want to do it again?"

We played it through five times straight. Each time she grew more comfortable, making it more and more her own. On the sixth time she owned it altogether, and I both heard and watched her find her voice.

And her song.

When she finished, her eyes smiled in concert with her lips. "Thank you." She gently closed my black book, handed it back to me, and slid her hands into her jeans. "Thanks for letting me sing your song. It's . . . yeah, just wow." She pushed the hair out of her face and looked at her watch. "I better get going. Long day ahead." She stepped off the stage and began walking toward the exit.

I hopped off the stage and walked after her. "Daley?" I shook my head. "I mean, Miss Cross."

She stopped. A hardened exterior had returned, and she looked like she had already begun fighting the day's battles.

"Can I ask you something else?"

"Sure. And it's Daley."

"Do you like the music that you play?"

She shook her head matter-of-factly. "Not really. But I sing it in the hopes that doing so will allow me to sing what I like one day."

I opened my book, tore out the perforated page, and handed it to her. "Your band shouldn't have any trouble. Everything they need is—"

She shook her head. "I can't. I mean, I couldn't poss—"

I held out a stop-sign hand. "You sing it better than I do. Unless you don't—"

"No." She clutched the paper to her chest. "I do. It's just . . . words like these are . . . I feel like I'd be stealing something sacred."

"It's yours."

"You must let me buy it from you."

I waved my hand across the stage. "Given my experience here in Nashville, I highly doubt anything will come of my dreams, but I think you should keep dreaming yours. I grew up in a world where music wasn't hoarded. It was shared. All the time." I chuckled. "My dad used to say it's like that proverbial candle that you don't hide. You set it on a table where everyone can see it. Where it gives light." I slid my hands into my pockets. "You're the only real light I've seen in a dark five years." I paused. "I write the music that I need to hear. Only when I give it away can someone else sing it back to me."

"That would make you different from most everyone else in this city."

"Music is an offering."

She held the song tight. "Where can I find you?"

"I'll be back here tonight. Cleaning up the

mess you and your band leave. Preparing for the next act." I pointed. "My day job is across the alley. Riggs's. I'm never far."

A gentle smile. "What do you do?"

"Try to make guitars sound like the voices that own them."

She laughed. "Figures." She pointed at my notebook. "You also wait tables?"

"No. Why?"

"The way you tuck that thing behind your belt at your back."

I turned it in my hands. It was worn, with tattered edges, and had taken on the natural curve of my lower back. "Old habit."

"What all do you write in there?"

"Stuff I don't want to forget."

A sly smile. This time I was pretty sure she was flirting. "You're being vague."

"Just songs."

"So you have more?"

"Yes."

Her voice softened. "You always this honest?"

"No. Sometimes I lie."

She eyed the single page in her hand, then extended it slowly into the empty space between us. "Speak now or forever hold your peace."

I wasn't sure about a whole lot in life, but I was absolutely certain that Daley Cross was made to sing that song. "Keep it."

I led her toward the door, unlocked it, and

pushed it open, holding it while she walked through. When she did, she brushed my arm with her hand, then my stomach. It was a purposeful touch, as curious as her questioning. Something in her wanted to know if I was real. It was also an unspoken acknowledgment that we'd just shared something that words couldn't ever encapsulate. No matter how long we stood there and racked our brains and tried to come up with a synthesis, there were no words for what we'd just experienced.

People who make music together know this. Talking about it never gets at the heart of what's been shared.

When she turned, the breeze caught her hair and pulled it across her face. She tucked it behind an ear. "What's your name?"

I extended my hand. "Cooper. But folks 'round here just call me Peg."

She raised an eyebrow. "Peg?"

"My dad used to say that my mom was his anchor. Like a tent peg. And I reminded him of her. The name stuck."

"Sounds like a tender love story."

"To hear my dad tell it, it was that."

"I'd like to hear more about them."

"That almost sounds like you're asking me out."

"It's the least I can do."

Something in me that had been frowning for a few years smiled. "I'd like that."

"After the show, then."

23

Riggs kept me busy most of the day. After lunch, he noticed my good mood. I think I'd been whistling. "You're in good spirits. Got a hot date or something?"

I shrugged. "Or something."

He smiled at me over a Martin he was working on. "Do tell."

I waved him off and stared out in the alley toward the Ryman. "You wouldn't believe me. Better just wait and see how it pans out."

I worked through lunch, but my mind was next door. When Riggs came back from lunch, he said the place was buzzing with people. A producer named Sam Casey was crazy about a new song that his new girl Daley Cross had sung for him early this morning. He heard it once, got on the phone, and immediately began making major changes to the set. Trucks were brought in. The place was crawling with electricians and audio-video people. Set designers from one of the top touring rock-and-roll big-hair bands had been paid a lofty fee to drop everything and oversee the overhaul.

I didn't know what limitations the Mother Church of Country Music put on its shows, but it sounded like this one would push the boundaries.

By the time I showered, slapped my face with aftershave, and walked through the back door of the Ryman around seven thirty, the seats were full and folks were standing up along the wall in the balcony. Word had spread, as evidenced by the number of cameras and glad-handing glittering celebrities. I'd only seen it like this a few times before, and that usually involved folks who'd been in the business awhile. This could be one to remember.

When the show started at eight I was mopping up a spilled Coca-Cola in the foyer. From there I moved to the men's upstairs bathroom where a toilet was in the process of shooting stuff the wrong direction. Not pretty. That kept me busy the better part of an hour, so by the time I exited the men's room, Daley only had a couple songs left.

I stood in the balcony against the back wall and watched the whirlwind of lights and sound envelop her. She looked as though she was struggling to find purchase amid an avalanche of stimuli. The heels she was wearing couldn't have been comfortable, and her clothes looked more appropriate for a Super Bowl beer commercial than a girl standing on a stage singing a song. After seeing her so relaxed, so comfortable early this morning, it was tough to watch. It was like watching a voice I'd heard walking around in skin I'd never seen.

Sure, it was technically perfect, and I was sure a

lot of people would go crazy over it. The media had found their next darling. But selling out had never been too attractive to me. And, sadly, Daley Cross was selling out right before my eyes. I exited the balcony and made my way backstage, where I knew I'd be needed as the show came to a close.

Daley had played fifteen or so songs, including a few well-known covers that endeared her to some of the older members of the audience. The concert ended, the applause faded, and I heard Daley's voice. She was breathing heavily. "Thank you. Thank you very much." A pause. "Phew. I need to start working out if I hope to make a career out of this. The guys in that booth up there are about to kill me." She put a hand on her hip. "Does it look hard? It feels hard."

The audience laughed.

"Sure glad my mom wouldn't let me quit dance lessons. I'm exhausted. And I need to apologize to you folks in the front; I think my deodorant wore off an hour ago." More laughter. She lifted her head and spoke to the folks in the sound and lighting booth. "Guys, could you bring the lights up, please? I'd like to make sure everybody didn't leave six or eight songs ago. Right now you've got the sun shining in my eyes." The lights were adjusted. Daley smiled at the audience. "Oh, hi." She sounded surprised. "You're still here."

A guy in the audience screamed, "Daley, we love you!"

She was quick to respond. "You should see me at four a.m."

The same guy responded, "Your place or mine?"

Everybody laughed. She strolled across the stage. "Guess I walked into that."

The crowd quieted. She slid a stool onto the stage and sat down. "These shoes are killing me." She looked at the glittering headliners seated in the first few rows. "I don't know how you all do this. I mean, is there a secret?" More laughter. "Matter of fact . . ."

There was a pause while she took off those ridiculous heels. Daley stood and walked down the steps to a young girl in the front row. You could hear her voice away from the microphone talking to the mother. "Mom, is this okay?" Daley's voice returned to the microphone. "Here, baby, you keep these. In about five minutes you'll be big enough to wear them. Maybe you can teach me how to walk in them." She hugged the girl, walked back up onstage, and shook her head. "They hurt my bunions."

More laughter and energetic applause as the star onstage became one of us.

"I'm a California girl. Grew up barefoot on the beach. See no reason to change now."

Another voice in the audience shouted, "Take it off!"

She laughed and aimed her face in the direction of the voice. "This is not that kind of show." She pointed. "But if you head that way down Broadway you might find what you're looking for."

She possessed a seasoned stage presence for someone so young and had those folks eating out of the palm of her hand. "If you're wondering what's going on, I'm stalling while the guys do whatever they're doing back there." The spotlights circled the stage and highlighted several men dressed in black working furiously.

"Over the last several months some very talented people have taken me under their wings, and we've worked really hard to find the right sound. Right song. Or songs. Some you've heard here tonight." She paused for applause. "During that time, I've listened to several hundred songs penned by some of the best songwriters in the business. During this process, I learned something interesting about myself. My management team was listening to those demos trying to find the sound that could identify me to you. The type of sound that when you heard it, you'd immediately think *Daley Cross* and then sing along.

"Me, on the other hand? That wasn't my primary motivation." She glanced at her producer. "Sorry, Sam."

Back to the audience. "I was listening not for the song that identified me to you, but identified me with me. I was looking for a sound, a song, that resonated within me. Something that would take on a life of its own inside me. That's not as easy as it might sound, and as a result, I haven't been sleeping much."

The same guy in the balcony interrupted her. "I can help with that."

Daley didn't skip a beat. "Does your parole officer know you're here?" She waited while the laughter died down.

As if on cue, the lights dimmed, save a lone hazy spotlight on Daley. The image brought to mind that single swaying lightbulb the night of the storm and how it circled above the piano. I thought of my father and Big-Big and how I wished they were here to see this. Then I thought of the money, the truck, and Jimmy, and I knew they would not be.

"I'm going to sing one more song. It's new." For some reason Daley turned her head just then, taking her eyes off the audience, and looked to her right, where she spotted me standing in the shadows just offstage. She continued speaking to the crowd, but she was looking at me. "I hope you like it." The way she said it suggested that I would not.

The lights cut to black, and Daley walked off the stage, where she was met by a woman wearing a headset and holding a shirt in one hand and a headdress that resembled a tiara in the other. She accomplished an eight-second costume change and then stood just a few feet away from me as the intro began to play. When the lights began to flash and thunder crack, Daley turned to me, grabbed my hand, and whispered, "I'm so sorry."

What surprised me was how someone so confident in the spotlight had become so fragile in the dark. The transformation was immediate, and I wondered which was the real Daley.

Compared to other venues, the Ryman stage is not that big. Originally designed for a preacher and a choir, there's not a lot of room to maneuver. Nor was it originally wired to handle large productions. The stage had its physical limitations, and from where I stood it looked like the guys in the booth were pushing them.

The manufactured thunder and lightning lit up the back of the stage, along with a giant video screen showing a dark storm rolling in. Smoke machines blew white smoke from both underneath and above, blanketing the stage in a cloud. Fans created wind, swirling the smoke. When they'd achieved total whiteout, Daley walked to the center of the stage, where the wind tugged at her hair. She stood in the storm waiting for the smoke to clear and the music to crescendo.

She never got her chance.

The increased load of lights, electric, smoke, and wonder overtaxed the already overworked motherboard and, with one giant cluster of sparks and bang, blew every fuse connected to light and sound. In response to what sounded like the first cannon shot at Armageddon, the stage went black. Immediately, the yellow-tinted emergency lights lit the auditorium. Daley stood on a silent stage in a clearing cloud staring out at a snickering audience. A voice a few rows from the front said, "Reminds me of my ex-husband."

The band exited the stage, leaving a disbelieving Daley alone with the audience and a few remaining sparks. A music critic with a camera snapped a few photos. She spoke around her camera: "Honey, you're only as good as your last song." She slung the camera over her shoulder and said to no one in particular, "It'll be awhile before she recovers from this one."

Daley tried to speak into the microphone, but it too was dead. So she stood there, frozen, unsure what to do.

The only word to describe the activity backstage and up in the sound booth was *pandemonium.* The same cold breeze that had blown through the Ryman earlier this morning blew now across the stage. Daley crossed her arms to ward off the chill.

The only light in the balcony came from the On Air sign above the radio broadcast booth. Evidently the panel that handled radio transmission hadn't been affected, and the microphones hanging from the ceiling were still capturing the sound onstage and broadcasting it across radio waves.

There was still hope.

I walked out onstage and found a tearful Daley just seconds from meltdown. I lifted the stupid-looking tiara off her head and pitched it back behind the drum set. Then I took off my flannel shirt, exposing a stained white T-shirt, and wrapped the flannel shirt around her. I said, "You want to sing that song?"

Her eyes were darting five different places at once. "Yeah, but—"

"Yes or no." I glanced at the people walking out. "You've got about three seconds."

Her eyes searched mine. "Yes."

I pulled up two stools and slung her guitar around my neck. Then I turned to Daley, whose eyes had grown large and round. I leaned in close so she could hear me. "Just take my words and sing them back to me."

Her hand bushed my arm. Another touch. A sonar ping. She nodded.

My fingers hit the strings and I began making a series of seven repeating whistles that grew louder —like the wind. In my mind I heard the echo of my father . . . *The great players aren't great because of all the notes they can play, but because of the ones they don't play.*

Given years of practice, and the mystery of the beautiful, cathedral-like acoustics of the Ryman, I created a cacophony of noise to grab everyone's attention. Whistles by their very nature do that. And while I might have stopped the exodus, it was Daley who turned the people around and pulled them back into their seats.

That was the night the world changed.

24

Daley rang the last note off the balcony to roaring, raucous applause. She'd turned them. Done what no one thought she could. She'd won them. Every one. When we walked off the stage, she was mobbed. I was met by a single person. A man. Her manager.

He smiled at me, and I immediately did not like him. Nor did I trust the look in his eyes. I gathered he was the one responsible for the attempted adulteration of my song. He extended his hand. "Sam Casey."

"Cooper O'Connor. Folks call me Peg."

"So I've heard." He nodded toward the stage and said, "How'd you like to sell that song?"

Daley wrapped her arm inside mine and pressed her chest against me. She was floating. Cloud nine.

I looked at her. Back at him. "It's not mine to sell you."

He looked confused. "What do you mean?"

"I can't sell you what I already gave away."

He clearly wasn't expecting that. "Some would call that naïve."

"Others would call it selfless. Kind, even."

"Twenty years in this business, and *kind* is not something I've experienced."

The last few years flashed before my eyes. He had a point. "Five years in, and I tend to agree with you."

"You have others?"

"I do."

"Are they as good?"

"Some are better."

He lowered his voice. "Could I hear them?"

I glanced at Daley, then back at him. "You have any openings in the band? I can play guitar and piano. And thanks to an evil, beady-eyed woman back home, I'm probably better at the latter. My vocals aren't too bad."

He laughed. "Funny you should mention that. We just happen to have an opening in all three of those areas. You're hired."

Okay, maybe he wasn't so bad. He put his hand on my shoulder. "Why don't you two come around for dinner this weekend. We have a lot to talk about." He turned to walk away, then paused. "Oh, and if you have any plans for the next year, you may want to cancel them. You might be traveling. Do you have a passport?"

"No."

"Get one. Expedited."

With a crowd buzzing around us and effusive congratulations coming with every hug and handshake, Daley pulled me aside, pressed my hand to her heart, and kissed me on the cheek, then again on the corner of my mouth. And it was there, backstage at the Ryman, that her trembling, tear-soaked, salty, warm lips answered my question of which Daley was the real one.

My boss told me I could have the rest of the night off. Actually, she said I could have the rest of my life off. She hugged me and said, "Come see us sometime." It was a much-needed acknowledgment and, coming from someone who'd seen the best in the business, I took it to heart.

It was only after Daley and I had walked out onto Broadway in search of dinner that the thought occurred to me. Everything had happened so fast, and given that I'd been up most of last night and this morning, my days and nights were all backward.

I turned to Daley. "What night is this?"

"Thursday."

I whispered, "Ryman Radio."

"What?"

"He was right."

"Who was right?"

The rush came in a flood. When Daley asked me why I was crying, I couldn't tell her. I hit my knees on Broadway, and couldn't talk at all.

The morning headline read "Cross My Heart," and the picture of the two of us covered the front page. It had been taken near the end of the song when Daley hit the highest note she could, popping a vein out on the side of her neck. The picture did a great job of depicting the power and strength of her voice. The story described in detail the electrical explosion that left her unamplified, without a band, "vocally naked" before an imposing audience. The writer quoted many of the stars who said they couldn't believe she'd gathered her composure and pulled it off. Others said they'd have walked off the stage. All praised her courage and resilience. The story talked about her "incomparable voice" and said the song had perfectly showcased her "unparalleled range" and labeled her "the next great one."

One local media outlet had managed to film our performance. Given that the Ryman AV feed had been blown, the grainy video was offered to multiple news outlets around town, and was then picked up by the national outlets. The poorly shot nature of the video only added to the mystique. By late afternoon, the story and the song were everywhere.

When I came into work the next morning, Riggs was reading the paper, wearing a smile wider than his ears. He looked at me over his reading glasses. "What're you doing here?"

I was tying on my apron. "Working."

He shook his head, laughing. "No. No, you're

not. Sam Casey's courting you. Get out of here. I can't afford you anymore."

"You're firing me?"

He took the apron out of my hands and hung it up. "Absolutely."

"Why?"

He was still laughing. " 'Cause you been lying to me." He tapped me in the chest. "Also to yourself. And to everyone else."

"What!"

"I knew you could play. I didn't know you could *play*. And sing? Where did you get pipes like that?"

"You're really firing me?"

Riggs put his hand on my shoulder. "Son, I'm trying to tell you what everyone else knows and you'll figure out soon enough. Your life is about to change. Go live it. Bring me your guitars when you need some work done on 'em."

I pointed upstairs. "And that?"

"Stay as long as you like. When you're on the road, I'm going to sell tickets to all the tourists. 'Peg Lives Here.' With a voice like yours, the girls will eat that stuff up. I can retire off ticket sales."

Riggs was a good man. He'd helped me when no one else would.

"Well," I said, "could I collect my last paycheck? I'm gonna need it to get from here to there."

Daley and I became inseparable. She showed me the high-rent world of Franklin, where Sam had put her up in a four-thousand-square-foot condo complete with gate, twenty-four-hour security, gym membership, and leased Mercedes. The world on a silver platter.

When she wanted to see my paper-plate world, I hesitated. Looking back was painful, and I didn't want her to know. She hooked her thumb in my belt loop and pulled me to her. Wrapping her arms tight around my waist, she said, "Tell me."

So I started at the beginning. Colorado. Mom, Dad, Big-Big, the tents, the storm, Miss Hagle, and my growing discontentment with my father. I told her about my high school band and about the fight with Dad. Stealing the money, the truck, and Jimmy. She was driving, so I directed her to the motel where I'd stayed my first night in town and where I'd hid the money. Then to the parking lot along the river where I'd slept in the cab of the truck. The Laundromats. I bought her a dog at the Sudsy Schnitzel. We parked under the overpass and I showed her where I'd slept. The woods. The soggy mattress. The dog park where I bathed. The street corner where Jimmy was stolen. Printer's Alley. Riggs. And finally, the Ryman.

When I finished, Daley was holding a handful of tissues. She couldn't stop the tears. The further we went down my story, the more they flowed. It was tough watching those beautiful eyes cry. Outside the Ryman, she just shook her head. She whispered, "How'd you do it?"

One of the things I came to love about Daley was the degree to which she empathized with others. Something in the hardwiring of her heart felt with acute sharpness what others felt. If you cried, tears dripped down her face. If you laughed, the ends of her mouth turned upward. It was both her greatest strength and deepest weakness.

I pulled out my wallet and unfolded the map Dad had wrapped around the money I'd stolen. It was frayed and white in the creases. "Hope is a tough thing to kill."

"Hope for what?" she said.

"That I can find a way home."

Saturday night found us winding down the drive of Sam Casey's fifty-acre Brentwood estate, bordered by the Harpeth River, and knocking on his massive door at his ginormous house. Bernadette, his siliconized, tucked and lifted, made-to-order bride, answered the door holding what was obviously not her first glass of red wine. She ushered us in and quickly disappeared with a little white yap dog into the kitchen where she was barking at the chef and the server.

The house was a showpiece. Where most homes have pictures or artwork, Sam had decorated his house with records. Gold and platinum records. Awards and recognitions were stacked on every shelf. His house was a museum to himself. What he'd conquered. What he owned.

I said, "These all yours?"

He feigned indifference. "Gifts from my artists."

I tested him. "Strange that they didn't keep them."

He made eye contact. "They love me. And who can blame them?" He pointed to one record after another. "When I found her, she was waiting tables in Tuscaloosa. This one was a rodeo clown. Car salesman." He sipped some brown-colored liquid from a crystal glass. "You two stay in this business long enough and you'll find that it's a jealous mistress. You turn your head for a second and she's gone." He made a fist. "Keep a tight grip. Tight all the time. Otherwise, somebody will come like a thief in the night and steal your trophies."

Dinner consisted of our choice of steak, lobster, or fish. I ate all three. After-dinner consisted of expensive brandy and a dessert that his chef prepared in front of us—which included setting it on fire. I had three helpings.

Finally he took us out back. We walked beneath the portico and into a second building some distance from the house. His recording studio. He patted the heart pine that glowed amber red in the recessed lighting. "Found this in Virginia. Two hundred years old. Used to be a stop on the Underground Railroad. Hid slaves in a cellar. Had it taken apart board by board, numbered, and reassembled here around one of the best recording studios in Nashville." He pointed to the sound-board. "Aren't very many of those."

He took a sip of his drink. "I've recorded more number one hits in there than I can count." He shook his head. "If those walls could talk." He looked at both of us. "Next week I'm going to record one more."

25

What Sam thought would take a week took less than a day. Evidence of the chemistry between Daley and me. She brought her guitar and her voice, I brought me, and Sam sat behind his motherboard and slid knobs up and down. Oz controlling all the levers. Smiling on the other side of the glass.

After the fourth time through, he pulled off his headphones and said, "I believe that'll do it."

I didn't like Sam and I didn't trust him, but when it came to sound production he had a gift. Listening to the playback, it was obvious he'd captured the essence of Daley.

Her first single hit radio stations the following week where, thanks to the hype from the Ryman show, it immediately jumped to number one. And stayed there.

Unbeknownst to me, Daley had credited me as the songwriter. She told Sam that while I'd given her the song to sing, it was mine. With my first royalty check, I bought a D-28 from Riggs with a price tag of twenty-two thousand. He sold it to me for fourteen.

Along with the guitar I sent my dad a check for fifty thousand dollars. I wanted to tell him what had happened. I wanted to tell him about Jimmy. I wanted to tell him about Daley. I could not. Some things must be said face-to-face. I simply wrote, *Dad, I'm sorry.* I tracked the package and con-firmed it was delivered two days later and Dad had signed for it. The thought of that brought some comfort.

Daley's "Cross My Heart" tour started the following month. We were gone a year. We opened for one big act after another. Pretty soon the fans were coming to see us. We performed in fortysomething states, in several countries, and on most every nighttime talk show. We even helped bring down the crystal ball in Times Square. Somewhere in there I turned twenty-four, but I can't remember where. Life was a blur.

Back in Nashville, Daley won Best New Entertainer, Female Vocalist of the Year, and, wonder of wonders, we won Song of the Year. It was tough to argue with a song that had gone five times platinum, giving Sam more glitter for his foyer. The emcee called us a match made in heaven. "If you want to hear what angels sound like when they sing, just listen to these two."

Later that night, to my surprise, I won Songwriter of the Year.

I stood on that stage, a trophy in each hand, looked out at all those beautiful people looking at me, and felt a deep and growing inner sadness. I was on my way. Daley and I both were. I had everything I could want.

Except what mattered most.

I stepped up to the microphone and remembered the Ryman, night after night, empty save my echo. "I'd like to dedicate this to my dad . . ." I swallowed.

Daley saw me wrestling with getting the words out. She knew the truth, so she walked onto the stage from the side and spoke for me. "He's not here tonight."

I gathered my composure. "Dad, I did what you said. I . . ." A tear spilled down my cheek. "I let it out."

That brought them to their feet.

After the show Daley went to dinner with the band while I disappeared down Broadway, let myself in the stage door of the Ryman after midnight, and played to an empty house. Halfway through the song, I cracked. Couldn't finish. I found myself facedown on the stage, sobbing at the top of my lungs.

I felt a hand on my back. Daley. No words. She just sat and held me and let me soak her shoulder. I'd been holding that inside a long time.

When I had gathered myself I said, "I need to go home, Dee. There's some things there . . . things left unsaid." I looked at her. "I need to clean up a really big mess."

She brushed the hair out of my face and kissed my nose. "Can I go too?"

That's when I knew.

The next day I walked into a jewelry store in Franklin that Riggs recommended and told them Riggs had sent me. When they found out what I was doing and who I was buying it for, they rolled out the red carpet, and the prices listed on the tags were immediately cut in half. As you can guess, I didn't know squat about diamonds, but I'd like to think that when I gave them my credit card and bought that $9,946 ring I got a good deal. The salesman told me all about quality and cut and brilliance, and by the time I left I could have written an essay on the reflective qualities of light through diamonds. But that wasn't why I bought it. I bought it because it looked like Daley.

Sam brought us in from the road and told us it was time to cut an album. Then he looked at me. "Now, about those songs."

Songs were not the problem. I had more songs than I could count. Sam, on the other hand, was. I still didn't trust him as far as I could throw him, but I couldn't argue with his ability to produce, so I played my cards close to my chest. Admittedly,

I was green, and five years repairing guitars and cleaning toilets at the Ryman didn't mean I knew much about the music business—but I was not completely stupid when it came to people. And Sam betrayed what he thought about us in his eyes.

To Sam, Daley and I were little more than train cars passing in the night. He'd ride us until we wore out or something better came along. His pasted-on, backslapper smile didn't fool me. Nor did the red carpet he continually rolled out for Daley. She had grown up with nothing, her father hadn't given her the time of day, and Sam used this void to his advantage. He gave her nice things, played the affectionate uncle, and kept her in his back pocket. Daddy Warbucks.

I knew we needed him, and for the moment he needed us. But Sam wanted to take Daley where Sam wanted Daley to go, and I had a pretty strong gut feeling that when Daley got there she wouldn't like where he'd taken her. But he was pretty well entrenched in that soft spot in her heart, so trying to convince her otherwise was an uphill trudge. Given that, and knowing a tug-of-war was coming with Sam, I showed the songs to Daley first. I let her pick the sound she wanted. I knew we were in trouble when she was afraid to make a decision.

"We need to ask Sam."

I will admit I had become protective. Maybe overly so. But in my defense, I was not trying to make Daley into who I wanted her to be. I was trying to encourage Daley to find the freedom to be Daley. Something no man had ever done. I stopped her.

"Dee, if you were going to sing with me alone at two a.m. in the Ryman, what would you sing?"

Without skipping a beat, she picked out eight songs in my notebook. She chose well. Each of those songs fit her voice, showcased her growing range and control, and allowed her to begin directing her own brand. Most importantly, because many of them were ballads, they allowed her to communicate the depth of emotive truth for which she was becoming famous.

Daley was playing before sold-out shows because she made people believe. And these songs would only add to that. We decided to walk into Sam's studio with these eight. I knew he wouldn't like that, but he couldn't argue with what I'd written.

Sam was no dummy. He knew I was holding back. He wanted more control. Further, his facial expression suggested that he didn't like the direction these songs were taking Daley. I knew there was an inherent tension between what he knew to be successful and Daley's desire to be her own person. That's healthy. When it becomes unhealthy is when you use your success as a continual argument for someone else's selling out. There's got to be some give-and-take, and with Sam it was all take. Talking with Riggs, I discovered Sam had sold out long ago. But since everything he touched turned to gold, or platinum, nobody argued with him.

In the end we convinced him to cut a "deluxe" record with eight new originals and four live cuts from concerts we would play in the next few months. We even tossed around the idea of adding in a cover or two if we happened to really like one of the live versions. Daley seemed pleased, but something in the back of my head was bugging me. Sam had given in too easily. I could tell he knew something we didn't. I just didn't know what it was, and I didn't have enough experience to figure it out.

Our last request was something I was pretty sure Sam would never agree to. Prior to the digital age, music was a shared experience and recorded as one. Meaning bands or artists and musicians would gather in a single room, much the same way they do onstage, and play. They might play a song five or ten or fifteen times through, but they did it together. The recordings captured not only their sound but their chemistry. Their shared experience.

But that had all changed.

Daley and I knew from experience that what happened onstage would be difficult to reproduce in the studio, given how records were made. More often than not, artists would lay down tracks separately. That meant that when

257

recording an album, musicians seldom played together. The drummer would lay down a beat, then maybe on another day the bass player would fill in with his lead, followed on another day by the guitarists, who might record rhythm first and then lead. The last things to be recorded were the vocals.

That made for a very dissected experience. Nothing like the stage. Further, it meant that if the record company was using studio musicians, the person singing might never meet the person playing drums or bass or guitar. The producer takes these disparate parts and then mixes them together. That means he decides how the music will be heard. He dictates the experience.

It's how 99 percent of music was made by then. And neither Daley nor I liked it. Daley's real gift was communicating emotion, and that happened best when we played together. Sam hated her dependence on this, but he couldn't deny the power of the chemistry. To our surprise, he agreed to record it our way. That's when I knew something was amiss.

We scheduled the recording for the following week. And Daley and I scheduled a trip home to Colorado the week after.

26

Having one thing left to accomplish before we left, I took Daley on a drive. We headed out of town, through the horse farms, hay fields, and rolling hills.

She laid her head back. "Where're we going?"

"You'll see."

We spent most of the afternoon just driving. Her hand in mine. We laughed. Talked of concerts.

"Remember when . . ."

"What about that guy . . ."

"What were we thinking?"

Band members. Broken guitar strings. The Eiffel Tower. Big Ben. The Statue of Liberty. San Francisco Bay.

When she was comfortable in someone else's presence, and I mean like DNA-comfortable, Daley had a habit of singing to herself. Different melodies she'd string together. Some of the most beautiful songs I've ever heard weren't songs at all. I was pretty sure she wasn't aware she was doing it. Most of that afternoon she twirled her hair around one finger and sang. The anxious, fragile girl I'd met in the Ryman had been replaced by the radiant woman beside me. I'd grown used to her presence, her tenderness, her touch. Even her smell. Sometimes, when I was with her, I'd just close my eyes and breathe.

For dinner that night, I took her to my favorite restaurant. The Sudsy Schnitzel. When we walked up to the counter I said, "Let me order." She loved an adventure, so she smiled and found a table.

I prepared mine with onions, peppers, and spicy mustard. I prepared hers with cabbage, onions, and that strange cheese that smelled really bad. I arranged both on two plates, set out two napkins, two drinks. Then I found her in a corner next to the glass where we could watch the guys wash and wax Sam's Mercedes.

She took one whiff and said, "Wow! That's special. What on earth did you get me?"

I told her the story of the old man in the green Cadillac. "Every week he came here. Still in love." I slid my hand beneath hers. "Dee, right now life is pretty good for us. The world is rolled out on a silver platter. But I've known it when it's not. I've known good and bad. I've known loneliness and I've been known . . . What I'm trying to say and not doing a very good job of it is this: I don't know what'll happen in the future. Can't promise you much. Don't know where we'll end. But just like the old man in the Cadillac, I know that I will love you a long, long time from now. Sixty years from now, I want to be sitting here ordering these same horrible dogs and laughing with you. Watching you twirl your hair around your finger and listening to your lullabies."

I placed the ring in the palm of her hand. "I'm giving you all that I have. All I'm ever gonna have. I'm giving you my song." I slid the ring on her finger. "Will you sing it back to me?"

The following week was a lot of fun. Sam feigned happiness, even threw us an engagement dinner at his house. I knew better. He'd been at this game a long time. And he'd never lost. That's the message he sent whenever I walked in his front door. I kept my eyes open.

On Monday morning we walked into the recording studio. The entire band. By Thursday evening we'd cut seven of the eight songs. Daley was elated. Sam seemed happy enough. Everyone agreed that we'd wrap Friday and then spend the weekend listening to takes to decide which we liked.

Thursday evening we finished work and Sam had barbecue brought in, spread across his back porch. Everyone had left the studio except me. I wanted to restring Daley's McPherson, let the strings settle overnight to be ready for tomorrow morning. I'd fallen in love with that guitar.

Problem was I needed strings. I opened the case and found nothing. I knew I could get anything I needed from Riggs, but he was a forty-five-minute drive away, and I figured Sam had to have some-thing lying around. I mean, this was a recording studio. So I started digging.

I opened drawers and rummaged through closets.

Along one wall he had custom-built instrument closets. Each instrument had its own sliding drawer or closet, depending on size. Everything from electric violins to Gibson mandolins and banjos to Fender and Gibson electric guitars. He had one whole wall of Martins. Another of McPhersons.

I may not have liked Sam, and trusted him even less, but he and I had one thing in common: an affinity for nice instruments. We'd been so busy during the week that I hadn't had time to play but a few of them. I began sliding the drawers in and out, looking to see if anyone had tucked a set of strings alongside one of the guitars.

Nothing doing.

Last I opened one of the large storage closets where everything that didn't have a place was kept out of the way. Music stands, boxes of electrical stuff, a stuffed deer head, Styrofoam cups, packing blankets. In the back he'd stacked the cases that went along with all the guitars. I wound my way through the stacks and started opening guitar cases. No strings.

I sat down. *You mean to tell me that in one of the most successful recording studios in Nashville, there isn't a set of medium strings?*

Sam's office was a separate two-story building fifty feet away, connected to the studio by a winding walkway. Downstairs was the conference room and upstairs was his office. I walked the flagstone path to the door, found it unlocked, and let myself in. I glanced into the heart-pine-paneled conference room and then went up the open staircase to the office.

If I thought Sam's *house* was a museum, I had another thing coming. His office was his own private Hall of Fame. Warm leather. Recessed lighting. An oak desk half the size of the room. A pecky cypress conference table with twelve chairs on each side lining one wall. A gun safe discreetly tucked away in one corner. The walls had custom-built cutouts, each with its own individual lighting, where he kept his most prized awards. Pictures with presidents. More than a dozen Grammys. Two Oscars for contribution to two different soundtracks.

Interestingly, there were no pictures of wives. Or children. Or grandkids' paintings. Nothing. Everything centered around Sam. I walked around to take a closer look and observed that he was always in the middle of the pictures. The word that came to mind was *narcissistic.*

Behind his desk, a door led into a smaller sitting room. A couple of leather couches. Looked like his personal music room. Or where he kept his most prized stuff. The back of the wall was mostly glass and looked out across the pasture and horse farm. A beautiful view. On either side, facing each other, were a couple of glass cases filled with three guitars. Two electrics on the right, one Gibson, one Fender; and one acoustic on the left. I couldn't see any reason for their significance. No plaque. I eyeballed the electrics with mild interest. What kid-at-heart doesn't love a good electric guitar? But it was the yellowed spruce top and signature Martin head-stock of the acoustic that caught my attention. I flipped on the light switch and my knees nearly buckled.

Jimmy.

I stood there staring. My breath fogging up the glass. The glass was locked, so I ran my fingers above the trim boards of the case on both sides and found a small key that fit the lock. I unlocked it and slid the glass open. Jimmy appeared unhurt, relatively unplayed since I last saw him. I lifted him gently off the rack and ran my fingers up and down his neck and headstock like Helen Keller running her hand under the water at the Alabama pump house.

Years ago I'd developed my own way of stringing a guitar. Once I'd fastened the string end securely beneath the bridge pin, I would wrap the string twice around the tuner peg, then separate the strings and run the loose end between those wraps and then through the hole in the tuner, then tighten and tune. That meant that as I turned the tuner, tightening the string, the tension pinched the strings even tighter, allowing the guitar to stay in tune longer. Or so I told myself.

Lots of guys did this. The thing that made my technique a little different was that when finished, I snipped the string ends smooth to the touch so they wouldn't snag anything. Most guys left a tag.

I ran my fingers across the tuners. The string ends had been cut smooth. Based on the dull color of the strings, the smooth ends, and the fact that the strings sat a little higher off the neck, I came to think that Jimmy had not been played in a long time. Meaning Sam had somehow acquired Jimmy and then hung him up here and forgotten about him. Which meant he had no desire to play him. He just desired that someone else not play him. And that someone else was me.

Jimmy, too, had become a trophy.

I sank my fingers into him, and while the strings had lost their life, Jimmy had not. His deep, boxy, mellow, resonating sound came to life, and a slide show of memories paraded across my eyelids. From watching Dad walk forward from the rear of the tent or weave through the aspens, to all those hours I spent playing that guitar in the backseat of the truck while Dad and Big-Big taught me licks, the pictures flooded back. Some were grainy, black and white. And some were Technicolor and 3-D. All were tied to a tether on my soul. I turned him over, held his headstock up to the dim light, and read the words my mom had engraved when she gave Jimmy to my father on their wedding day.

To me, Jimmy was not simply wood, glue, and string. Many nights I'd slept with one arm draped across his neck. He had been my teddy bear. My mom's whisper. The arms of my father. The plumb line. Now he was my ticket home.

I felt a seething anger. How did Sam acquire Jimmy? When? How long had he had him? Why? Did Sam thump me in the head himself? He struck me as someone who paid others to do his dirty work. I had so many questions, and yet I knew that if I asked any of them, if I showed any interest at all in what was apparently one of Sam's most prized trophies, Jimmy would disappear and I'd never see him again.

What to do. I had to either steal Jimmy or find Sam in his office, confront him, and take Jimmy in plain sight. But I had to do all that without interfering with the recording of our album and Daley's career.

I'd picked a fight with the schoolyard bully before and was all too happy to do it again, but punching Sam in the teeth would not help Daley I had to outsmart him, not outpunch him. I had to find a replacement for Jimmy and make the switch without being seen. It would be years before Sam would even notice he was gone.

27

I spent early Friday morning rummaging through Riggs's old Martins. When he asked me what I was doing, I told him I was looking for an older-looking D-28. Something yellowed. He slid one out of a rack, opened the case, and handed it to me. A late sixties or early seventies model. I was shopping not for a particular sound so much as a color. I held it to the light. Close enough.

I paid him four thousand dollars and began thinking about timing. My best bet would be later today, after we'd finished recording and everyone was celebrating on his pool deck. Better yet, later that evening, after Sam had been drinking. Ninety seconds was all I needed.

We wrapped the recording Friday afternoon to champagne, cold beer, hot dogs, and burgers. I manned the grill and kept my eye on Sam.

With one arm around Daley, he lifted his glass and began his toast with a listing of new tour dates. He then toasted Daley, her voice, and her connection with the audience, which was, he said, unlike anything he'd ever seen. The sky was the limit. Then he toasted the band and their hard work. Lastly, he toasted me.

"I've been in this business a long time, seen a lot of great ones, but I've never seen anyone mix a guitar with words the way Cooper O'Connor does." He looked at me. "The way you match the guitar with words and her voice . . ." His eyes subconsciously glanced at the small of my back. "It's uncanny." He looked from me to Daley and back to me. "There's no telling how far the two of you can go." He lifted his glass. "To all the great things to come."

For a minute there I almost believed him.

By ten o'clock everyone had mellowed. Sam was circulating the pool deck, talking with Bernadette, moving in and out of the house, taking phone calls—proving that he was never not working. When somebody called from out of state, I saw my chance. Sam disappeared inside and I said to Daley, "Be right back."

I scooted around the side of the house, popped the trunk on Daley's car, grabbed the new-old Martin, and then walked through the woods toward the office. I let myself in through the back door to the conference room, shot upstairs, and made my way through his office in the dark. I walked around his desk, through the open door behind, found the key, unlocked the glass door, slid it open, exchanged guitars, locked it back up, and hid the key. Then I exited his office and caught a faint whiff of propane gas. Which I'd not smelled upon entering. I hurried back down the stairs and through the conference room toward the back door, where the smell grew stronger.

And where I bumped into Sam.

The single outside light shone down on his silhouette. His steely eyes were focused on me and the guitar case. In his right hand he held a gun. He lifted his arm, pointed the gun at me, and said absolutely nothing.

Then he pulled the trigger.

As his forearm flexed, pulling the trigger on the revolver, I lifted Jimmy across my chest. The blast blinded me as the bullet pierced the case and entered Jimmy's spruce top, exited his Brazilian rosewood back, and then entered me, where it sliced into my chest cavity.

I have a vague memory of a flash of light, a large explosion, of pain in my ears, searing heat in my throat and eyes, of something falling onto me that was too heavy to move. When I opened my eyes, the world was on fire. My chest felt like someone had shoved a hot poker through it. The smoke was so thick I couldn't see. I tried to scream. I tried to move.

Jimmy lay next to me. I pulled him to me. Wrapped my left arm around him. Trying to protect him from the heat. I remember clutching him, knowing that we would both die in that room. I felt around behind me, between my back and belt, but my notebook was gone. The thought of it burning somewhere in this room saddened me. More than the hole in my chest.

I thought of Daley, heard her voice, saw her face. I would have liked to spend a lifetime with her. My last thoughts were of my father. How would he hear the news? How would he take it? Would he drive down here and bring my crispy body home? Bury me in the aspens next to Mom? What would he put on my tombstone?

Cooper "Peg" O'Connor
Dead at Twenty-Four
Such Promise
Such Pain
Such a Waste

My throat felt like someone was filleting it with a small knife. I couldn't stand much more. I tried again to get up, but the stuff on top of me was too heavy and my right hand was useless and wouldn't do what my brain was telling it.

I wanted to die with my eyes open. To see what it looked like when I limped from this world into the next. But the smoke burned my eyes. One ear heard nothing. The other was ringing.

Then I heard a strange sound. Almost familiar. A man's voice screaming my name. At first it was faint. Then closer. Then a shadow appeared. I didn't know who it was or where he'd come from, but a figure wrapped in a blanket hovered over me. I remember the blanket brushing over me and cooling my face, and I realized that it was soaking wet. When they say people in hell want ice water, they're not kidding.

The man lifted whatever was holding me down with one hand and picked me up with the other. He threw me over his shoulder, grabbed Jimmy with his other hand, and carried me away through the flames. Stuff was cracking, falling, smoke was billowing. I was coughing and spurting blood out the hole in my chest and I'd never been so hot in my entire life. But the guy was just striding like it was Sunday. Not a care in the world.

The world went black.

My last conscious thought was, *Dad, I'm sor—* but the words never made it out my mouth.

Not enough air.

28

The sound woke me. An incessant beeping from a machine above my head. I blinked and tried to adjust to the light, but the world was white and bright and fingers-on-chalkboard noisy. Tubes and wires were running into and out of most every part of me. I was draining and dripping everywhere.

A man walked between me and the light overhead. A stethoscope hung around his neck. The beeping stopped. His voice sounded muted. "How you feeling?"

I tried to talk, but my voice was nowhere to be found. I mouthed the word *alive,* but no sound came.

He patted my leg. "When you got here, you were not."

I tried to say something else, but it never made it out.

He continued, "You want the good news or bad?"

I figured I already knew the bad. *Good.*

He smiled. As if that somehow made it better. "You'll live."

I found little comfort in that. Given that we were talking, I thought we'd covered that. I pushed hard and almost whispered the word. "Bad?"

His face changed. "You'll live"—he paused, choosing his words—"differently." He eyed the whole of me. Wondering where to start. The way a mechanic does after you've just taken your fifteen-year-old car in for a diagnostic.

"Something pretty big fell on your hand and broke most every bone."

I tried to move my fingers, but they felt thick and obstructed.

"Whatever was burning in that building was toxic and extremely hot. Fried your throat and voice box. You're going to have to learn to talk again. I highly doubt you'll ever have the same control you once had over your voice."

That would explain the strange lump in my throat.

"We reconstructed your eardrum, but hearing loss is a certainty. And we stopped the bleeding in your chest and managed to get the bullet out, but it did some considerable damage." He turned and shined a red laser at an X-ray. I recognized a rib cage and spine, which I assumed were mine. "We'll talk more about that in the days ahead."

I was pretty groggy. Coming out of a rather deep haze of medication. His words were echoing off the inside of my mind without landing anywhere. I motioned for a pad of paper, which he handed me. The injury to my right hand forced me to scribble with my left, so the words were barely legible. *Where's that leave me?*

He sighed, sat on a rolling stainless steel stool, and scooted up next to the bed. "You'll never sing again. Might not even talk. Probably never play an instrument that involves your right hand. You may never hear out of your right ear again. And then there's your liver." He continued to speak, but my mind was having a tough time making sense of what he said. The words bounced around the inside of my skull like a marble.

I lifted my head and tried to look around, but the room was spinning, so I laid it back down and closed my eyes. "Jimmy?"

He leaned in closer. "Who?"

I mimicked playing a guitar.

He laughed. "The guitar you were latched onto when they brought you in?"

I nodded.

"Never seen that one before. Had to pry the case out of your hands." He continued, "It probably saved your life. Had it not been there, I doubt we'd be having this conversation. It's right over there, in the corner." His eyes took on an inquisitive slant. "You know the guy who pulled you out?"

I shook my head.

"Sam something-or-other. He's been in here several times with that girl. The singer. He's her producer. Everybody on the hall wants his autograph. Hers too."

My whisper was angry. "Never happened."

He glanced up at the TV. "He saved your life. It's on all the networks."

I let it go. The truth would take too long.

Whispering so much had dislodged some mucous in my throat, causing a painful, stitch-stretching, spastic cough. He held a plastic bowl beneath my chin, which I half filled with crimson mucous.

I looked around me and patted the bed with my left hand like an old man searching a coat pocket.

"You looking for something?"

I used hand signals to accentuate my broken whisper. "Small black notebook. Rubber band holding it together."

He shook his head. "Haven't seen it. I'll ask around, but I doubt it survived." A pause. "That was a hot fire."

"Heart pine."

He leaned in closer. "What's that?"

I whispered, "Two-hundred-year-old kerosene."

He nodded. "That would do it."

I stared at the ceiling as the tears gathered in the corners of my eyes. Somewhere in these first foggy moments, I realized several things: my songs were gone and my playing days were over, but it was the last revelation that hurt the most.

Daley was better off without me, and I was going to have to leave her without explanation—which would hurt her the most.

29

The story was all over the news. Sam feigned torment and acted deeply distraught. The ten stitches in his forehead added color to the picture.

In the aftermath, two stories emerged. What Sam told the public. And what Sam told Daley.

The truth, however, was in neither.

In the first story, Sam told authorities and pretty much everyone with a camera that he and I had been working on postproduction when we encountered a man robbing his office safe. He confronted the man, and the man shot me, hit

Sam in the head with something heavy, and then evidently lit a propane bomb to cover the evidence.

Sam woke to flame and fire, gathered his senses, and carried me to safety. The thief escaped with eighty thousand in cash and his wife's jewelry. Through crocodile tears, which the camera did an excellent job of highlighting, Sam lowered his voice and spoke of how he considered me the son he never had. He spoke of my promise. Of all the lost possibilities.

Authorities were still looking for the unidentified man, whom Sam couldn't see well enough to identify. Just said he was big. Film taken by media crews showed an inconsolable Daley clinging to my smoking clothing as I was being loaded into an ambulance clutching a guitar case.

It made for fantastic news.

They brought me to Vanderbilt Medical. The nurses said Daley had been at my bedside 24/7. She'd helped turn me. Bathe me. Change my wound dressings. The ever-benevolent and affected Sam spearheaded my care. He brought in the best doctors. Burn specialists. Surgeons. A hand specialist. Throat specialist. They stuck me with needles to shoot stuff in and they stuck me with needles to draw stuff out. I began to feel like a raw pincushion.

This care for me did two things: it endeared Sam to Daley and it sold a lot of records.

But as they weaned me from medicine and began slowly waking me from my medically induced coma, Sam suddenly found reasons for Daley to be on every talk show across the country. She became the poster child for how to overcome unspeakable personal tragedy and make it through. Camera angles flashed back and forth between her engagement ring, pictures of us performing onstage, and her present-day watery eyes. Daley was fragile, on the verge of cracking, and Sam took advantage of every tear that fell from her beautiful face.

I sat in bed, watched Daley make the talk show rounds in New York, and caught snippets between naps. The unknowns were many. Interviewers asked her, would I be able to walk her down the aisle? Could I speak? Sing? Play? How much of me had been burned? Would we be able to have children? Had I suffered oxygen deprivation? Did I have all my faculties?

An empathetic Sam even sent her to and fro on his private jet so she could return quickly to my side. In a brilliant coup d'état, he secured a *60 Minutes* exclusive. If he tried over the next million years, he'd never get media exposure this good.

Interestingly, no mention was ever made of my missing notebook.

But if I thought this entire charade showcased his talent, I had another thing coming. The ever-resilient and inventive Sam had two more tricks up his sleeve. The first was to "reluctantly" release the album. Out of respect for me, he stated publicly that he wanted to wait until I could play again so that we could tour, but then a copy was leaked to the media. He vowed to find who did it. "They'll never work anywhere in this town again."

It went platinum in two days. And platinum a second time by the weekend.

That didn't surprise me. But the second trick I never saw coming. Sometimes you bump into a better poker player. And Sam was just better.

Pain had become my constant companion. My skin still felt like it was on fire. Much of me was raw, including my vocal cords. Moving cracked open scabs. Lying still caused thicker scabs. Surgery had reconstructed my eardrum, but the only thing I could hear was a constant muted ringing.

My pessimistic and constantly frowning doctor said, "Any ability to hear will take months to return, and only if the grafts hold." A forced smile. "So don't hit your head on anything."

"I'll try not to."

"But even if you wear a helmet for the next year, you can only expect at best about a 10 percent return. For all intents and purposes, you'll be deaf save certain low-end frequencies. There was just too much damage . . ."

I tuned him out. *What kind of a guy goes into medicine who only knows how to give bad news? I mean, there has to be some good news around here somewhere.* I started wondering if he actually enjoyed it.

Given the risk of infection, they kept me in the burn unit, which gave me a good bit of solitary time to think. The truth was painful but clear. I couldn't sing. Couldn't play. Couldn't talk. My throat felt like someone had cut out my vocal cords. And while all this was settling in my foggy brain, my doctor returned with more bad news. He sat on a stool with wheels and scooted over next to the bed. "I have your labs."

I heard the words he spoke, but they didn't really sink in.

"So when you hear your heart pounding like Niagara in your ears, or cough and find both blood and what looks like coffee grounds . . ."

I whispered, "Until then?"

"Live your life."

"Like an inmate on death row."

He tilted his head side to side. "That's one way of looking at it."

"How would you look at it . . . if you were lying here?"

He didn't answer.

I stared out the window, across a brilliant blue Nashville skyline, and rasped, "How much time do I have?"

He wouldn't commit. "That's anybody's guess."

I stayed quiet for a moment, lost in the view, until he tapped me on the knee. "You still here, Cooper?"

I turned toward him. My voice had grown hoarser. "You should probably call me Coop."

He nodded, realizing that he knew more about my physical person than anyone on the planet. He folded his hands. "I keep wishing I could walk in here with good news, but—"

"Me too." There was little good and we both knew it.

"You've got some visitors waiting to come in, but I wanted a chance to talk with you first."

My voice had checked out so I reached for the pad by my bed and scribbled, showing how my left hand moved more slowly than my brain. *They know any of this?*

"No."

I'd like to keep it that way.

"Understood."

He patted me on the foot and walked out, and a few minutes later Daley and Sam walked in. She'd been crying, and when she sat she kept a safe distance—which struck me as odd. Sam stood at the end of my bed, a smug look on his face.

Finally Daley spoke. "Cooper, why?"

She called me Cooper. *Why'd she call me Cooper?*

I looked from her to Sam and back to Daley. I didn't like where this was going. I turned the pad to a new piece of paper and scrawled, *Why what?*

She blew her nose. A lot was coming at me fast, but it was here I noticed she wasn't wearing the ring I gave her. She said, "Why'd you do it?"

My eyes were still staring at her naked hand. I forced a whisper. "Do what?"

"Sam is willing to brush it under the rug. Keep it between us. But just give it back."

I tried to shake off the fog. More Sanskrit. *Give what back?*

She looked at Sam, pleading, *Let me try and talk some sense into him?*

Ever forgiving, he smiled in soft understanding and patted her shoulder.

"All the stuff you and your friend took out of the safe?"

So that was how he was going to play this.

That's what he told you? I wrote.

"You deny it?"

You believe him?

She pointed to his head. "Explain that." She pointed to me. "Explain any of this."

I tried to write faster. *What'd he tell you I took?*

She looked to Sam and then back at me. "The eighty thousand cash. And Bernadette's jewelry."

I'd never been a poker player. Didn't really like cards. But lying in bed with tubes running out of me, I realized I was playing poker with Sam whether I liked it or not, and he was only seconds from running the table. I scribbled angrily in block letters and held up the paper to Sam. *YOU TELL HER THIS?!*

He played the empathetic and forgiving uncle. "Coop, we've got a lot of good things on the horizon. In a couple of months you'll be making some healthy royalties." He acted like he was doing his best to take it easy on me, be understanding, let bygones be bygones. "Some of that jewelry belonged to Bernadette's grandmother. They got it out of Germany before the war."

If I could have climbed out of bed and ripped his smirking lips off his face, I would have.

The thing that Sam understood, far better than I, was this: all he had to do was appeal to the fragile place in Daley that had been wounded by her dad. If he played the I-am-the-one-person-on-the-planet-you-can-trust card, then she'd turn on me. Her experience with men would convince her that she couldn't trust me when it mattered most. Aside from his strategy being as painful as the physical torment my body had suffered, it was brilliant.

I sat there, letting story number two sink in. Sam had played both hands perfectly. He'd told the media one story, which made him look like the loving Daddy Warbucks and in turn helped sell millions of records. Behind closed doors, he'd told Daley story number two. Both stories endeared her to him and separated her from me.

I stared out the window. *What defense do I*

have? What can I possibly say? The pain in my side registered. *And even if I could convince her that Sam is lying, what future does she have with me?* Finally my brain cleared and I asked myself, *What's best for Daley?*

I did not like the answer.

Sam helped Daley stand and then tapped me on the foot. "Bernadette would be grateful if you'd return everything. All is forgiven. Water under the bridge." Then he waved his hand across the hospital room. "All this is on me. We've got the best doctors. No need for you to worry about paying any of it back." He tugged on Daley's arm and said, "Come on, Dee."

He'd even started calling her by my nickname for her. She patted his hand, holding his one hand in both of hers and looking up at him. "Can I have a minute with him?"

"Sure, baby. I'll be right outside if you need me."

I'd known hardship in my life. Nothing like this. I wanted to puke.

He left, and Daley stood at the foot of my bed. Tears falling down. Arms crossed. The same cold wind. A safe distance. Finally she shook her head and palmed her face. Smearing the tears more than wiping them. Her face spoke betrayal and pain. The truth was simple. I'd lost.

She managed, "How—?" Her voice cracked and her throat choked off the words. "After all he's done . . ." She reached into her pocket, slowly set the engagement ring on the bed, and walked out.

The smell of Coco Chanel was still wafting across me when Sam walked back in.

He stood next to the bed. Towering. Finally he leaned toward me and his mouth took on a smile, but there was no good in it.

"I heard you play when you were seventeen and traveling with your dad's ridiculous tent circus, and I knew I'd never really heard anyone play like you. We courted you, tried to record you, even sent you a Fender with your name on it, but your dad would have none of it. Eighteen months pass, and I walk out of a bar where one of my acts is being upstaged by a punk on the street corner. People were actually leaving the bar to hear the kid on the street. I thought, *Let me take a look.* And there you were. Playing the guitar your father made famous. The one you'd stolen. You looked so happy, so in tune with 'Jimmy,' that I was all too happy to pay someone to take him from you." He chuckled and his eyes darted to the corner. "One of my favorite trophies."

He tapped himself in the chest and I smelled whiskey in his whisper. "I choose who makes it in this business. Not you. Not your talent. Not your dream. Not the gift in your fingers." He laughed again. "Did you actually think I would let you have Daley?"

I wanted to respond, but the world was coming at me too fast.

"Leave a forwarding address so we'll know where to send the wedding announcement." He stood and ran his fingers along the inside of his belt. "Oh, and—" He pointed a thumb at Jimmy. "You can keep the souvenir."

His words shot through me, doing more damage than his bullet. He didn't just want Daley's music. He wanted Daley.

That was the last time I saw Sam Casey.

Six weeks later I walked out of the hospital and limped to the mailbox. I had written the letter left-handed, which took some time and made it difficult to read.

Music washes us from the inside out. It heals what nothing else can. It's the miracle we call song. May the song you sing forever heal the hurt you feel.

I love you. Me.

I stuck my thumb in the air and made my way west. I stopped when I hit the Pacific.

30

A year passed. Then a second. I had no destination in mind. Wandered a lot. Rented a shack on the coast in Oregon. Watched the tide roll in and out. Wasted the better part of a year there. My voice returned enough to whisper and even groan out a hoarse moan. Finally it returned enough to make me sound like a five-packs-a-day smoker. My hand healed somewhat, and feeling replaced numbness. To force my fingers to move, I made myself brush my teeth and write. Anything to tax the muscles and nerves. Writing was the tough part. Initially I wrote block letters. Then cursive. Followed by single short words. Just a few letters at a time.

Playing any kind of instrument was out of the question. Not that I wanted to.

My hearing returned slowly. At first my ear just itched. Then I could hear the ocean. Months later, the waves on the rocks. Finally, seagulls in the distance.

Provided I existed at a subsistence level, I had enough money to survive a few years, but eventually I'd have to get a job. I hired myself out for weeks at a time. Until I got bored or just couldn't take it any longer. I worked for a tree surgeon hauling limbs in northern California. Bused tables near the Canadian line. Washed dishes in Wyoming. Worked custodial at a Nevada motel where I vacuumed the halls and cleaned rooms. Worked the grape harvest in the Columbia River Valley of Oregon. After almost three years I'd gained enough strength and coordination in my hand to do a few pull-ups and even floss my teeth. The guy at the motel sold me an old Jeep that burned oil but got me from place A to place B. I drove it up the coast, through Washington, and then south. Eight years, six months, and three days after I'd left, and nearly three years since Sam shot me, I found myself sitting at the stop-light in Buena Vista. My house sat eight miles to the right.

My hair had grown down past my shoulders, I'd not shaved in a few years, scars covered my neck and shoulders, my skin was tanned, my eyes were harder, my movements slower and more deliberate, and my hands calloused from running chainsaws. I'd come back different. Patched up. Pieced together. Very much broken.

When I crested the hill and pulled into the drive, I found the cabin dingy and in disrepair. Weeds had grown up under what I guessed was my dad's truck. The bus sat off to the side of the garage. One tire flat. I cut the engine and climbed up on the porch. I smelled coffee through the open front door. I knocked and, to my surprise, Big-Big appeared out of the shadows. His hair had turned white as wool. His feet shuffled. He saw me, his face lit, and he spread his big arms, wrapping me in them. My cocoon against the world.

I stood there and let that man hug me a long time. Finally he stood me up straight and looked at me square. "Coop—" His lips tightened. Half a breath escaped. He'd been holding this. Even now, it was tough to let out. I knew what he was going to say before he said it. "Coop . . . your daddy? He dead."

Big-Big and I spent the day on the porch. He told me that Dad had not tried to continue without me. He knew better. Not that he couldn't. But that his heart wasn't in it. He'd be lying to people. Sold everything but the bus. He knew it had been me when I called. That gave him hope that I was alive and at least thinking of him.

I asked, "Big-Big?"

He didn't look at me. "Yeah, boy."

"What'd he die from?"

Big-Big stood from my dad's rocker, poured out the rest of his coffee over the porch railing, sucked between his teeth, and wiped the tears soaking his face. "His heart just quit working. That's all."

I had a feeling there was more, but I wasn't sure I could bear it.

"Where is he now?"

His eyes turned up the mountain. Then he pointed back at the road that led up to the cabin. "The procession be three mile long. Folk come from five states. Busloads." He shook his head. "Beautiful day. I said what I could, but he always better with words. Never had no problem knowing what to say." The wind cut across us and lifted up through the aspens. The leaves smacking each other.

"I go up and talk to him most every day. Carry my coffee." He waved his hand across me. "I miss him mo' now than befo'."

"Does he ever talk back?"

He studied me, then reached into his breast pocket and pulled out a letter. My name was written on the front. A lump appeared in my throat at the sight of my father's handwriting. Big-Big handed it to me and then motioned toward the mountain. "He left you this. Now, go on up and let him speak to you."

I clutched the letter, weaved through the aspens, and sat down in the grass between my mom and dad.

Dear Son,

You left tonight. Drove out of the Falls. I stood on the stage and watched the truck's red taillights get smaller and smaller. I'm sitting here wondering whether I should've let you go. Wondering if I should've gone about all this the way I did. Maybe I was wrong. I don't know. I know my heart hurts. I imagine yours does too . . .

I don't know what kind of dad I've been. I know you've grown up without a female influence, and I wish you had known different. I wish you'd known your mom.

You might be better prepared when you get where you're going. She was better at a lot of things. Teaching you tenderness was one of them.

I don't know when you'll get this, if ever. But if and when you do, I want you to know that some of the happiest I've ever been has been watching you play your guitar. When you play, you come alive. Music is the language of your heart, and you speak it as well as anyone I've ever known.

Maybe I've been overly protective. Maybe I should've let that scumbag keep the tapes you made in the gas station. Maybe I should've done a lot of things differently. But then I think about your gift and I want to protect it, and not let it fall into the wrong hands. What you have is special, more special than you know, and when you think back on me, I hope you see that I was trying to protect you from the folks who just wanted to profit off you.

That night, the night of the storm, you were afraid to get up because you saw Blondie sitting on the piano. I believed you, not because I could see him, but because I could hear him. Hear them. Son, I've been hearing them for years. Every time you play, I hear angels. I don't know if you can hear them, but there's an entire chorus attached to your fingers. And they make the most beautiful sound. The only two times I haven't heard them were the night in Pedro's and when that snake-oil salesman recorded you. It may take you awhile to realize this, but the purpose of your gift is not to make you the focus. It's to point those within earshot. Direct them. To reflect, not absorb. Anybody can stand on a stage and demand another's affection. It's the nature of the spotlight. But few will choose to deflect it. When you see people with their hands raised, you'll understand what I'm talking about. Rightly or wrongly, I want you to spend your life making music where the angels sing along. Being a reflection. I think that'd be a life well spent. I failed to say that before now, and for that I'm sorry. If I may offer one excuse—I've never raised a son before. Please allow a few mistakes. I'm figuring this out as we go.

After last night I had a feeling that you would leave in anger. And I was guessing you'd take whatever we had, so I gave you all I had. Think of it as my investment in your career. So is Jimmy. Take care of him. You make him sound better than I do by a long shot, and your mother would have liked that.

I'm asking you to hear me when I say this: I know you're angry right now, but please let these words break through that hardened outer shell. Let them filter down and come to rest on your heart. This is the truth about you and me as much as I'm able to know it. And when it comes to the truth, people have a right to know it. Always. No matter how much you think it might hurt, the truth is the only thing that both cuts us free and holds us tight. When you think back to us, remember this—the memories I hold of you are good and tender. All of them. Even tonight.

When you think back to the stage tonight, to our last words and your leaving, don't let the picture in your mind be the angry one. I'm not angry. Never have been. Never will be. You can't hit me hard enough to cause me to close my arms to you. Period.

Being eighteen isn't easy. Neither is finding your own way in this world—especially when your dad casts a big shadow.

One last thing. When you get where you're going, chances are good you will hear a lie that is real popular these days. It goes something like this: If you don't make it, if you don't succeed, if everything you set your hand to doesn't prove to me that you were right and that you can make it on your own, then you have lost your right to come back. Your only ticket back into my good graces is some certificate of success. As if the world will give you one, when you've proved to everyone that you've made it on your own. That's a lie from the pit of hell. Always has been. But it's the end of the lie that's the worst part. The end of the lie says that there is a place that's too far to come back from. That somewhere in the distant future, there is something you could do or someplace you could go or some hole you could fall into that would disqualify you from ever coming home. And once you've stepped over that line, there's no coming back.

Don't listen to that lie.

Here's the truth: No matter what happened on the stage tonight, no matter where you went when you drove out of here, no matter where you end up, no matter what happens, what you become, what you gain, what you lose, whether you succeed or fail, stand or fall, no matter what you dip your hands into . . . no gone is too far gone.

You can always come home.

And when you do, you'll find me standing right here, arms wide, eyes searching for your return.

I love you.

Dad

I ran my fingers through the grooves of the stone etching of his name and tried to say what I'd rehearsed so many times, but I could not.

The emotions that I'd stuffed for so long began looking for an exit. The wave started in my stomach where it swirled, then erupted, giving me enough time to turn my face. Anger, sadness, shame, and regret spewed across the ancient and silent forest floor. The pain turned me inside out, exited me, and took most of me with it. The wretching lasted several minutes. When finished, I sat back on my heels, wiped my mouth with my shirtsleeve, and realized that I was now twenty-six and fatherless.

The anchor of my life had been cut away.

PART III

31

The fire dwindled, leaving white-hot coals. My skin had dried and I was shivering less. Big-Big touched my shoulder, then left as quietly as he came, leaving me alone with my memories and Dad's letter. My core body temperature had started to rise, but I could not control the shivers. I never could. I stared at the water a long time, thinking about my dad dying right there. Drowned due to a heart attack.

I wondered about his last few minutes. Had he known only the pain of a heart attack, and was he dead before he hit the water? Or had he known piercing chest pain first, followed by the slow pull of the water and the inability to extract himself from the river, followed by the suffocating inability to breathe? Even now, at forty-four, I found that question tough to stomach. Dad had been strong as an ox. If his heart had quit, it quit because it had been broken. Truth was, I'd broken it. And that was the toughest part of all.

Throughout the night, I read and reread the letter a dozen times. It spoke to questions of the heart in ways that only my dad could, like salve on a burn. It also produced a painful longing to hear his voice just one more time.

The next morning was Friday. I slept in,

showered, spent some time with Jimmy on the porch, then drove to Leadville, where I expected to spend the afternoon. But when I got there, the old man was a no-show. No crowd. No open guitar case. No song in the air. Nothing but soggy cigarette butts on the street corner.

I stepped into the bar across the street and asked the bartender, "You seen the old man plays guitar across the street?"

"You mean Jube?"

"I don't know his name."

"Died. Week ago. Right there on that street corner. Guitar in hand. Case full of tips. Smile on his face."

I turned to walk out, then stopped. "You happen to know where they buried him?"

He pointed. "Two blocks. Turn left. Cemetery at the end of the road. He's in the back right corner, up on a hill. You'll see the fresh dirt."

"Thanks."

The cemetery was fresh cut. Well maintained. Wasn't hard to find his headstone. The sun was going down when I walked up. There were no dates. His stone simply read:

Jubal Tyre
Loving Father
for eighty-five years his soul made music
"This people have I formed for myself;
they shall shew forth my praise."

I stood there a long time. Looking at the words *shew forth*. King James English with its archaic spelling had always been tough to wrap my mind around, but my dad had preached on that very verse. He was always good with visuals when he taught, so he brought a broom onstage and said that "shewing forth" wasn't something you did when you were trying to get a dog out of the yard. He demonstrated, scurrying around the stage. *"Shoo! Shoo!"* He then brought out a twelve-foot stepladder and climbed up to the second rung from the top, where he cupped his hands together like the town crier. He said in his loudest voice, *"Shewing forth* means to announce beforehand. Declare. Shout it from the rooftops. Without apology." He paused. Made sure he had their undivided attention. Then he'd add with a sly smile, "Or sing at the top of your lungs!"

I thought about the old man on the street corner. He fit the job description perfectly.

When I turned to go from the cemetery, I found a boy standing behind me. Maybe twelve. He was holding a guitar. Resting it on his shoulder like an ax. It was the Gibson I'd given the old man.

He looked up at me. "Mister, you know him?"

I slid my hands into my pockets. "We met once."

He held up the guitar. "You the man who gave him this?"

I nodded.

He stared up at me. "My grandfather said that

the man who gave it to him might be the best guitar player he ever met." He extended it. "You want it back?"

I studied him. "Can you play?"

He glanced at the stone. "My grandfather showed me a thing or two."

Interestingly, the kid did not seem inclined to prove to me that he could play. Which told me everything I needed to know. The tips of his fingers on his left hand were calloused. Evidence that he'd been playing a good bit.

I pointed at the mound of dirt. "He give it to you?"

He nodded. As if the memory was both pleasant and painful.

"You keep it," I said.

We stood there several minutes, staring at the granite staring back at us. Finally I asked the kid, "What happened?"

He spoke matter-of-factly. "Drunk himself to death. Body shut down."

"I mean, before that. Years ago."

The kid shrugged. "He loved my grandma, but he loved the road more. Momma says one of her first memories was standing on the curb watching him climb on that bus. Grandma called it the jealous mistress. He'd stay gone for months at a time. Send postcards. Make promises. Sometimes he'd send money." The kid paused. "When my mom left for college, Grandma disconnected the phone and burned all his clothes. He came home to an ash heap and a key that didn't fit. So he climbed inside a bottle and never climbed out."

I nodded and mumbled to myself, "Some people wear their shame."

He glanced at the scars on my neck and hand. "You wearing yours?"

I nodded. The kid was smart, and I liked him. "Yes."

"What happened to you?"

"I was young and full of myself, so I turned my back on somebody who loved me a whole lot. Fell in with some bad people when I got where I was going."

"You ever turn back?"

I chuckled. "Yes."

"What happened?"

"When I got home, my dad was dead. That was eighteen years ago."

"Did you love your dad?" The kid's eyes were round and bright and pure.

I nodded once. "Still do."

He shook his head. "I never met my dad."

I turned toward the kid. "That's his loss."

"That's what my mom says." The space between his eyes narrowed, and his expression became one of curiosity. "If you had thirty seconds and could say anything to your dad, what would you say?"

I didn't answer. "What would you tell your dad?"

He shrugged. "I'd tell him that we don't really like bologna and that when it gets toward the end of the month, Mom adds water to the milk. That when it gets cold I steal firewood from our neighbors and don't tell Mom, but I think she knows because she doesn't look at me when I walk back in the door. I'd tell him that I won the talent contest at school three years in a row. That I make good grades. That I can read at a college level. And I'd tell him that Mom cries some nights after I've gone to bed. I can hear her through the wall." He glanced up at me. "I'd tell him stuff like that."

I squatted down, putting me closer to eye level with the kid. I sucked between my teeth. "I'd tell mine I was sorry."

The kid nodded, turned around, and started walking off.

I called after him, "You need a ride home?"

He shook his head and pointed at a shack up on the hill. White smoke rose out of the chimney and a woman stood on the porch, a shawl wrapped around her shoulders, watching us. He'd walked a few steps farther when I said, "Hey, kid?"

He turned and looked at me.

"What's your name?"

He pointed at the headstone as if the answer were self-explanatory. "Jubal."

● ● ●

It was after dinner when I pulled into Riverview. Mary was in bed. Dozing. I scooted up next to the bed and watched her sleeping. After a few minutes her eyes opened and one eye focused on me. Her voice was a hoarse whisper. "How long you been there?"

"Few minutes."

Without warning, she grew animated. "Oh—"

She tried sitting up. I helped slide her up and propped a few pillows behind her back. The ammonia smell told me her diaper needed changing.

"You hear the news?" she said.

"What news?"

"Daley's playing the Falls."

"When?"

"Few weeks."

"How'd that happen?"

"That video of you two at the Rope went viral. I still can't figure out how come I wasn't invited."

"It was sort of a spur-of-the-moment thing."

"That's no excuse. Anyway, she got to this casino and started playing a bunch of new songs nobody's ever heard before. Just her and her guitar. Like really great stuff. Her shows started selling out. They're recording a live album at the Falls. Bringing in a choir."

I knew what was coming next.

"You'll take us?"

303

"Us?"

She waved her hand up and down the hall. "Us!"

I chuckled. "Big-Big too?"

"Of course."

I was pretty sure I wouldn't be alive in a month. But I squeezed her hand. "Sure."

32

Tums, Pepto-Bismol, and Alka-Seltzer had ceased providing any medicinal benefit, and the shock of cold-water submersion remained the only remedy for the ticking inside me. My episodes were becoming more and more frequent, the acrid taste seldom left my mouth, the rushing in my ears was constant, my appetite was pretty much gone, and the amount of time required in the water to stave off the impending rupture had become longer and its effect shorter. In short, my options had dwindled and what few I had didn't do much.

Given this, I stayed close to home. Close to the creek. Given the acidic nature of coffee, I quit drinking Honey Badgers and started sipping some sort of herbal peppermint-ginger concoction with honey. I snacked on Nilla Wafers and bananas, drank milk, and reread my father's letter. I napped a lot, but never more than an hour at a time because I had more control over the outcome if I was awake.

On Friday I drove to town, parked along the tracks, and ran a few errands. I walked into the beauty shop and paid Mary's hairdresser to make a house call Saturday morning and do something special.

Then I visited the town attorney, where I made sure Mary would be taken care of. I left money for Frank to pay his bills, with enough left over to allow him to quit skimming and take his wife and daughter to the islands while there was still time. At my request, my attorney had researched Jubal Tyre. I started a college annuity for him and left his mom enough to buy more than bologna for the rest of her life. It would never replace an absentee dad, but it would help. Everything else went to Daley.

I picked up my new dark-blue suit at the tailor and some mail-order black Allen Edmonds dress shoes at my PO box, and paid my remaining bills. Then I walked into the barbershop and got my first real haircut in twenty years. When the barber asked me what I wanted, I smiled. "I need to look respectable. Or at least presentable." When I walked out without hair down to my shoulders, I felt naked.

The town of Buena Vista was buzzing. Posters hung on every pole, national news trucks had parked on Main Street, tall antennae telescoped above the skyline, food trucks had appeared, traveling BBQ pits filled the air with tantalizing smoke, and the hotels were full in every direction for thirty miles. Whatever media marketing campaign Daley's producer had orchestrated had worked. In my thirty-five years of experience with the Falls, I'd never seen the town swell like this. Buena Vista was bursting at the seams. College kids taking an early weekend break, middle-aged bikers with their wives on mirrored Harleys out of Denver and the Springs, four-wheel drives pulling RVs, hitchhikers, and locals—the town looked like parade time on the Fourth of July.

I stood at the gas station, filling up the Jeep, and smiled at the traffic jam and colorful crowds walking the sidewalks on what had become a beautiful though brisk fall day. West of the Collegiates, a few snow clouds crept closer, which could make for an enchanting weekend. Daley could not have chosen a better or more scenic venue or time of year.

I had done my best to slow down everything about me. My movements. My pulse. Even my decisions. "Just one more weekend," I told myself.

Though I knew better.

The ticking was louder. Niagara closer. The angry storm on the horizon of my life now stretched as far as I could see. Soon the swirling world I'd been able to hold at a safe distance for twenty years would be the sideways-spitting fury in the face, ripping my tent pegs out of purchase. Where the lightning struck without warning and set my world on fire. Where no bench would hide me and no strong right arm would scoop me out like an excavator. Stopped at the light, I stared in my rearview mirror and heard the thunder rumbling over my shoulder.

The light turned green. I drove through the intersection and felt an odd swelling at the base of my throat. I coughed into my handkerchief and stared down at a puddle of bright crimson. The next wave started in my stomach and traveled upward, where the taste hit my mouth and I coughed again, this time spraying blood across the inside of the windshield.

Life had been reduced to minutes.

Heading west on 306 toward Cottonwood Creek, I shifted into third and redlined the Jeep above 7,000 rpm. Two miles out, I braked at nearly a hundred miles an hour, turned right onto 361 without flipping, sped downhill, spotted the creek, and aimed the nose toward the water as the roar of Niagara deafened my ears. I veered off the highway, avoided a giant cottonwood, jumped the bank, launched the Jeep airborne, and crashed nose-first into the rushing creek. The thirty-six-inch BF Goodriches dug themselves into the smooth river pebble-and-sand bottom, where the water rolled just beneath the front bumper. Steam rose from beneath the hood, but given the snorkel air intake, the engine idled smoothly. The Jeep settled, I unbuckled and fell out into the creek. The shock to my system stopped my ability to breathe. The water grabbed my clothes, pulled me down, and bounced me gently along the bottom. I waited.

When my head broke the surface, the water rolled me upright and I began both breathing and choking. The water here was just above knee-high. I bobbed, turned, flipped, rolled, got sucked under an overhanging tree, and then the water widened and the depth decreased to eight or ten inches. I felt my butt and legs drag the bottom, and my shoulder bumped into a large rock a little bigger around than a basketball. I hooked one arm around it and then wedged my foot between two smaller rocks on the bottom so that my body wouldn't wash downstream and dump me into the Arkansas. If it did, they'd never find me.

The seconds ticked by. The bank was ten feet away, but it might as well have been a million. My teeth had quit chattering and the needles in my skin had quit stinging.

Over two decades I'd survived dozens of these episodes. Maybe a hundred or more. I quit counting long ago. Depending on the amount of time required in the water to push back the tide, lucidity would come and go. The trick was to remain clearheaded enough to stay in the water as long as required while still being able to crawl out and get someplace warm and dry. Usually the initial shock stopped the hemorrhage before a total rupture occurred. But that was the key. Everything depended on the below-freezing temperature shock stopping the hemorrhage. And all that had to happen before my electrical circuits shut down completely.

It was a waiting game.

Something stung my nose and eyes, which were the only part of me sticking out of the water. When I opened my eyes, I realized it was snowing. I smiled. I liked the thought of that. Dying in the snow. Wrapped in a blanket of white.

The walls began closing in. My last thoughts were of Daley. I would have liked to see that concert.

Wouldn't be long now.

Suddenly my peaceful, silent departure, accented by falling snow and the gentle rippling of sub-freezing water, was disturbed by the high-pitched whine of a small engine, the sound of sticks and large limbs breaking, panicky screaming, and finally a big splash and someone thrashing through the water.

I felt hands under my armpits, and someone was dragging me toward the bank. Water washed over my forehead, but between waves Daley's face flashed above me, silhouetted against a gray sky spitting snowflakes. She dragged me onto the pebbled beach and cradled my head, slapping my face and screaming at me. And while I could see her mouth moving and read the frantic expression on her face, I could hear very little and feel even less.

The blood had puddled in my mouth. I coughed, spraying us both in crimson puree, and managed one word. "F-f-f-f-ire."

Daley's complexion grew even more ghostly. She set down my head, disappeared over my shoulder, and the next sound I heard was the unmistakable hum of the Jeep's engine. Evidently Daley drove the Jeep downstream, climbed the bank, and parked it next to me.

Locals know that conditions in Colorado can change with little notice. Sunshine one moment. Snow and ice the next. Given an inability to predict when that will happen, most of us keep a box in the back of our vehicles with enough necessities to allow us to live in a snowbank for a few days if needed. Daley tore through my emergency box and quickly made a pile of whatever she could find. She pulled the five-gallon gas can off the back of the Jeep, soaked the wood, then loaded the flare gun, stood behind the Jeep, and shot the flare into the pile.

I watched with sedated amazement, thinking she was rather resourceful and quick-thinking. As if she'd done all this before. She then returned to me, dragged me across the hard ground, near enough to feel the warmth of the fire, and started ripping off my wet clothes. When she had me down to my underwear, she unrolled my sleeping bag from the back of the Jeep, stripped off her own wet clothes, and then zipped us both inside the bag where she pressed her chest, stomach, and legs against mine. She was shivering too, but she managed to rub my arms and back with her palms in an attempt to generate warmth, friction, and possibly blood flow.

When someone has been submerged for any period of time in water that feels colder than freezing, the first thing to come back is the perception of cold. And pain. Both return at once. Second are the gross-motor shakes, which are the body's involuntary and violent response to the flow of oxygenated blood and electrical stimuli into the limbs and extremities. The last step is an unstoppable shivering and an inability to get warm.

It's not pleasant.

33

An hour passed. Much of which I slipped through passing from conscious to unconscious and back to conscious. When the color had returned to my face and my head had stopped rocking violently back and forth, Daley extracted herself from the sleeping bag and added more fuel to the fire.

Anything she could find. The result produced a roaring and hot bonfire. Further, she grabbed a tarp from the box in my Jeep, strung it like a tent over us to keep the snow off, then slid back into the sleeping bag and placed her chest to my back and wrapped her icy feet around my calves. Some-where in there I dozed off again. When I woke, our clothes were suspended above us, beneath the tarp, drying. Inside the bag, her arms and legs were wrapped around me, placing me in a cocoon of her making. I took it as a good sign that my legs told me she hadn't shaved her legs in a few days.

For several minutes I lay there drinking in the smell of her. Sweat mixed with Coco Chanel. The touch of soft skin. Letting her body warm me. When I finally opened my eyes, I found her looking at me. The quiet expression on her face told me she was a little scared and a little mad, and I had some explaining to do. As she stared at me, I realized that the peroxide blonde of a month ago had been replaced by her natural amber brunette. Daley today looked like Daley twenty years ago. She spoke softly. "You lied to me."

I knew she was talking about our conversation at the bus stop. "I never actually lied."

"You didn't tell me the whole truth."

"I didn't want to hurt you."

"Cooper, I been hurting for twenty years. Hurt is a way of life." She adjusted one arm, wrapping tighter around me. "Either tell me what you're afraid to tell me, or so help me I'm dragging you back into that river and holding your head under until you decide to talk."

From the moment I'd met her onstage at the Ryman, I'd always loved her strength. And even after two decades, she still had it. I swallowed, knew I wasn't going to die right that second, and so I backed up and started at the beginning.

"In the aftermath of the fire, Sam spun two stories. In the first, he and I discovered a guy robbing his office. The guy shot me, thumped Sam on the head, torched the office, and disappeared like a ghost. Then, at great risk to his own life, Sam mustered the inner strength to drag us both from the raging inferno."

Daley nodded.

"That was the public version. And, incidentally, that's the version I heard from the doctor when I woke in the hospital."

She nodded a second time.

"The second story, supposedly the true one, is the one he told you in confidence—in an apparent selfless attempt to keep it quiet and help me. In story number two, Sam discovered me and a second mystery man robbing his office safe and a rather expensive Martin guitar. He confronted us, the conversation went south, my so-called partner shot me, thumped him in the head, and, again at risk of his own life, and despite the fact that I'd just betrayed him, Sam rescued me from the fire while my unnamed partner left us both to bake to a crisp. Gone missing was something like eighty thousand in cash and Bernadette's mother's jewelry, valued somewhere north of two hundred thousand. This ringing a bell?"

"Yes."

"But what if neither was true?"

She waited.

"After I left, and you walked into the recording studio, how were the songs?"

"Good."

"And after that?"

"Not so much."

"And what happened between those two dates? Between you and Sam?"

"Sam made advances. I said no."

"Did he all of a sudden find new girls to replace you?"

"Yes, but he was always signing new talent."

"And the songs they sang? Were they any good?"

She nodded. "Very."

"Where'd he get those songs?"

"Sam's genius was that he always had his finger on the pulse of the city. Sam had writers everywhere."

"After the fire, a lot of noise was made about his money and his trophy wife's jewelry. But what was the one thing you never heard about after the fire?"

She shook her head. "I don't know, Coop. It was a long time ago. What are you getting at?"

"What was the one thing you never saw me without?"

"A notebook."

"Even now, have you seen me without it?"

"No."

"Doesn't it strike you as odd that the most valuable thing lost in that fire was never mentioned by Sam, and yet you knew as well as anyone it was the one thing he kept trying to get his hands on?"

"But . . . the fire took everything. You barely escaped alive."

"Don't you find that the least bit convenient?"

"But why didn't you speak up?"

I continued, "Let me open door number three. Sam discovered you, cared for you, and 'made' you. His plan was working out great, until the night you first sang at the Ryman. Then the world heard you sing my song. Sam's no dummy. Where there's one, there might be more. So he encourages you to get to know me, and then he gets close to us. He sees me constantly writing in my little black book and he sees a gold mine. Dollar signs. Problem is, I'm attached to it and I'm attached to you. What's more, he realizes that the source of the song in you is the pen in me. So now he needs to hatch a plan to get you and the notebook and get rid of me all in one fell swoop.

"Sam was just biding his time until he happened to find me alone in his office, where I just happened to be stealing Jimmy. He couldn't have scripted it any better. He saw the perfect chance, shot me, blew up the evidence, then 'rescued' me. You know the rest. When the smoke clears and I'm lying in the hospital with my skin peeling off, he's effectively crippled my ability to make any type of music. Further, he's stolen my songs. And yet he knows there's one thing more important to me than those songs. You. Further still, he knows that I know that you have no future without my songs. And you would have no future with me. He was banking on the fact that if I loved you I would concede that he could give you a better future with my songs than I could with a burnt and broken body."

Her head was shaking slowly side to side. "Why didn't you come to me? Tell me everything?"

"Turn the lens, Daley. Look from the hospital bed. What kind of future could I possibly give you? The best thing for you was for me to keep quiet and let Sam spin you a career with the songs I wrote. Not to mention, I couldn't talk or hear or play or go to the bathroom by myself . . . so how could I have explained any of this?"

She filled in the blanks. Rolled the tape forward. "Then I refused him and he took your songs else-where."

"Right."

"But that doesn't explain the mysterious third man. You never denied his existence, and you can't tell me that Sam gave himself that cut on his head. That was a huge gash."

I shook my head. "That's a piece to the puzzle that I may never find. I believe there was a third man, but I can't prove it any more than I can prove any of this. Sometimes in my dreams I see a man running through the fire wrapped in a blanket. Running toward me. But I can't move. And the flames are reaching up around my neck. I can't breathe and I wake up choking with the sheets wrapped around my face . . ."

The pieces were falling into place in Daley's mind. "So . . . there was never any money? No jewelry? From the beginning, all this was about . . . your songs?" Her eyes searched mine.

"And you."

"Until I refused him."

"Yes."

The truth of the past settled in Daley's heart and pushed out the tears that had been there a long time.

"Let me fill in the rest," I said. "That particular notebook held seventeen songs. And because I'd become rather good at the Nashville Number System, Sam didn't need me to play them to figure out how they sounded. I'd done all the hard work. Then you turned him down and he moved on, giving my songs to four different artists who turned them into twelve number ones and five platinum records."

She turned to me. "And you couldn't prove they were yours."

"Couldn't play. Couldn't sing. Couldn't argue ownership." I paused. "I thought if I left quietly, Sam would take those songs and spin them into three or four records for you. Maybe five. Solidifying the next ten to fifteen years of your career, if he was smart. Which he was. I lay in that hospital bed and knew the best thing I could do was get out of the way. So I left. Quietly. A year went by. Followed by another. And I began hearing my songs on the radio, but it wasn't your voice singing them. By then it was too late."

Daley stared out across the street. More of the truth settling in. "You've written seventeen number one songs spanning five artists?"

I said nothing.

"But you never contacted me."

"Would you have believed me?"

"At the time, probably not." She stiffened. "But none of this explains why you've stayed silent for twenty years. Twenty years, Cooper. That's a long time to hold my love."

The time had come. "Dee, when Sam shot me, the bullet entered my liver. The good news is that the liver can heal itself. The bad news is that the bullet acted like a flying razor blade. By the time they got it out, the damage had been done.

The resulting scar tissue was severe. In cases like mine, the liver thinks it's been abused and responds with cirrhosis. Even my initial lab results in the hospital confirmed this. As has every one since."

"Like an alcoholic's?"

"Exactly. But cirrhosis doesn't require alcohol. Just damage. And of that, I have plenty. The scarring and hardening causes what the medical community calls 'bleeding esophageal varices.' "

She rose up and rested on an elbow. "What's that in English?"

"All our organs send blood to the liver. When the liver is damaged or scarred, blood can't flow through it like it's designed. That pressure backs up, or reroutes the blood flow. The first place is to the base of the esophagus." I tapped the top of my sternum where my esophagus meets my stomach. "The problem there is that the veins in that area are thin and not designed to handle the pressure, allowing for the possibility of unpredictable rupture."

"Meaning?"

"Meaning I'm a walking time bomb. No one can say when it will go off because they don't know how my liver will react. The doctors once thought I could heal up and live a relatively normal life, but the last twenty years have proven otherwise."

Her lips tightened. A vein appeared below her

right eye. Evidence that the truth was starting to sink in. "And your chances?"

I shook my head. "Slim." I paused, staring at the river. "To none. Given my experience over the years, and the taste that rises in my mouth, my liver has reacted negatively. That means the varices can erupt suddenly and without warning, and I can find myself coughing up blood without enough time or cognitive ability to dial 911."

She shook her head. "There's got to be something—"

"There's nothing. If it happens, it happens. But I'll never know it 'cause I'll be dead before my head hits the floor. I either go live my life or curl up in a fetal ball and wait."

"But why here? Why the creek?"

"The doctor at Vanderbilt told me there was a study, if you can call it that, of a scientist working above the Arctic Circle. He said his research partner had cirrhosis. The medical community had given up on him. This doctor was able to prolong the guy's life by prescribing that he jump daily into freezing water for a certain number of seconds, and eventually minutes. The shock to his system removed blood from his extremities, slowed his heart rate, and, they thought, forced healthy regeneration of his liver. It also gave the veins at the base of his esophagus time to heal and strengthen."

"And you believed this?"

"I found the study. Called the scientist."

"What happened to the other guy, the one with cirrhosis?"

"Died of pneumonia."

All of this was coming to a sudden halt inside her brain, where it was starting to make sense. "I was afraid you were going to say that." She bit her bottom lip. "How long do you have?"

I shrugged. "I had about ten seconds until you showed up."

She leaned into me, pressing her flushed face to mine. The puzzle pieces were settling inside her mind. "This is why you never spoke up. To save me the pain of knowing this."

"It seemed rather selfish to ask you to fall in love with someone who might be here tomorrow and might not."

"You ever stop to think that decision wasn't up to you?"

"I didn't want to hurt you any more than—"

She managed a broken whisper. "I never stopped hoping."

"I'd like to think that."

Daley's necklace had spilled onto my chest but I'd paid it little mind. The silver chain hung long enough to place the pendant in the middle of her chest. Over her heart. She shifted slightly and the pendant sparkled and now lay flat across my own heart.

But it was no pendant.

"I went back to the hospital, but somebody else was lying in your bed. Went to Riggs's, but your apartment was cleaned out. Went home and waited, but you never showed. A few days later, this appeared in my box." The necklace held the engagement ring I'd given her twenty years ago. She wove her fingers in with mine and placed her hand on my chest. She said it a second time, shaking her head. "Never stopped hoping."

Daley didn't wait for me to respond. She hooked her legs around me, pressed her chest against mine, and locked her hands behind my neck. "I've lost twenty years. I don't want to lose another twenty minutes."

"Dee . . . I sip Pepto-Bismol like water. Eat Tums like Skittles. My bedtime cocktail is four tabs of Alka-Seltzer chased with Nilla Wafers. I've tried every tonic known to man. Despite everything, I'm just postponing the inevitable. I can't hold it back and I'm not in control of this."

"We'll go see a specialist."

"I've been to Denver. Massachusetts. Rochester. They all say the same."

Tears dripped onto my chest. "It's my choice."

"You realize what you're saying?"

"Cooper, I choose you."

"And what it might cost you?"

"I realize what it has cost me." She placed her palm on my cheek. "Why won't you let me love you?"

I wanted nothing more. "It's not that."

"Then what is it?"

"Daley, this does not end well. We could be walking through the grocery store, you look away for one second, and when you turn around I'm nothing but an ugly puddle on the floor. You could kiss me good night and wake up next to rigor mortis. You could—"

She tried to crack a smile. "I've wanted to kiss you good night for twenty years."

"I am a dying man, Dee. You need to hear that. Let it sink in. I don't want you to fall in love with me, because—"

She was crying harder now. "Because why?"

"Because I won't be here to hold you when I'm gone."

She pressed her finger to my lips and tried to smile. "We're all dying, Cooper, and I'm already in love with you. Sending me away won't change that." She kissed me, holding it a long time and smearing salty tears across my face. "You once told me that music washes us from the inside out. It heals what nothing else can." She placed her hand flat across my heart. "Did you tell me that?"

"I did."

"Did you mean it?"

I nodded.

"Really?"

"Yes."

She straightened. "Then let's find out."

"And if it goes badly? If the worst happens?"

When she spoke, the sound started in her stomach. "I will not let the fear of what might be rob me of the promise of what can." She pressed her forehead to mine, slowly shaking her head back and forth. Her body was warm. Her breath blanketed me. Her right hand pounded gently on my heart. She said it a second time. "The fear of what might be will not rob me of the promise of what can."

I shook my head. "And just how do you plan to go about that?"

"I'll sing your song back to you."

I wrapped my arms around her, cradling her. Twenty years of tears dripped onto my chest. I pressed her head to my chest and whispered, "My father would have loved you."

34

I looked at my watch. Daley's concert started in less than an hour. When I tried to sit up, the world was spinning like a top. I wasn't sure how much blood I'd lost in the river, but I had a feeling it was more than usual.

"We'd better get you to the Falls."

"Forget the concert. I'm taking you to a hospital."

"Dee, I've been to a hospital. There's nothing they can—"

The reality was starting to take hold. "So you just live this way? Waiting?"

"Yes."

"Then I'll wait with you."

"Not a good idea."

Her lips tightened. "You don't scare me, Cooper O'Connor. And I'm not going anywhere."

I stood up. Wobbly but upright. The sound in my ears told me that while the storm had passed, I was simply standing in the eye. The other side was coming, and I wouldn't escape it. I thought it best to create some distance between Daley and myself, but I wasn't sure how to pull that off.

"I haven't been back to the Falls since the night I left. I'd like to see it." That much was true. "And I'm feeling better. I think it's passed for now." While that was not.

Daley wrapped her arms around me like we were dancing. "Let's get you some dry clothes first."

The Falls was packed. Sold out. Mostly middle-aged couples. Lovers. Hand in hand. Daley's team was frantic that she'd not shown up sooner. She walked me to the front row, where Big-Big was seated with Mary and several others from Riverview. She set me in a chair next to Mary. "If you get to feeling poorly, just wave and—"

"I'll do no such thing."

325

She put a hand on her hip. "How's this going to work if you don't ever do what I tell you to?"

It struck me as she was standing there flirting with me that she seriously thought I'd improve with care. That I could get better. That there was hope. That we could grow old together.

I would have loved spending my life loving her.

I forced a smile, and Daley disappeared backstage. The space between Mary's eyes narrowed and a wrinkle appeared when she turned to look at me. She placed a twitching palm on my cheek. "Cooper?"

I was shivering. "Just caught a little something."

Big-Big looked down at me. Concern in his eyes. "You going to make it?"

I nodded and wrapped my second Mellie tighter around me. "I'm good."

Half an hour passed as members of the choir appeared, but we had yet to see a single member of her band. I saw Daley talking with the guy who I guessed was her new producer. He couldn't hide the worrisome look on his face. Daley listened, crossed her arms, and walked off slowly, nodding. Ten minutes later I saw them speaking again, and the look on her face had worsened.

I stood, wobbled, gathered myself, and walked toward them. "What's up?"

"Storm in Denver. Socked in the Front Range. My band is sitting in a bus alongside the road. Can't get out."

"You have no band?"

Daley shook her head. "They're canceling the show."

I glanced out across the amphitheater. "These folks may not like that."

She nodded and looked at me. Her McPherson stood upright in the rack on the stage.

"We could go old-school," I said.

She ignored me and pressed her palm to my forehead. "You look pale."

"I'll feel better once we get started."

"I don't think that's a good idea."

I turned to the producer and pointed at the McPherson. "Can you plug a wireless pickup into that?"

He looked at Daley, wanting an explanation. She said, "He's offering to fill in for the band."

"For the whole band?" He looked dubious. "And just who might you be?"

Daley spoke for me. "This is Cooper O'Connor. He's the songwriter."

He did not look impressed. "Which song did he write?"

She looked at me. "All of them."

He studied me but spoke to Daley. "He doesn't look well. Are you sure he can—"

I answered for myself. "I need five minutes and"—I turned to Daley—"I want a favor."

She smiled. "Anything."

I told her what I wanted, slung her McPherson

around my neck, and started walking toward the bathroom. I doubted it'd do any good, but once there I drank the remainder of a bottle of Pepto and shoved an entire roll of Tums into my mouth.

Outside I heard audience applause, followed by Daley's voice on the microphone. She said, "Folks, I have some bad news. My band is stuck in a snowstorm somewhere outside of Denver. My producer suggests we cancel the show."

The audience booed loudly and shouted disparaging remarks about the producer's mother and what he should do to himself.

Daley laughed. "I told him you'd say that."

The audience stopped booing, and a few started clapping and whistling.

"So we're going to do something a little different tonight."

Sensing all was not lost, the audience began clapping loudly.

"If you guys can handle it, we're going to do this entire concert with just a piano, a guitar, and our voices. That way if we really screw it up, you'll be able to hear all the mistakes."

The audience laughed and applauded.

Big-Big walked into the bathroom and found me with the empty Pepto bottle in one hand and Tums wrappers in the other. He raised a single eyebrow. "You know what you're doing?"

"No." I threw everything in the trash and

began washing the blood off my hands. When I finished, I faced him. "I need a favor."

"You need to be in bed."

I frowned. "You think it'd do any good?"

"No, but it'd make me feel better. Like I wasn't so helpless."

"If you want to help me . . ."

Big-Big's eyes began to water as I told him about the folder from the attorney and that I'd like him to make sure it was handled. Make sure Mary had everything she needed. Tell Frank who his boss was. Visit Jubal and his mom. Take him one of my guitars. And check on Daley from time to time.

Lastly I said, "If what I think is about to happen, happens . . . don't let Daley see." I paused. "It won't be pretty."

"And all those people out there?"

"Just get me off the stage."

He looked away, shook his head in defeat, and then nodded. His voice was deep, gentle, and wound its way to my soul. "Cooper—"

I turned. His face glowed an amber brown. "Sir?"

"I been here afore."

I smiled. He had. "We had some good times here, didn't we?"

"We did. All three of us." He wiped his face with a handkerchief and said, "I need to tell you something. Something I should've told you a long time ago." He reached into his pocket and pulled out an envelope.

"You had been gone three, maybe fo' years. It was quiet 'round here. Your father had aged. Wasn't preaching no mo'. We were sitting one night listening to the radio, sipping coffee like we always done. Then we heard a voice whisper into the microphone. The voice said, 'Sing my song back to me.' He knowed right away it was you. Never even finished his coffee. Drove to Nashville that night—"

"My dad was in Nashville?"

Big-Big continued, "He rented a motel room and tried to find you. He wuz gone a few weeks. I didn't hear nothing from him. Then all of a sudden he drives up. Said you were touring around the world with some girl name Daley. He'd bought her record. We sat on the porch many a night listening to your guitar behind her voice. He smiled a lot that year. Then he heard you were back. Cutting a new record. He was so excited he was about to bust. So I say, 'Why don't you go see him.' That was all the encouragement he needs. He drives back down there. Gone a few weeks.

"Then one morning I'm watching the national news and this beautiful face pops on the screen talking about you and a fire and how they're not sure you're going to pull through . . . Next thing I know your dad come driving up the road.

He could barely lift hisself out of the truck. And I knowed it by the look on his face. He was bad sick. Limping. Coughing. He fell through the door. I done what I could. Slep' on a cot in his room. Brought the doctors up. They tended to him best they could. He tried to hold on but he was in a bad way . . ."

The pieces of my life's puzzle were slowly coming into focus. "Big-Big?"

He didn't answer.

I asked again, "What killed my dad?"

He turned, hiding his face.

"Big-Big, please."

"Complications."

"From what?"

Big-Big turned his head and looked at me. "A fire."

"A *fire?*" The word was out of my mouth about the time the truth of it settled in my heart. I managed, "Big-Big?"

He sucked through his teeth, cleared his throat, and kept talking. "He fought hard. Went up every day and soaked in the creek. Sat there 'til he turned blue. And he wuz getting better too, for a time, 'til the infection took to his lungs. I heard him sitting at his desk one morning. Hacking. All manner of stuff coming up. I knew it'd gotten worse and we needed to get him to a doctor." Big-Big swallowed and pursed his lips.

He spoke more softly, his voice muted by

memory and pain. "On that day . . . he were in there, sitting at his desk like he do. Writing. But then he started to coughing. Tough time catching his breath. So he got up and came to me. Told me what he wanted. Asked for my word, so I gave it. He handed me a letter and then turned and walked up to the creek. I axe him if he want me to go with him and he just shake his head and smile, so I watch him go. He say he be back directly."

Big-Big turned the envelope in his hands. My father's handwriting was unmistakable.

"I heard him coughing as he walk up to the creek. Then he quit. Just went quiet. I thought I better go check on him. So I hurried up, but that hill is steep and I'm heavy and I had to stop to catch my breath. By the time I got there, it was too late. He gone. I searched all day. All night. Walked every inch of that creek. Found him two days later." He pointed toward the Falls. "The current got aholt of him. Took him a lot father'n I thought. Washed him over. I found him resting with his hands folded across his stomach in that pool down yonder at the Falls."

I tried to speak, but no words came.

He nodded knowingly. The tears puddling. "He asked me not to tell. Asked me for my word."

"But . . . how could you? All the tears. All the dying you've seen me do."

He didn't look at me. "I told him that people should know the truth when it involves they eart. They love." He leaned down and kissed me on the forehead and said, "Twenty years this has been acid in my gut. Eating me from the inside out." He spat and forced a laugh. "But you know how he can be."

"Why now?"

"He told me to give this to you only if—"

"If what?"

Large tears trickled down Big-Big's face and fell off his chin. "If your heart was at stake. If knowing the truth might somehow make the difference between life with love . . . and life without."

Big-Big's bottom lip was quivering. "You ain't the only one been hurting these twenty years. Every time I see you, I see him. And every time I hear you sing . . ." Big-Big shook his head, blew his nose into a white handkerchief, refolded it, and placed it back in his pocket. "I never seen a father love a son the way he love you . . ."

He suspended the letter in the air between us, his finger resting on something inside the envelope. "He looked for three days. Sunup to sundown. He found it in some rocks where the last few rays of sunlight were reflecting off the water . . ."

When I opened the letter, my hands were shaking. It was dated the day he died.

Dear Son,

As I write this letter, I am not getting better.

Some sort of infection in my lungs I can't shake. Three rounds of antibiotics aren't touching it. I've been working on this letter for a week, but every time I read it, it doesn't say what my heart wants to say so I tear it up and start over. But time is short. Please allow your old man a few final words.

I don't know if you know this, but I came to Nashville. Wanted to tell you that I'm sorry. See your smile, hug your neck, hear your voice. Wanted to tell everyone I met that you're my son. I tracked you down one night at dinner with Daley. You two were standing in a garden outside the restaurant waiting on a table. I'd never seen you so happy. So grown up. The smile on your face. The laughter in your voice. The tenderness in your touch.

Then there was Daley. The way she looked at you, held your hand, locked her arms in yours and leaned into you, how she kept admiring the ring you gave her . . . Reminded me of your mother. Your mom was a real touchy-feely person. Her hands were like sonar pings or antennae. She liked to know where she was| in relation to me. Said I was her anchor line. It's easy to see you are that for Daley, and I think your mother would have loved her.

I got close enough to overhear you two talking about cutting a record at your pro-ducer's studio, fellow by the name of Sam something-or-other. I figured I'd let you two enjoy your dinner and we'd meet up another night. I wanted to do something nice before I left, so I paid for your dinner and asked the maître d' to bring champagne and roses. I'm hopeful he did.

It wasn't tough to track down Sam's house, so I waited until Friday night when I knew you'd be finished working. I was hoping to catch you alone. Give you and me a chance to talk. If you were still angry, I wanted to be able to leave quietly without causing a scene. I saw my chance when you disappeared into that building out back.

Then I heard the explosion.

When I got to you, you were covered in blood, your clothes were on fire, and you were pinned beneath one of the rafters. I didn't think we were going to make it out. Only words coming out of your mouth were, "Dad, I'm so sorry . . ." That's when I knew I should've come to Nashville long ago.

Son, there's nothing to forgive. Not one single thing. I forgave you the moment you drove out the drive. You can't hit me hard enough to make me hate you. Truth is, I'm the one should be sorry.

I know I can be overbearing and imposing. I know I cast a long shadow. If I made you feel like I was holding you under my thumb, holding you back from your dreams—I'm sorry. Really. Forgive me. That's not my heart for you. Maybe my way of protecting you and pulling for you wasn't the best way. Maybe I could've done better. Maybe I should've done things differently.

If Big-Big has given you this letter, then something has happened in your life to cause him to think that what I've just told you, despite the pain of it, might help you in some way. You should know that I asked him to keep the knowledge of my sickness and cause of my death a secret. Made him give me his word. If this makes you angry, blame me. I was trying to protect you from thinking you were somehow responsible for me. You're not. And before you start arguing with me, no power on earth could stop me from running through fire for you. Not now. Not ever.

Now that you know, let me tell you what I'd have told you two at dinner that night. I know—I've always known—that what you have—the gift that is in you—is special. Unlike anything I've ever heard. Most of my favorite memories center around you playing and singing. Starting with the night of the storm. The sound that comes out of you is the most beautiful thing I've ever heard. Something about it is not of this earth. And while music may take you from BV, the Falls is and always will be your musical home. I know it may be tough, but don't let whatever you're wrestling with keep you from that. Sometimes we have to sing through the scars. Sometimes a song is the only thing that heals the broken places in us. Only thing that breaks the chains on the heart. Jimmy taught me that after your mom died. Take care of him.

If you have found yourself in a storm where the sky is black and lightning has set fire to the world around you, if you are afraid, hurting, or maybe your hope is sucked dry, then remember that fearless kid who emptied himself on the piano bench and . . . let it out. Don't let the fear of what might be rob you of the promise of what can.

I love you. Always have. No gone is too far gone.

Love,
Dad

Taped to the bottom of the letter was my oak ring.

35

I could not believe Dad had found my ring. How long had he looked? Is that what Big-Big was talking about? Three days? Where did he find it? When I threw that thing off the stage, I threw it with some anger, and when it disappeared out into the night sky, I knew it was gone forever. I slid it on my finger now, and what I felt was not guilt, or shame, or hurt, or pain, but ownership. Identity. Belonging. Holding Dad's letter in one hand and wearing the ring on the other, I felt something I'd not felt in a long, long time.

I remembered that dinner. The candlelight. Laughter. It was one of our happiest moments, but I'd always thought Sam had sent the champagne and roses. I felt guilty for giving Sam credit for my father's kindness.

Daley walked up onto the stage beneath the spotlight. She was so comfortable before an audience. She wore faded blue jeans and a white button-down. Comfortable in her own skin. No pretension. *Take me or leave me, but either way I'm here to give you the best I have.*

She'd hurt awhile, but she'd be okay. She was strong.

She stepped up to the microphone. "I want to introduce you to the most talented singer-songwriter I know. He wrote every one of my songs that is any good. You might have heard him twenty years ago when I debuted at the Ryman. But to introduce him, I want to ask a man that knows him better than anyone. Mr. Ivory 'Big-Big' Johnson."

Big-Big walked up the steps, and his presence alone commanded a hush. Five thousand people fell pin-drop quiet as a six-foot-six, broad-shouldered giant of a man with ebony skin, piercing eyes, snow-white hair, and a wide and gentle smile stood in front of the microphone.

Big-Big wiped his forehead with his handkerchief and then cleared his throat. As he began speaking, a cameraman appeared to my left and a live shot of my face appeared on a huge screen behind him. I was looking at Big-Big onstage, who was looking at me at the far end of the audience. When he pointed and began speaking, most every head turned toward me.

"I remember when that boy were young. I do. He was only three. Maybe four. Little towhead with hair falling down over the greenest eyes I ever seen. Quiet. Curious. Tender. But don't confuse tender with weak, 'cause one day when he was a little older, I seen a bigger kid shove him and take his ice cream. Take his lunch money. He didn't take to that. He jumped up, wiped the tears out of his eyes, and come unglued. Got his lunch money back. I remember laughing. Apple don't fall far. He see black and white. Ain't no gray. Even then he had thick shoulders. Stocky kid. Square jaw. Came 'bout to my waist. Big hands. Remind me of a puppy with big paws.

"When I got out of prison, his daddy, the man who built this place, invited me to breakfast, where he fed both my stomach and my heart. Then he offered to put me to work. Only man who ever took a chance on me, and given my history I didn't deserve a chance. This is back at the camp meetings. In the heyday. When the fireflies lit the fields. Before most of you were born. This boy would stand beside me beneath the big top, offstage, in the shadows. At first it made me uncomfortable. I'd think to myself, *Can't this white boy see the color of my skin? Don't he know where I been? Don't he know what I did?*

"If he did, he didn't care. He just stood there, one hand hanging on my pants pocket, bracing for the impact, staring onto the stage where his daddy was speaking. Bible in one hand. Sweat in the other. Speaking 'bout setting captives free. 'Bout making all things new. 'Bout finding what was lost. Sometimes when his daddy voice get loud and booming, that boy would grab my hand. I'd look down and think, *God must be good,* 'cause what I held in my hand was the goodest thing I ever knowed. And while everybody be focused on his daddy, that boy seem distracted. Like he listening to something ain't none of the rest of us can hear. Like with one ear he be listening to this world, but with the other, he be listening to some other.

"Then the boy get older. And pretty soon I be sitting at the piano and I look out in the crowd, down below the lights, and thousands done come. They camp out in the rain. Pack the tent. People standing outside in the dark. They come to hear the man. His daddy, he had a gif'. Ain't never seen nothing like it. I remember the very first night we gathered in this very spot. On this ground. Pastor be talking 'bout the war in heaven. How the dragon done been cast down like lightning. How he at war with the woman. He in a great big fury. And then outside the tent, it got evil dark. Clouds done block out the moon. Can't see my hand befo' my face. And then high up in the sky, out of nowhere, the lightning crack. And hit the tent. That boy and me, we jump fo' feet in the air and he wrap his arms 'round my leg. And he be shaking like a leaf. And me too. The hair on my arms stood porcupine straight. Smoke filled the tent 'cause that lightning done struck the canvas. Split it down the middle. Heaven open wide. E'rybody got saved then. Them that weren't was, and them that was got it again. But that boy, he just stood behind me. Peeking 'round me. Eyeing the piano. And when that smoke filled that tent, and people be screaming and calling on the Lord, that boy hide beneath the bench. Ball up. Then his daddy crawl over next to him. Reach in with one arm, pull him out. Set him on the bench. Whisper in that boy's ear. So that boy, while the world be on fire and falling down, while people be screaming and fighting and hating one another, he stretch out his arms and he touch those keys. Run his fingers across the ivory like he reading what they had to say. Like they be having

341

a conversation but ain't nobody else can hear it.

"Then I look up and the tent be on fire above the boy where the lightning hit, but the boy, he don't care. He still talking to the keys. People be running out. Screaming. Tripping over chairs. Trampling one another. Chaos. I'm thinking his daddy be right and we're be watching the end of the world. But not that boy.

"See it now like it was yestuh'day. See it clear as a picture. That wide-eyed boy look up at his daddy. His daddy be staring down, smiling. Waiting. Whole world coming down 'round him and he be smiling down. It be the end time. Armageddon. He closed his book, pull the handkerchief from his back pocket, and wipe his forehead. Firelight flickering off his cheek. Smoke billowing. Then he refold it and tuck it in his pocket. He nodded and whispered, 'Go ahead.' He glanced at the keys. He say, 'Let it out.'

"That boy didn't move. He shouted above the roar of the storm, 'How you know it's in there?'

"His daddy never hesitated. 'I saw Him put it there.' That boy be shaking, so his daddy he say, 'Son . . . let it out.'

"You believe what you want. You call me crazy. Call me a liar. But I was there. A few feet away. Seen it with my own eyes. Don't know where he got it, don't know how it happened, don't know nothing 'bout nothing. What I do know is that boy, he look out at those people, then back at those keys, and he done what his daddy done told him. He opened his mouth and fingers and he let it out.

"And when he did . . . that when the thunder done come.

"That be the night when the thunder come."

The night of the storm replayed in my mind. For a split second I felt stinging rain on my cheek, smelled a pungent earthiness that only comes after the rain, sensed the song in my fingers. A growing tickle crowded my throat, forcing me to cough into my handkerchief. The blood was darker, and mixed with what looked like coffee grounds.

Daley had miked both me and her McPherson with wireless mikes. Making me untethered, allowing me to wander. While I waited for my entrance, a man appeared to my left. Broad-shouldered, dark jacket, he took a seat in the back row. Shoulder-length, sun-bleached blond hair. Something familiar struck me about his posture. The way his broad shoulders hung relaxed. The look of his hands.

He was reading a book, and I circled him from a few feet away, trying not to stare, but he noticed me and looked up. His skin was tanned, face chiseled but gentle, and his eyes were a piercing emerald green. I looked closer in disbelief. It'd been two decades since I'd seen him. He'd not aged at all.

I circled him and tapped his shoulder, then backed up. "Hey."

He said nothing. Just nodded.

I said, "It's good to see you. I've missed you."

"You've been missed." When he spoke, I remembered his voice.

"I looked for you in Nashville."

"I know."

I leaned in closer. He smelled of rosemary and something else I couldn't place. Maybe tea tree oil. "What made you come back?"

He closed the book and stood, staring down on me. "What makes you think I ever left?"

"You've been here this entire time?"

"Not exactly."

I coughed. More blood and coffee grounds. He saw it too. One of his eyebrows rose slightly. I wiped my mouth, refolded the handkerchief, and stared at the stage. I asked, "You think I'll make it through this?"

He didn't hesitate. "No."

The sound in my ears was growing louder. I stared out at all the people, at Daley alone on the stage, at Big-Big, and then down at the guitar. "I'd like to finish what was started in me."

"Why?"

I didn't know how to answer him. "Last time I was here, I said some things." The reflection of the ring caught my attention. "Did some things—"

He glanced at the stage. "I remember."

I swallowed. "Those things left scars. On the inside. I trip over them a lot."

He did not look impressed with my revelation. "And?"

"Sometimes I think if I could go back and start over—"

"There are no do-overs."

"I just thought—"

"You just thought what?"

"I thought that the only way I know to get rid of them is to offer up what I held back."

"Which is?"

A shrug. "My song."

"Shouldn't you have thought about that twenty years ago?"

"Yes. And every day since I left here has hurt more than the one before."

He closed the book and slid it behind him, between his belt and his back. Then he reached out and placed his finger in front of my mouth. Holding it there. He said, "Stick out your tongue."

"You want me to stick out my tongue?"

He tilted his head slightly and waited.

When I stuck out my tongue, he touched it with the tip of his finger. It was the first time he'd ever touched me, and when he did, it felt hot. Like fire. With his hand so close, I noticed the calluses on the tips of his fingers—like mine. He gestured toward the aisle in front of me. "Go ahead."

I pointed at the calluses. "You play?"

He faced showed no expression. "A bit."

I took a step and stopped. "We should play sometime."

He leaned down. His face inches from mine. "We used to." His breath warm on my face. "I've been waiting twenty years for you to say that."

"Really?" I scratched my head. "How come you didn't say something sooner?"

"I've been screaming at the top of my lungs."

"How come I never heard you?"

He touched my chest, just above my heart. "You haven't been listening."

"Good point."

"Thank you."

"Can I ask you one more thing?"

His tone was matter-of-fact. "You can ask."

"If this goes badly—"

"If?"

I backtracked. "Okay, *when* it does, will you please stand between Daley and me? I don't want her to see—"

"It's a little late for that."

"If my dad were here, he'd tell you that it's never too late. That nothing disqualifies us. That no matter where we end up, no matter what mess we make, we can always turn around. Come home."

"So you were listening?"

I shrugged.

"Why does this matter?" he asked.

I looked at Daley standing on the stage. "She's been hurting a long time. I'm the source of a lot of her pain. I don't want to hurt her any more than I already have."

A tear cascaded down his face and landed on my cheek. He glanced at Daley, then back at me, and nodded.

I took a step toward the stage, then turned back and spoke louder. "I'm sorry about before."

"Me too."

Between us there were words still unsaid, but when I looked for him again, he was gone. Every few minutes a shiver would ripple through me. My thawing out continued. I was pretty sure I could make it through the concert and pretty sure I would not make it through the night. I needed to plan an exit that did not include Daley.

That said, I wasn't dead yet, and there was music to be played.

Big-Big's voice had just finished echoing off the cliff walls. I remembered that angry storm and Dad walking from the back toward the front with nothing and no one but Jimmy. In memory of that, I started tapping out a rhythmic percussive beat on the top of the guitar.

My tapping and fingerpicking brought five thousand to their singing-whistling-clapping-shouting feet. I walked forward slowly, remembering how Dad had done it. Taking his time.

Weaving around people. One spotlight framed Daley on the stage. The other shone on me. As I walked closer to the front, the choir started humming. Then I heard the piano bleed in. Big-Big's timing, his touch. His sausage-size fingers were playing a melody around me. The effect of that tapestry was all encompassing. But while there was beauty in it, it held little glory, and no majesty, until Daley opened her mouth and let her words rain down.

I climbed the stage. Mesmerized. One side of me played. The other side watched her empty herself. The smile on her face was the final expression of an emotion that enveloped her entire body. Every muscle, impulse, heartbeat had a singular focus—the song erupting out of her. As my fingers played the chords and picked the strings, the floodgates inside me opened and began letting out the song I'd held back for twenty years.

36

An hour in, Daley paused long enough to take a breath, and a natural break occurred in the set. Out of the lull some guy yelled, " 'Son of a Preacher Man.' "

Daley looked at me and shrugged. "I'm game."

I stared from the stage to the venue the Falls had become—the place my father built. "I think

Dad would be okay with that," I said aloud to myself.

"What'd you say?" Daley asked.

"I said, 'You're beautiful.' "

The voice in the audience had sounded familiar. I scanned the front row and found a guy in a hoodie. He was sipping on a soda, eating a hot dog, and his feet were propped up on the stage. Close enough for me to catch a whiff of the dog. The smell was familiar . . . cabbage and some nasty-smelling cheese.

I leaned down. Blondie looked up at me from beneath the hood. I said, "That was you?"

No response.

"But I thought you said you weren't in Nashville."

He took another bite, smearing mustard across the corner of his mouth. "Never said that."

"You did too." I pointed to the back of the audience. "You just said—"

"I said, 'What makes you think I left?' "

"Exactly."

"Cooper, I wasn't talking about a place."

I scratched my head. "Then what were you talking about?"

"I wasn't talking about a what or a where. I was talking about a *who*."

I was about as confused as I could be. "You are making no sense whatsoever."

He took another bite and hopped up onstage. He

brushed past me and whispered, "Some have entertained . . ." Then he sat atop the piano just behind me, opened his pocketknife, and began whittling. "Therefore since we are surrounded . . ."

I shrugged. "I've heard this one before. Lots of times."

He stopped whittling and tapped me on the edge of my ear with the tip of his pocketknife.

"You might have heard it, but were you listening?"

In a matter of seconds, Blondie's face transformed to look like the old man in Dietrich's Wiener schnitzel car wash, then the policeman who woke me in the street after I was mugged and Jimmy was stolen, then the bouncer in Printer's Alley who gave me the sheet music denoting the Nashville Number System, and finally to the little kid with his father in Leadville who asked for my autograph.

He leaned close enough for me to feel his breath on my face. "What makes you think I left you?"

"You were with me all along?"

"Don't let it go to your head. You're not any more important than anyone else, but the gift in you . . . well, that's another thing entirely."

"Do you talk this way to everyone?"

"How's that?"

"So flippantly."

"What makes you think I talk to anyone else?"

"But you just said I'm not special."

He shook his head. "Never said that."

"Yes you did."

"Nope. I said you weren't any more important than anyone else."

"Same thing."

"No. It's not."

I stepped closer. My face inches from his I spoke through gritted teeth. "Why are you here?"

He smiled, stood, and took off his sweatshirt. "It's about time you asked that question."

I was about to object when Daley started singing in that raspy, powerful voice that would melt most men in the audience. She further grabbed my attention when she inserted my name in the first line. It was true. I was, in fact, the son of a preacher man, and by her own admission I'd been the only one to "reach" her. Just before the last chorus, she leaned across the guitar and kissed me beneath the spotlight. I don't know who loved it more, the audience or me. From there we played a mixture of covers and her own stuff. Or, I should say, *our* own stuff. We sat on stools and accepted requests while Blondie sat on the piano and whittled.

During a lull I pointed at the pile of wood shavings at his feet. "Nice mess."

He eyed the pile beneath him. "It's not nearly as bad as the one you made."

"Touché. But do you have to do that right now, right here?"

He hesitated. "When I'm not babysitting you,

my day job is instrument repair. Lately you've required a lot of my time, so I'm behind."

"Really?"

He nodded matter-of-factly.

"What's that you're working on?"

He held up the piece of wood in his hand. "When finished, it'll be the neck and headstock to a guitar."

Evidently I'd entered an area he didn't mind talking about. His work.

"It's a custom fit. Rather time-consuming. I take some measurements, then do some hand-fitting to make sure it works perfectly with the player's hands." He lifted it so I could see it. "This one happens to belong to your dad."

"You talk to my dad?"

His face was expressionless. "All the time."

"Can you tell him something for me?"

"Yes, I can, but no, I will not."

"Has anyone ever told you that you're not real accommodating?"

He never looked up from his work. "Accommodating you is not my job."

"Well, you have a unique way of determining what is your job."

He glanced at me out of the corner of his eye. His look was one of tolerance but not necessarily interest.

I tried again. "Will you please tell him something for me?"

"No."

"Why not?"

He pointed at the audience with his knife. "Tell him yourself." As he said that, something in my vision changed. It was like sitting in the optometrist's chair, and the doc is flipping those lenses in front of your eye and asking which one is better, one or two? And as you answer, the picture gets sharper and sharper until everything clicks into focus.

In front of me, I saw the audience that had bought their tickets. Those folks, like me, had come in through the gate. And then in a blink, the image went from one to two—and five thousand turned into more than I could count or guesstimate. And standing near the front, with a guitar slung over his shoulder, smiling wide and eyes intent on me, stood my dad.

I had not expected that.

Daley and I were sitting on stools, near the edge of the stage. Turned slightly toward each other and facing the audience. She smiled and put her hand on my knee, proving once again that she, like my mother, was a touchy-feely person. Her eyes smiled with as much mischief as her mouth. She turned toward the audience.

"Coop won't tell you this, but he's written eighteen number one hits. Five of which were mine." She turned to me and raised an eyebrow. "You have anything new you'd like to share with us?"

I muted the strings and spoke into the microphone. "Twenty-five years ago this month, I stood on this stage with my dad, and in my infinite stupidity and ignorance, I told him I wasn't going to sing his stupid songs anymore, or travel with his stupid tent revival circus, or do pretty much anything he wanted. Then . . . I balled my fist and struck my father in the face. Hard as I could. Split his lip. The same father who had loved me really well and never withheld any good thing."

The audience responded with silence.

I walked a few steps to where my dad had been standing. "And while he stood right here, bleeding onto the stage, I took off the ring he'd given me and threw it—along with my identity—as far as I could into the river."

The silence of the crowd allowed the peaceful roll of the river to flow over us.

"Adding insult to injury, I stole everything he valued, including his life savings, his truck, and the guitar my mom gave him as a wedding gift."

If I did not have their attention before, I had it now.

The next admission was the most painful. My voice cracked. "I never saw my dad alive again."

The entire audience came to a halt. Even the folks walking to and from the bathroom or concession stood still.

"That night I drove to Nashville, where I learned I was really nothing special and I promptly lost everything I'd stolen. Money, truck, guitar, everything. Five years later I was shot in the chest and left to die in a building set on fire. For twenty years I have not known who pulled me from the flames. Until a few minutes ago."

I held up the letter my dad had written me. "It was my dad. I don't know how he found me, but he did. He rescued me when I could not. I'd like to tell you the story has a happy ending, but . . . the price for my trip out of the flames was high. Dad died from burns to his body and the toxic effects of smoke in his lungs."

The expressions on people's faces had eclipsed pity. It was more akin to understanding. To empathy. They were wiping tears. Intently listening. And what I saw for the first time was not only the impact of my story on others but how it resonated with their own. While their details were different, a lot of those folks staring up at me shared the same hurt, the same regret, same heart-ache, and somehow, in hearing the truth about me, they learned they weren't alone. That they weren't the only one to walk away from someone they loved, and who loved them.

I gathered myself. "When I left here, I didn't just take my dad's stuff. I took me. My most selfish act. And that hurt him the most."

I walked to the edge of the stage. My fingers rolling gently across the strings. "For twenty years I've been trying to figure out how to tell a dead man I'm sorry. Sometimes I climb up in those hills behind us and stare out there and ask God why He keeps me around. Why not just be done with me? Zap me with a lightning bolt and be done with it. And then I hear a song. And I know that what I'm hearing doesn't start with me. It can't. There is no way on this earth that something so beautiful can come out of something so screwed up. So black-hearted. But somehow it does, and because it's beautiful and I don't want to lose it, and because there is still a part of me that would like to share it, I write it down." I shook my head as the tears dripped off my chin. I wiped my face. "So here I am at the end of myself, asking just what do I do with the music in me?"

Big-Big quietly played chords on the piano. The choir hummed. Daley swayed beside me. The collective voice of the choir grew louder over my shoulder. Blondie and his friends had moved closer to the stage. I turned, and my dad was standing next to me. I slid the notebook from the small of my back, opened it, and handed it to Daley. Slowly I raised both hands as high as I could reach. A mirror image of my father.

"This is a song . . ." My voice cracked. "This is a song . . . about what I hope to find when I get where I'm going." I played the opening chord. "It's called 'Long Way Gone.'"

So I played. And for the first time since I left this stage, I sang at the top of my lungs.

Somewhere in the first verse, Daley's voice rose beneath me. And then showered over me.

When I finished I rolled into a song everyone already knew, and by the time I sang the second line, "Tune my heart to sing Thy grace," they were singing back at me at the top of their lungs.

We sang all six verses, and reaching the last verse, we muted all the instruments and sang a capella.

"Prone to wander, Lord, I feel it
Prone to leave the God I love
Here's my heart, Lord, take and seal it
Seal it for Thy courts above."

When we finished, people were leaving their seats and moving forward. Crowding the stage. Ten thousand hands waved in the air. It was a good song. Daley would go far with it. I think my dad would have liked it, and he was right, there's just something about old hymns.

The world seemed muted. My heartbeat was in my ears. The acrid taste had returned. I had pushed it too far. I felt the rupture and knew no river treatment would help. I only had a few moments.

Blondie stood off to my left. Close to Daley. A cat ready to pounce. My dad stood nearby, playing alongside me. If I was going to die onstage, I wanted to die with a guitar in my hand. Playing. I put the capo on the fifth fret and started strumming a G-D-Em-C chord progression. The words were muddled, and I could tell the audience knew something was off. I tried to sing the first verse but all the words got jumbled and I lost the tune. The world took on a sepia color and everything moved in slow motion.

Daley stared at me. A wrinkle between her eyes. Big-Big stood from the piano and stepped toward me. When the blood spilled out my mouth, I remember looking upward, then falling backward, and the only thing I could hear was a million voices singing over me.

I watched me from above me. It was quiet up here. Chaos below. I lay on the stage. Motionless. Eyes growing dim. There was a good bit of blood. Daley was screaming. Her guitar had been sprayed red. I felt bad about that. She was holding me. Her shirt was stained.

Big-Big was leaning over, crying. Shaking his head. I heard him screaming, "No," real loud. He looked angry. And he too looked like he was talking to someone who wasn't there. Then I saw him pick up my body and carry me off the back of the stage toward the waterfall. He walked my limp rag-doll body across the pasture into the darkness, away from the lights, and waded into the river where the water rose above his waist. Walking upstream. Finally he just stood there in the falls, letting the water rain down on him and me both. Washing over us. I could see his chest heaving. Letting out deep moans. Screaming at the sky. His voice seemed a long way away. He was saying, "I told you I'd look after him and I ain't done real good."

My body turned blue and pale, the light left my eyes, and the crimson trail stopped pouring out my mouth. He held me there several minutes. Finally he walked out of the water and laid my lifeless body on the ground in the lush grass, where Daley cradled me. Pulled me to her chest. Trying to rock me back to this world.

But she could not.

Long way gone.

Behind me, I could hear sirens and see flashing red and white lights.

To my right, Blondie appeared. He was lined up in a perfect row with all the others. Stretched out as far as the eye could see. He'd changed his clothes. He was wearing white, barefoot, his hair was swaying, he was sweating. I heard the faint, fading echo of music. Like the last note of a measure. Blondie looked as if he'd just finished one dance move and was waiting on the music to start for the next. Off to one side stood a bunch of folks holding musical instruments. Most I'd never seen. Dad had a guitar around his neck. Oddly, it had ten strings. Next to him was a vacant spot. I was about to step into the spot next to Dad when Blondie held up his hand and waved a single index finger. "Not yet."

I looked down at me, at Daley, at Big-Big, at the chaos and frantic movements, but all I heard was the most beautiful singing coming from the voices around Blondie. I pointed down at me. "But I'm dead."

"You were dead." He paused. The book he'd been reading in the back row of the audience he now held in his hand. It was a black notebook. Like mine. He'd scribbled some words on the inside. His handwriting was the most beautiful I'd ever seen. He tucked it between my belt and back and then reached inside me and took something out. Something dark and painful. Then he squared up to me, pressed his lips to mine, and exhaled. The breath filled me. Warmed me. He said, "Now you're alive."

At that second the world of light that I'd been standing in became dark, and I felt cold like I'd never known. Except my lips. Which felt warm. Moist. And they tasted salty. That only meant one thing.

Daley's tears.

And somewhere in that darkness, I heard the whisper of my father.

For obvious reasons, the opening of my eyes caused a bit of a ruckus. Paramedics appeared a few minutes later, placed an oxygen mask on my face, inserted a needle in my arm, and started asking me questions I couldn't answer then and can't answer now. I'll tell you the same thing I told them: I was doornail dead. Looking down on myself. No pulse. No nothing. Then in a blink, I felt grass beneath me, felt cold, and tasted salt. Then I started getting warmer and turned from blue to a better shade of red. I don't understand that. One second I was gone. The next second I was not. I have no words for that. I do know this— somewhere between here and there, whatever had been broken in me was made no longer broken, and however it happened, I didn't cause it and I didn't deserve it. I'm not certain about a whole lot, but I know two things without a doubt: I'm alive and I didn't fix me.

As I was riding in the back of the ambulance, with Daley's arms wrapped around me, Blondie appeared. He sat next to the paramedic who was squeezing the IV bag to force fluids into my system faster. It was the first time I heard a softness in Blondie's voice. He said, "You don't have to understand this. But you do have to live."

I woke in front of the fire in my cabin. Wrapped in a sleeping bag with Daley intertwined around me like a vine. I could not have extracted myself if I'd wanted to. Big-Big sat on the couch. One leg crossed over the other. He was sipping coffee, waiting on me. When my eyes focused, he stood, ran his fingers along the inside of his suspenders, and then looked down at me as he wiped his forehead with his handkerchief, which he then folded and refolded.

"Look here, you little squirt, I told your daddy I'd look after you." He set down his coffee cup and turned toward the door. Palm down, he sliced his hand sideways through the air. "I'm done." He stood staring out across a cloudless blue sky. "No mo'. I'm getting too old to be caring for you. It's time we start doing this t'other way 'round."

"What way is that?"

He laughed. "The way where I don't go in the river no mo'. Nothing but a crazy man go in that thing. It's too cold. You'll catch the pneumonia."

He pulled open the door and looked at Daley. "Three o'clock?"

She smiled and pointed at the porch. "We'll be here."

Big-Big shut the door and I heard his truck engine fade off down the mountain. I asked, "Three o'clock?"

Daley nodded matter-of-factly. "And not a nanosecond later."

She snuggled closer, which I hadn't thought possible moments before. "What's happening at three?" I asked, though I had a feeling I knew the answer.

She closed her eyes, pressed her ear against my heart, and tapped her finger on my chest. "The beginning of you and me."

Epilogue

It was Sunday evening and a Christmas Eve snow feathered the street, muting the excited voices and giving an amber reflection to the flickering gaslights. I'd asked Frank to be in charge of parking cars. Tanned from the islands, he'd gladly agreed.

The town was quiet and shut down save the Ptarmigan Theatre, which was packed to overflowing. We'd brought in a few dozen extra chairs, but they had filled quickly. Those without a seat stood along the sides or in the back two and three deep. Mary sat up front. Wrapped in a blanket and a new Mellie that Daley had bought her. Her new BFF. She was beaming. Big-Big sat with one leg crossed over the other. Content and full of life.

Daley and I were recording our second album in a free concert. A live acoustic version of both old and new. Our producer, a midthirties sound genius named Andy, had brought in the best engineers from Nashville and LA to capture what he called the "exquisite acoustics" of the old stone walls. Given the success of our first album, *Live at the Falls*, anticipation was high. At five minutes to seven, the orchestra was seated and tuning. The choir stood backstage awaiting their entrance, swaying in purple velvet robes that would have made my dad smile. Andy wanted to create an environment as much as a sound, so in the days prior he had installed a lot of indirect lighting, giving the room a warm, firelit feel.

Daley sat on the stage talking quietly with folks in the audience. Answering questions. She loved this part. I, on the other hand, was looking for someone who didn't want to be found. But I had an idea where he might be.

I pulled up my collar to shield me from the cold and walked out the fire exit into the alley behind the theatre. My no-show had built a fire in the fire pit and stood warming himself against the single digits. Over the last year, when we'd finished our lessons, we'd do this. Standing by the fire had become our thing. The place where my heart poured into his. And his into mine. Snowflakes hung in his black hair. He heard me coming but didn't look. I stood next to him warming my hands. "Hey, big guy. How you doing?"

Jubal shook his head once and didn't take his eyes off the flames.

I'd been where he was. No need to rush him. They'd wait for us. When he looked up at me, I said, "You scared?"

He nodded. The confident and verbal kid I'd met at his grandfather's graveside and the kid I'd gotten to know over the last year had been replaced by a muted, squirming boy looking for an exit. A bench to crawl under.

A minute passed. Finally he whispered. "What if I freeze up? Forget everything?"

I shrugged. "We'll start over."

"What if I freeze again?"

I chuckled. "We'll start over again."

"What if—"

I gently tapped his temple. "Song doesn't come out of here." I tapped his chest. "It comes out of here." I inched closer to the fire. "Your heart will remember what your mind forgets."

"How do you know?"

"Music just works that way."

"You ever get scared?"

"Not now."

"Were you ever?"

"Once."

"Where?" He was stalling, but I understood.

"First concert." I pointed south. "The Falls. My dad found me hiding under the piano bench."

"What'd he do?"

"Set me on the bench, lifted my chin, and told me that, no matter what, he was proud of me. That I could do no wrong. That all I had to do was open my mouth and let out the breath I'd been holding my whole life."

"Did you?"

"Yep."

One side of his mouth turned up.

"Can I tell you a secret?" I said.

He nodded, but he still had his back turned toward the door.

"You don't have to play tonight."

He looked both relieved and confused. "Don't you want me to?"

"Of course. But the world won't come to an end if you don't."

"So I can stay here?"

"Yep."

"You won't be mad?"

"Nope."

"What about Miss Daley?"

"She won't be mad either."

His shoulders relaxed. When I turned to go, he grabbed my arm. "That's it?"

I turned around. "Jubal, can I let you in on another secret?"

He waited.

"The secret is that we *play* music. We don't *work* music."

His nose wrinkled. "What do you mean?"

"Making music isn't something you have to do. It's something you *get* to do. It's fun."

"You won't be mad if I mess up this recording and tick off that guy back there with the head-phones looking at all those lights?"

I looked at him with a wrinkle between my eyes. "Where did you get the idea that you had to be perfect? I didn't teach you that."

"But all those people on the TV shows always get raked over the coals by the judges as soon as they finish singing or playing."

"Is that where this is coming from? TV? I'm going to talk to your mom about canceling the cable."

He laughed.

I said, "Let me set the record straight on something. You're not playing for judges. If anyone in that room tonight listens to you and doesn't like what you play, they need to go suck on a lemon."

He liked that.

"And further, if they utter one negative word about you, it's got to go through Daley and me to get to you. Jubal, you might as well understand this now. Music is a gift. We make it to give it away. All those people in there, they might not know it, but they need what you got, because you're the only one out of something like six billion people on the planet who has your song. God chose you. Not your grandfather. Not me. Not Daley. Not anyone else. So you can bottle it up and drink it all alone out here by the fire if you want, but before you let the fear of failure keep you from walking in there and playing, you should know that some of those people in there are sick. Some have been burned. Broken. Left out in the cold. Some are wrestling with painful words spoken over them by someone they love or

367

walking around in chains of their own making. A few are dying inside. Whatever the reason, when you sit down in front of them and say, 'Let me play a song for you,' you're giving them something that no amount of money can buy."

He looked confused. "What's that?"

"Hope."

He considered this.

"Think about it. It's Christmas Eve and there's a couple hundred people sitting in what was once an old, abandoned church. Waiting on three people to walk up onstage and make some noise." I inched closer. My voice barely a whisper. "You know why they're in there?"

"Yeah, 'cause you and Miss Daley are really good."

"Nope. There are lots of people that are really good."

"Then why?"

"Because they are all living with the singular hope that maybe tonight, in this place, under this blanket of snow, within the sound of our voices, God can take their pain and give them something in return that makes all the broken and dying stuff new and alive again."

"You really think it's that important?"

"I do."

He stared up into the snow. Then at me. His big, brown eyes as curious as his question. "Can He?"

"He did with me."

He looked surprised. "Really?"

"Yes."

"How?"

"Before I met you, I'd made a pretty big mess. He took the ashes of my life and gave me something beautiful in their place."

"You tell me about it sometime?"

"Sure."

He nodded as if he understood. "Uncle Coop?"

I smiled. "Yes."

His lips grew tight and his face took on an unashamed confidence I'd grown to love. "You think my grandfather knew that?"

"Don't know. What I do know is this—the kind of music we were made to play breaks chains. It walks deep inside us and everyone within ear-shot, drives a stake in the ground, and silences the thing that's trying to kill us. And I think your grand-father knew a good bit about that. I think that's why he did what he did, and I think that's what he was doing when I met him, and I think that's why he gave you that guitar."

"I wish he were here."

"Me too."

Jubal turned and began walking toward the entrance. When he got to the door, he pulled it open and spoke around it. "Okay, but if I screw this up, it's your fault."

He disappeared inside, and I stood there laughing while the snow settled on my shoulders.

On the other side of the fire stood Blondie. He was sucking on a Tootsie Pop. When he spoke, he pointed it at me. "Nice job."

"I had a good teacher."

He stuck the sucker back in his mouth and gave me an approving nod. "That you did."

I turned. "You coming?"

He stepped around the fire, alongside me. "Wouldn't miss it."

I nodded toward the door Jubal had just passed through. "Can he see you?"

Blondie motioned with his sucker while one end of his mouth turned up. "Not yet."

I laughed. "This ought to be good."

When I walked onto the stage, Daley brushed my arm and stomach with her hand. Another sonar ping. I loved it when she did that. I took my seat opposite her, and she turned toward the audience.

Daley stepped from her stool and stood next to Jubal, putting her hand gently on his shoulder. "Ladies and gentlemen, Cooper and I would like to introduce to you Jubal Tyre." She smiled. "He's the newest member of our band, and at twelve he's also the youngest."

Laughter and applause rippled across the audience.

"We've asked him to play and sing on this record for reasons that will soon become obvious." She returned to her stool and sat waiting on me. I turned on my mike and glanced at Jubal.

My voice echoed across the stone walls. "You ready?"

He smirked. "Waiting on you, Old Man."

More laughter. I set Jimmy across my knee, touched the strings with my fingers, and looked toward the back where Andy sat in headphones staring at a flashing board. "Andy, you ready?"

He adjusted a slide control and then gave me a thumbs-up. I studied the audience, letting my fingers roll across the strings. Jimmy's aging and rich voice rose out of his bullet-holed body and resonated off the rafters, where Blondie sat swinging his feet. The choir began parading single file into place, humming as they walked. While they made their way across the stage, Big-Big walked to the piano bench behind me, sat down, and began quietly constructing the scaffolding we would soon stand upon. Jubal began lightly embellishing the melody, filling the air above the piano. Mary, sitting just a few feet in front of me, stopped twitching.

I said, "Let's start at the beginning. The first date I had with my wife was an impromptu at the Ryman. She caught me with my hands on her guitar, so I wooed her with this one . . ."

Given Jubal's innate talent, one of the first songs I had taught him was "Let It Out." He started tapping out a percussive rhythm on the body of his guitar, I re-created the shrill sound of the wind with whistles, and Daley sang my song back to all of us. It was a good beginning.

Midway through I quit playing, the stage lights dimmed, and the spotlight singled on Jubal, who didn't seem to mind at all. It was fun to watch him come into his own, listen to the audience's surprise at his ability, hear the resulting applause, and then watch the smile spread across his face. I don't think he was scared anymore.

Over two hours we played all of Daley's number ones. Several songs off our new record. A few covers that had become favorites. We closed the concert with "Long Way Gone."

I said, "This last song was twenty-five years in the making, and the last time I tried to play it for a group of folks like you, it didn't go so well, so—"

The audience identified the song, laughed, and began clapping in anticipation. For many of them, it was the reason they'd come.

"It follows the course of my life. From promise to pain to . . ." I stretched both hands high into the air. Palms out. Reaching out as far as I was able. When I did, Blondie stood up on the rafters and pulled back the ceiling. I continued, "To coming home. It's called 'Long Way Gone,' and it goes something like this."

• • •

We walked off the stage to a standing ovation. Backstage we stood in a circle. The player's high. Even Big-Big. We'd had a lot of fun. While Daley and I felt like we'd taken a deep breath, Jubal's attention was elsewhere. He kept staring around the corner.

I put my hand on his shoulder. "You good?"

He pointed toward the stage. "What's up with that guy?"

"Who?"

He pointed toward the center of the stage where his guitar stood. "The dude playing my guitar."

The stage was empty.

I smiled. "How big is he?"

"Bigger than Big-Big."

Beyond the stage, they were calling for an encore. "Is he any good?"

Jubal nodded and frowned at the same time. "Better than you." A few seconds passed. He looked confused. "You can't hear him?"

I removed the notebook from the small of my back, handed it to him, and began walking back out onstage.

"What am I supposed to do with this? Ask him if he wants a cheeseburger?"

I smiled. "You'll figure it out."

We returned to the stage, where Jubal leaned against his stool and timidly picked up his guitar.

While I spoke to the audience, his head rotated on a swivel and his attention was focused on the choir. Blondie was sitting in the front row. Leaning back. Feet crossed in front of him. Arms crossed. A smug, satisfied look.

My fingers touched the strings and I began playing a song I'd only rehearsed for Daley. I played remembering my father's admonition that the great players are great because of the notes they choose not to play. Once through the intro, I leaned toward the microphone, then thought better of it. The same was true for too many words.

Daley and the choir picked up on the melody and began humming. Big-Big filled the air beneath us with chords. Between the visitor in the choir and the song I was now playing, which he'd never heard, Jubal was lost. Over the last year, as we'd learned and transposed songs from one key to another, I'd taught him the Nashville Number System. It was a fun exercise to begin a song in one key, modulate on the fly, and finish in a second or third. He'd gotten pretty good at it. I whispered around the mike, "Key of E. One, six, five, four."

Jubal started strumming and watched me for the changes.

Jubal had several musical gifts. One of which was the rhythm in his strum hand. He did unconsciously what some studied for years, never to perfect. I spoke into the mike but kept my eyes on him. "Folks, he's never heard this song before." Applause rose up beneath me. "Your career will be fun to watch."

I loved to hear that kid play.

I turned to the audience. "When I think back over my life, several images flood my mind. If you know my story, our story, you know that around this time last year in a concert at the Falls I had a bit of a health scare."

Up front, Mary laughed out loud. "You think!"

"Well, you would too, if somebody had tried to drown you in subfreezing water." I nodded behind me toward Big-Big.

"I don't pretend to understand all of what happened. But I do know this—this right here is just prelude. Dress rehearsal. The intro. One of these days each one of us is going to get called up and given the chance to join our voices in a song we've never heard, yet one we've known our whole lives.

"My dad used to give a sermon about how we were custom-made for music. How each of us is a walking instrument. I used to laugh at him and his ridiculous ideas, his animated theatrics, but now not so much. Dad was right. He was right about most everything. He loved to sing at the top of his lungs most anywhere. Didn't care a lick what others thought. We'd be walking down the aisle at the grocery store and he'd start singing "Frère Jacques" with the same emotional intensity as an aria from Handel's *Messiah*. I'd stand next to him and want to hide my face. Let a crack in the earth open and swallow me. But Dad just kept on singing."

I stood and nodded for Jubal to follow. Strumming louder, I said, "One of these days I'll get to sing with my father again. Get to hear his beautiful voice. Between here and there, we get to make music of our own. With that in mind, here's a new song. It's simple. Nothing fancy. Four chords and a bridge. I don't even think it has a title. I wrote it for us to sing together. To put our voices on a pedestal. Not just mine. So stand. Sing with me. Loud as you want." I glanced over my shoulder where Andy had projected the words on the screen. "This is a love song for my father . . ."

The End

No Gone Is Too Far Gone

I imagine he stunk. Clothes tattered. Hair matted. Beard stained. One shoe missing. Fingernails bit to the quick. The once-high chin now drags his chest. His eyes scour the ground—afraid to make eye contact lest he bump into a creditor. One missing front tooth. Another cracked. A puffy, purple shadow rests beneath his right eye. The chest full of gold chains are gone. Sold. Gambled. Stolen. And the ring his father gave him? Pawned weeks ago.

This silent and passive ending had a boisterous and in-your-face beginning. Not uncommon. It sounded like this: "I want what I want, when I want it, because I want it and I want it right now." His friends poured gasoline on the fire and he was soon spitting flames. Full of himself, he went to his father. Stared down his nose. Disdain spread across his lips. Always thought his father such a little man. He spouted, "I want my share. Now!" Given the culture, his demand was unconscionable. Sort of like saying, "You are dead to me. I want nothing more to do with you and your silly, pathetic life. I'll take what's mine. From this moment, you're no longer my father and don't ever speak to me again."

Amazingly, the father granted his request.

Pockets full, he turned his back and, surrounded by a fair-weather posse, walked away. Laughing. Skipping. Slapping backs. Sucking courage from a brown bag. Glorious sin on the horizon.

Behind him, the father stood on the porch, cheeks wet, a piercing pain in his chest.

The distance increased. Time passed. The boy lived it up. Drunk whatever. Smoked whatever. Bought whatever. Slept with whomever. Whenever. Wherever. He was a man with no control over his spirit. A city broken down without walls. A poor fund manager, and unwise in every way, his prodigal living was short-lived. Highlife led to no life.

To make matters worse, famine entered the story. Once the sugar daddy had been picked clean, the posse stampeded.

Broke, hungry, alone, and ashamed—but not quite humbled—he "joined" himself to another. Said another way, he sold himself as a slave. Don't miss this—he's a Jewish boy going to work for a Gentile farmer raising pigs. This is apostasy. He could not have been any more unclean. There were laws about this, and he had broken all of them.

Standing in that pen, surrounded by manure, maggots, and swarming flies, holding the slop bucket, he stands just one final rung from the bottom.

We pick up the story in Luke 15. Thirty pounds

lighter, it's easy to count his ribs. He is staring into the bucket with a raised eyebrow, watering mouth, and thinking, *That's not so bad. I could probably get that down.* The New English Translation speaks of "carob pods"—sort of a bean-looking thing with the consistency of shoe leather (v. 16). One of the only fruit-producing plants to actually produce fruit in that area during times of famine. It's a last resort—even for the pigs.

Can you see him scratching his head? Staring around to see who might be watching? This is where he steps off the ladder. Feet on the bottom—of the bottom. He has "attempted to pull fire into his bosom," and it is here that we see the third-degree burns. Not only has he sinned and fallen short, gone his own way, astray, he has missed the target entirely. To quote Isaiah, his righteousness is as "filthy rags." By "rags," Isaiah means used menstrual cloths. Let me spell this out. Left to our own devices—like our prodigal—the best that we can produce, absent a right relationship with the Father, is no better than a bunch of used feminine products. That may offend you, but that's Isaiah's point. Everything about the prodigal is offensive, and he is paying the price of his offense.

But notice what finds him. There in that muck and mire, sour stench, poor choices, and sin piled high, something swims past the reason-filter of his mind and into the still-tender, yet-to-be-calloused places of his heart. And it's not condemnation and finger-pointing shame. It's the memory of his dad. The love of the father.

Of all places for love to find him. (If you could see me, I am fist-pumping.)

Someone once asked me, "When is gone too far gone?" Here's my answer in a nutshell: There is no place on Planet Earth that the love of the Father —the blood of Jesus—can't reach. "His arm is not so short that it cannot save." This side of the grave, no one—and I don't care who they are or what sin or sins they have or are committing—is too far gone.

"But . . ." You raise a finger and shake your head in protest. "You don't know what I've done." You're right. I don't. What I do know is that "while we were still sinners, Christ died for us." That means at our worst, most offensive, suffering the consequences of our own shame and defiant choices, a long way from home, Jesus poured out His soul unto the death. Paul to the prodigals in Corinth said this: "He made Him who knew no sin to become sin for us, that we might become the righteousness of God." If ever God drove a stake in the ground, it's that.

Scripture doesn't say it, but I think our prodigal ate the pods. A guess, yes, but it may well be an educated guess because Scripture does say, "When he came to himself . . ." What better than the bitter, nasty aftertaste of the pod to shake some sense into him.

I love what happens next. So subtle yet so world-rocking. He turns around. Note: he is turning his back toward his sin and setting his face toward his father. Isaiah talked about this too. He called it "setting his face like a flint." Look up *repentance* in the dictionary and you will see a picture of this. The humbled prodigal manages a hesitant jog at first. Then a chin-raising trot. Lungs taking in air. When he reaches the hill a mile out from the farm, he is sprinting. Arms flinging sweat, a trail of dust in his wake. If you listen closely, you can hear the beginning of a sound emitting from his belly. Low. Guttural. It is the sound of pain leaving his body.

And here's my favorite picture in this story. It's the father. Still standing on the porch. Yet to leave his post. One hand shading his eyes. Scanning the horizon. Searching for any sign of movement.

Something atop the hill catches his eye. He squints. Leans. The space between his eyes narrows. The father exits the porch as if shot out of a canon. This picture always gets me. Son running to father. Father running to son.

Having closed the distance, the son falls at his father's feet. He is groveling. Face to toes. Snot mixing with tears. He can't even look at him. "Father, I have sinned . . ."

The father will have none of this. Scripture says

the father "ran and fell on his neck and kissed him." A more accurate translation is "covered his face in kisses." Pause here: I need this picture maybe more than all the rest: the father kissing the son of squalor who willfully betrayed him. Gave him the finger. How many times have I done this?

I cannot count.

The son protests, arm's length; he has yet to make eye contact. "But, Dad, I'm not worthy—"

The father waves him off, orders his servants, "Clothe my son! Bring me a ring! Carve the steaks! Raise the tent!" Servants scatter. The son stands in disbelief. "But, Abba . . ." The son has come undone. "You don't know what all I've done. I'm unclean. Please forgive—"

The father gently places his index finger under his son's chin and lifts it. Eye to eye. He thumbs away a tear. Holds his face in both hands. "You, my son . . . are my son. Once dead, now alive. All is forgiven."

If you're the parent or loved one of a prodigal, let me bolster your hope with this: the Father has yet to leave His post. His eyes still scan the horizon. And no darkness, no matter how dark, can hide the prodigal. Job said it this way: "For He [the Father] looks to the ends of the earth, and sees under the whole heavens." This hasn't all of a sudden changed in 2016. It's not like God's eye-sight has grown dim.

And despite the prodigal's total and complete depravity, the father is not interested in making him or her a slave. Even though that's His right. The Father is about total restoration. A complete returning to sonship. An heir with all rights and privileges thereof.

Maybe you're the prodigal. Surrounded by pigs and staring at the pods. Let me say this to you—I don't care what you've done, where you've gone, where you are, or who you've become, the truth is this: the sanctifying, redeeming, justifying, snatching-back-out-of-the-hand-of-the-devil blood of Jesus reaches to the far ends of the earth.

To think otherwise makes a mockery of the atoning blood of Jesus.

Don't believe me? This is Paul, speaking to the Romans. Like us, they'd ventured a long way from God. Earlier, Paul called them "God haters." He could do this because he knew a thing or two about hating God. He had held people's jackets while they bashed Stephen's brains out. He'd dragged Christians from their homes and executed them in front of their families. To these Romans and fellow prodigals, he said, "Our old man was crucified with Him, that our body of sin might be done away with, that we should no longer be slaves of sin. For he who has died has been freed from sin." See those words *"done away with?"* That means cut away. Disconnected from you. A yoke lifted off your shoulders. Permanently.

Oftentimes Paul said things two or three times. To reinforce his point. He said, "If God is for us, who can be against us? . . . Who shall bring a charge against God's elect? It is God who justifies. Who is he who condemns? It is Christ who died, and furthermore is also risen, who is even at the right hand of God, who also makes intercession for us."

The question is not whether we are guilty. That's a given. We are. Welcome to earth. The question is who stands between us and our guilt. Paul continued, "Who shall separate us from the love of Christ? Shall tribulation, or distress, or persecution, or famine, or nakedness, or peril, or sword? . . . Yet in all these things we are more than conquerors through Him who loved us." Paul paused here, and I think it's these words that echo out across eternity. That reach me here today as if they just left his lips. "For I am persuaded that neither death nor life, nor angels nor principalities nor powers, nor things present nor things to come, nor height nor depth, nor any other created thing, shall be able to separate us from the love of God which is in Christ Jesus our Lord" (Romans 8:31–34, 35–37, 38–39).

If you unpack this, nothing is excluded from this list. No exceptions.

Don't think I'm letting you or me off the hook. I'm not. Such unmerited grace is conditional. It requires something of you and me.

The requirement is that we turn back. Pivot on our heels and put one foot in front of the other.

If you're really broken, surrounded by the wreckage of your own mess, asking, "How?" you may need this spelled out: This means you are not your abortion. Not your affair. Not the reason for your prison sentence. Not the needle holes in your arm. Not the empty bottles next to your bed. Not the shame you see in the mirror. If I'm speaking to you, and you feel as if I've written this just for you . . . let me welcome you to the human race. You're officially one of us.

I am not suggesting that turning around frees you from consequences. Or even pain. You may still go to jail. May carry some scars. May well be infected with HIV and your wife may still leave you and take the kids. But none of this prevents your return to the Father, and neither the sin that brought you here nor the consequences you face determine your eternal identity or the Father's desire to heal your very broken heart and wrap you in His arms.

If you remain unconvinced, the writer of Hebrews offered this encouragement: "Therefore, since we are surrounded by so great a host of witnesses, let us throw off everything that hinders and the sin that so easily entangles. And let us run with perseverance the race marked out for us, fixing our eyes on Jesus." The Charles Martin translation reads like this: "Drop the bucket and run." Think about it: There is a host in heaven cheering you on. Pulling for you. Screaming at the top of their lungs. If you're wondering what kind of sound that might be, the word *host* is described by Daniel as ten thousand by ten thousand. That's a hundred million.

I can hear the rebuttal. "Yeah, but, Charles, you don't know . . ." Stop. Scripture promises us that "everyone who calls on the name of the Lord will be saved." When I read that, my eye focuses on the word *everyone*. And if you're one of those people who wonder how Scripture written two thousand years ago could still be true today, Jesus answered that when He said, "Heaven and earth will pass away, but my words will never pass away." When I read that, my eye focuses on the word, *never*.

"So," you ask with a disbelieving finger in the air, "Charles, are you seriously telling me that there is no place I can go that's too far gone?" I've just spent three hundred pages and a year of my life attempting to say that very thing. Yes, that's exactly what I'm telling you.

I don't care what the shameful voices in your head tell you, or the deafening lies that the memories whisper. I don't care if you're reading this from a prison cell staring at decades in the face, or from the plush comfort of first class staring out over the shimmering face of the

Pacific. We're all broken, all walk with a limp. Here is the truth about you and me: even when in a far-off country, wasted life, stripped bare, smeared, squandered, nothing but scar tissue and shameful, self-inflicted wounds, the love of the Father finds the son and daughter.

He finds us.

This inconceivable, mind-shattering, heart-mending, I-don't-deserve-it reality is the singular thought out of which this book bubbled up. This crazy idea that no matter what, we can always come home. That me and my shipwrecked life and my lifetime of baggage and bad decisions didn't and doesn't disqualify me from Him. Paul said: "Nothing separates us." Charles Martin says, "No gone is too far gone." They mean the same thing. There's hope for the broken, and this is true even if it's our own choices that broke us. Our hope, the very anchor of our souls, is standing on the porch. And His eyes are stretching out through time and space and they are singularly focused on you. On me.

Here's the deal—only Jesus gets to tell you who you are. Period. Any other voice is a lie from the pit of hell. When Jesus said, "It is finished," He wasn't kidding. Then and there, death and sin lost all legal claim over you. "You're no longer a slave." "Sin has no dominion." If the weight of you is crushing you, and you're wondering, *How can this be?* let me lead you to Colossians 2.

He, Jesus, "wiped out the handwriting of requirements that was against us, which was contrary to us. And He has taken it out of the way, having nailed it to the cross." And in doing so, He "disarmed principalities and powersohn, brother of Jesus, said this: "See what great love the Father has lavished on us that we should be called children of God! And that is what we are!" To the Romans, Paul said simply, "We are God's children . . . heirs with Christ."

You may not feel like a triumphant child of God right now, but this is the gospel of the kingdom of the righteous reign of Jesus Christ. Your enemy would have you wrap yourself in the muck and mire of rearview-mirror-shame, staple your chin to your chest, and focus on the pods. Then whisper in your ear, "You could probably get those down." Or worse, replay the video of your leaving—for the ten thousandth time. Faith punches that joker in the teeth, kicks that video to the curb, throws off everything that hinders, focuses on the figure on the porch, and runs like the wind.

Big difference.

If the thought of your encounter with the Father at whom you thumbed your nose causes you to tremble, don't. You can't tell Him anything He doesn't already know. When He lifts your chin—and He will lift your chin—you won't need to say a word.

The choice is yours. Cling to the bucket and eat the pods. Or turn for home.

"But when he was still a great way off, his father saw him, his heart went out to him, and he ran and fell on his neck and covered his face in kisses." What would it look like for the God of the universe to cover your face in kisses? This is the beauty and wonder and majesty, and I-just-can't-believe-it-ness of the love of Jesus.

And after He kisses him, the Father cups the son's face in His hands and speaks these words, through tears and snot and laughter: "Bring out the best robe and put a ring on his hand and sandals on his feet. And bring the fatted calf here and kill it and let us eat and be merry. For this, my son, was dead and is alive again; he was lost and is found."

Meaning?

No gone is too far gone.

Discussion Questions

1. Which character do you most identify with: Cooper, Daley, Cooper's dad, or Big-Big? Why?

2. "Music washes us from the inside out. It heals what nothing else can." Have you found that to be true in your own life? If so, share some of the lyrics and how they provided healing for you.

3. It's much more difficult for Cooper to forgive himself than it was for his father to forgive him. Why do you think that is?

4. Cooper didn't tell Daley the truth about the fire and the shooting when it happened, and he doesn't tell her again when they reunite in Buena Vista. Nor does he tell her about his illness. His reasoning is that he loves her too much. Do you think he made the right decision?

5. The old traditional hymns are sung and discussed throughout the book. What role do they play in the story? Do you have a favorite hymn? What do its words and melody mean to you?

6. Cooper's dad says, "Music cuts people free. It silences the thing that's trying to kill us." How does music cut each of the characters free in this novel?

7. In the sermon he delivers when Cooper leaves, his father challenges Cooper and the listeners at the tent meeting: "Question is, what and who do you worship?" How do you think that convicted Cooper? Did it cause you to consider what and who you worship?

8. What are some of the reasons Cooper creates in Nashville to justify not going home? Do you think they are valid? Can you identify with his struggle and his feeling that he has to make things right before he can go back to his father?

9. After Daley learns of Cooper's liver condition, she tells him, "I will not let the fear of what might be rob me of the promise of what can be." How do you think aspects of her story impacted her passion to be with Cooper, despite the fear? Are there times in your life when you have let fear rob you?

10. How does the theme of "No gone is too far gone" play out in each character's life? Do you believe that no gone is too far gone?

About the Author

Charles Martin is the *New York Times* bestselling author of twelve novels. He and his wife, Christy, live in Jacksonville, Florida. Learn more about him at charlesmartinbooks.com.

Facebook: Author.Charles.Martin
Twitter: @storiedcareer

Center Point Large Print
600 Brooks Road / PO Box 1
Thorndike, ME 04986-0001 USA

(207) 568-3717

US & Canada:
1 800 929-9108
www.centerpointlargeprint.com